SAND DOLLARS, SECRETS, & Starting Over

A LOVE IN *DESTINY* ROMANCE

BY

BAILEY THOMAS

Published by BTA Publishing

Cover and Interior Design: A Fabulous Production

(afabulousproduction.com)

Paperback ISBN: 978-1-967156-10-8

First Edition: September 2025

THE LOVE IN

DESTINY

ROMANCE SERIES

WHERE SMALL-TOWN CHARM
MEETS BIG-HEARTED ROMANCE

Contents

To my wonderful husband: Where you are is where I want to be.

In loving memory of my aunt, Catherine, who possessed a wonderful sense of humor and never hesitated to share her opinions.

In loving memory of Woodson and Harrison, who brightened our lives with love, laughter, and tail wagging.

In loving memory of my sister-in-law, your smile, laughter, and support will be deeply missed.

Chapter One

RAMONA FRITZ SQUEEZED THE green wedge that had been attached to the rim of her margarita glass into her drink. A fine mist dotted the air, its liquid coating her fingers. A burst of fresh citrus permeated the space. Is this really happening? she asked herself. Had she really lost everything in a span of a few hours? She wasn't a kid; she was a twenty-seven-year-old adult who had made a horrible mistake. What the hell was she going to do?

Her gut rolled from the knowledge that she'd been used and discarded like spoiled leftovers. She despised hindsight. Now, an unknown future stood in front of her, tapping its foot. The din from the crowd along with the stale smell of beer had her lifting her head. Laney Miller raised a matching glass, patiently waiting until she followed suit. The hard clank of glassware had the liquid inside almost sloshing over the rim.

"Fuck him," Laney said, full of indignation. Her eyes sparkled with mirth. In case Ram hadn't heard her, she repeated herself in a slow drawl. "Fuuuck hiiiim."

Yup, that was her best friend, whom she loved dearly and had been by her side for the last ten years. Laney didn't mince words and always had her back. Some people might not like her approach, but Ram always knew she'd get the truth from her. A true spitfire who stunned on the inside as on the outside, with her long, glossy black hair and chestnut eyes. From the moment they had met, their friendship blossomed.

"I've gotta leave, Laney," Ram whispered as she rested her head on the palm of her hand. God, her mistake would end up costing her dearly. Staying in Knoxville wasn't an option, as she wanted a fresh start, one that was free of him—the cheating, lying jerk who savagely upended her life right under her eyes. Some might say that running away wasn't the answer, but to her, it was self-preservation. Humiliation burned deep inside of her for being so damn stupid.

"I hate it, Ram, but I also totally get it. Sometimes we need to wipe the slate clean. So where do you wanna go?"

"Ugh, I don't know. It's not like I have a lot to pack, and getting a job shouldn't be too hard. There always seems to be an accountant position open. Do you want to come with me?" Ram asked, her fingers crossed, knowing that wouldn't change her friend's answer.

"Nope. My life is here...at least for now. You know I'll be there with you in spirit and for many visits." Laney paused. "Holy guacamole, I have an idea. Hold on a sec," Laney announced as she dashed toward the bar on a mission. After a bit, she returned with a map, which she affixed on the wall next to the picture of Ram's ex-boyfriend, George Warren.

Ram scrunched up her face, watching Laney. "Whatcha doing?"

Laney slapped a set of darts down on the scarred wooden high-top table and pointed at the wall, where the picture of him was now affixed to one half of the dart board and a map of the United States to the other half.

"Go on, pick one side and take aim. It's not every day that we get to maim the living free from prosecution. Or find a new place to live."

Laughter bubbled up from her gut as she stared at the photograph of her ex with multiple holes covering his face from their previous throws. Only Laney would come up with an idea this wild.

"Sometimes I think you were dropped off by aliens or something. Who does that, or more accurately, this?" Ram asked, moving her hand around their space. She tried to plaster her best "are you serious" look on her face, but the tears that were streaming down her face from laughter gave her away.

Laney scooped up the rest of the darts, depositing them on the table. "Do you have a better idea? I don't see you coming up with a plan of where you want to live, and you've got to get out of town."

None of this was funny. It was far from it, but it beat hysterically crying. Ram had no doubt that she'd do that later in the privacy of her apartment, where no one could see her blotchy face and red nose. She wasn't feeling too bad, in her opinion, considering that four hours ago, she learned that her boyfriend had drained not only her checking and savings account, but had also run off with another woman—his soulmate. He'd *actually* written that in the note he'd left her, the jackass.

Her bestie did have a point. Where was she going to go?

She blew out a frustrated breath. The embarrassment bothered her the most. How could she have been so blind? Or more to the point, that oblivious? She'd fallen for a stunning man who was charming, devoted, and selfish. He had made her the center of his attention, and she had soaked up every second of it. At first, it didn't make sense to her because she wasn't anything special—mousy brown hair, basic brown eyes, with some extra weight. Just a plain, ole average woman, in her book. Her body did not contain an ounce of supermodel beauty, so when that man took an interest in her, she fell right under his spell.

She had been so happy, but now she realized those types of relationships only existed in the movies or on television. She hadn't dated a lot in her life, so her pool of experience was limited, but you can be damned sure that dating wasn't in her future. Keeping what was left of her heart and dignity intact was her priority.

Ram grabbed the first dart and tried her best to aim it at the map. She even closed one eye, tossing it toward the wall only to see it bounce off and clatter across the worn linoleum floor.

"That's okay, Ram, we all miss on the first try," she said with a grunt as she bent to retrieve the dart from the floor. She cringed, listening to herself because she'd missed the mark on her freaking boyfriend, too.

Once again, her bestie demonstrated the proper technique before handing the sharp, pointed missile over.

At least Laney understood her need for change, even if it meant leaving her behind. Mileage wouldn't be a problem for their friendship; it only meant more adventures to come. She took the proffered dart from Laney, bumping her hip as she passed by her in the process for good luck. Good Lord, her athletic skills were limited, along with precise hand-eye coordination. Her skillset and hobbies were more creative in nature. She adored anything to do with flowers—like the Juliet rose, a unique, circular rose which costs $30 million to cultivate, or the sunflower, which moved with the sun and always faced east at the start of the day. That was her jam. If those facts were darts, she would be the queen of bullseyes.

"Are you forgetting that I don't have a sporty bone in my body?"

Her bestie rolled her eyes before raising her eyebrow elegantly and pinning her with a look that said, "Are you kidding me?"

"Oh, no! Sweetie, no one could ever forget that factoid, but I still believe in you. How else are we going to narrow down where you're going to live? Your destiny is in your hands. Don't you just feel the excitement?"

Well, Laney had a point. She didn't have any prospects or any ideas about where to live. All she knew was that she needed to put Tennessee in the rear-view mirror. If there was a small silver lining to this day, it was that her most recent paycheck was still in her pocket because her company had decided to move to a new payroll system that required two cycles of paper checks to be issued.

She patted her pocket, thankful that she hadn't made it to the bank yet or her ex would have stolen that too. She sucked down a deep breath. Exhaling slowly, she mimicked the pose Laney had just shown her. When she let go of the dart, she let out a woot because that sucker had landed right on her ex's crotch. They cheered, jumping up and down, celebrating like they had actually wounded that son of a bitch.

Ramona snatched the second dart off the table and aimed it at the map. She smiled as her belly fluttered. She balanced the cool metal between her fingers. She tried her best to repeat the exact process as the last one. It went wide, sticking in the wood paneling. She had one last chance to see where she'd end up. For some silly reason, it seemed more adventurous to allow the dart to choose her next home. Maybe this metal dart knew more about geography than she did and would land on the ideal place. Maybe even her forever home, if that place even existed for her.

"Okay, Ram, this is the last one," Laney said. "If you don't hit a location on the map, then it's my turn."

Ram picked up the last dart and stretched her neck from side to side. Then she lined it up, squinting with one eye to double-check her aim with the map, and let it fly. She watched as a burst of hope fluttered in her heart. It landed on Florida. She and Laney both inched forward toward the map, Ram's stomach tightening.

Laney's eyes went wide, and her lips formed a divine "O" shape as she pointed to the location pinned by her dart. "Holy smokes, Ram, you nailed Destiny, Florida. This is a sign; I mean, we were just talking about *your* destiny. And of all the places on this map along with your crappy aim, you've picked it. It's even on the ocean side!" Laney said, wrapping her up in a big side hug.

"I don't know what to say. Do you think it's going to be super expensive?" Ramona muttered, her mind running through all sorts of questions as she stared at the map.

Laney's arm tightened around her. "No, I think it's fate. You've got to stop second-guessing it. Don't mess with the powers of the universe, Ram. That's bad juju."

Laughter bubbled up from deep inside her, along with a sense of calm. Her friend was right. The decision had been made. Doubting it would be bad juju, and she sure as hell didn't need any more of that in her life.

Ram lifted her glass and dipped it toward Laney. "I'll miss you, Laney, but my destiny has been determined. You better be planning a trip to visit me soon."

"Oh, Ram, I'll miss you too," Laney responded as they clanked their glasses again. When she set her glass down, she twisted so she could reach into her purse until she pulled out a thick envelope and handed it to Ram.

When Ram opened it, she saw a wad of cash inside. Her gaze snapped to Laney's. "No, I can't accept this."

"Yes, you can. This is a little boost to help get you going. You'd do the same for me and you know it. Now take it, or our waiter is getting one hell of a tip tonight," Laney said, raising an eyebrow, showing that she meant business.

Ram crushed her friend in another hug, feeling her tears stinging her eyes. "I love you, Laney."

They stood like that for a few seconds. There wasn't a better person in this world than Laney, who had a golden heart, and loved unconditionally. So many memories had been made with this woman over the years. When Ram moved to Tennessee all those years ago, Laney was the first person she'd met when she pulled into the apartment building where Laney was the property manager. It hadn't taken long for them to connect and become best friends.

Not wanting to waste one moment, Ram focused on enjoying the rest of their girls' night out, googling together to learn more about her new home. After tonight, she would give notice to her job, pack up her apartment, and drive to Florida.

R AM STOPPED AT THE red light and opened the driver's window to take in a whiff of the salty, brine-filled air. Big, white, puffy clouds dotted the blue sky. On the right side of her truck, she saw a wooden sign that read "Welcome to Destiny." Beneath it, made entirely of flowers and plants, was a spectacular display of a sailboat and anchor. Whoever did the design had some talent.

She flipped her wrist, checking her watch, and was pleased that she had arrived ahead of schedule. It had only taken her a little over eleven hours to drive from Knoxville to Destiny, which sat on the panhandle of Florida. Though she was tired, the drive had reinvigorated her. She was happy that she had decided to leave in the wee hours of the morning, so she would arrive in the afternoon.

When the signal flashed green, she continued forward until the tops of the sails and masts of the boats docked in the marina came into view. To her left, a place called The Tipsy Pelican seemed interesting to her, and she made a mental note to check it out when she had some time. A bit further down, she noticed the Conch Shell Café.

She already loved the seaside charm of the town. This entire place reminded her of several Jimmy Buffet songs. So far, so good, she thought to herself, making a list of things of everything she wanted to tell Laney when she called her later. If Ram didn't give her a call, her friend would send the cavalry out to look for her.

At the next light, she turned down a winding road that ran parallel to the harbor, making her way to the Sapphire Hotel. The drive was breathtaking. At the end of the road stood a stunning building surrounded by water views that certainly fit into the Crown Hotel Group's line of prestigious properties. This was where she planned to stay while she got the lay of the land on her living and work situations. She had forgone setting up any interviews until she got to town, wanting a mini-vacation before she started the next chapter of her life.

She had barely pulled her truck into the circular driveway when one of the valets standing off to the side in teal uniform greeted her. "Good day, ma'am. Are you checking into the hotel?"

She stifled a giggle because these two men were probably used to vehicles that didn't scream "I'm on the run with everything I own." It was a fair question, since the back of her pickup was tarped and loaded high with her possessions. Since this place was far from a roadside hotel, she was sure she was the anomaly for the day. She handed her key to the valet. "Yes, I am. Park this up front for now, please."

When he nodded his agreement, she headed toward the main doors. Instantly, air-conditioned air wrapped around her body, cooling her warm skin on this humid June day. Moving further inside, she caught a strong floral scent. When her eyes adjusted to the inside lighting, she noticed at least thirty buckets of flowers, tropicals, and greenery in all varieties all over the lobby, including roses, lilies, exotic ginger, red anthurium, birds of paradise, hala leaves, and so many more flowers.

Off to the side of the desk, she noticed an older woman dressed in a bespoke skirt and blazer, holding a phone to her ear with one hand while pinching the bridge of her nose with the other.

Nearby, a young clerk wearing a hotel uniform greeted her with a broad smile. "Welcome to the Sapphire Hotel. How can I assist you?"

"Hi, I have a reservation," Ramona replied, digging into her purse to pull out the paper that held her confirmation code.

"May I get your first and last name?"

"Ramona Fritz," she replied, watching the clerk's fingers dance across the keyboard.

"Excellent! We have you in a king room on the fourth floor, with you checking out a week from this coming Monday."

"What do you mean no one can turn these buckets of flowers into arrangements?" the woman off to the side barked into the phone. "I certainly did not intend for buckets of raw flowers to be delivered. I ordered bulk flowers to save money with the expectation that they would arrive arranged. Why else would I purchase the glass bowls? The event is tonight, and no, there isn't a florist in this area. Are you kidd--"

A muffled grunt slipped past the woman's lips as she snapped the phone receiver into its base. She smoothed back a wayward strand of hair before turning towards the clerk with a smile plastered on her face.

"When you're finished with our guest, will you join me in the back office?"

Ram's initial reaction was to jump in with an offer to help. The words were on the tip of her tongue, but she swallowed them down. Indecision wracked her brain. Would they find her annoying, like her mother had when she lived with her? Or would offering her assistance help show her new community that she was worthy? That she could be a part of this community.

"Excuse me," Ram blurted out, leaning into the desk so that the older woman would hear her. When the woman paused and turned back, Ram continued. "Forgive me for intruding, but I overheard your conversation. I can help with arranging all these flowers for tonight. I mean, if you're willing and need extra hands?"

The woman's smile brightened, even though it didn't reach her eyes. "The company didn't finish the job, and I do need a speedy fix."

Ram hooked her thumb toward herself. "Flowers are my love language. When I was younger, I learned all about them because my mother liked them. In many ways, I was her in-home florist. Anyway, that's a ton of flowers that must be trimmed and sized for those low glass bowls."

So much for staying out of it, Ram thought to herself. She watched the woman weighing her options against the unknown person standing in front of her before she finally extended her hand. "I'm Brenda. I appreciate your offer—there aren't many guests who would offer to jump into the fray."

"I'm Ramona Fritz, but please call me Ram," she returned, shaking the woman's hand. "I may be a guest this week, but hopefully next week, I'll be one of Destiny's newest residents. This magnificent hotel is my temporary home until I figure out where to live."

"Okay, you've intrigued me." Brenda moved around the front desk and ushered her toward the sitting area that had become a flower and greenery storage. "There are forty-five centerpieces and five taller arrangements for the raffle and buffet tables that must be ready before six o'clock tonight. Would you walk me through how you'd arrange them?"

Ram rubbed her hands, mimicking her excitement. She eyed all the buckets, asking a few questions before she arranged her selections from the buckets in her hand.

"For the vases, I'd stick mostly to the tropical and adjust the heights to make it dimensional. Meanwhile, for the tables, I would group the flowers following the three-five-eight rule."

"I like it! I don't understand that rule, but should I?" Brenda asked.

"Oh, sorry, no. It's just a standard rule florists use when doing arrangements. You use three different kinds of flowers, five stems of greenery, and eight filler flowers. Of course, all good artists bend the rules when needing to dazzle our customers."

"That's marvelous." Brenda's smile finally brightened up her face. "You're a lifesaver. What tools or supplies do you need to get these whipped out?"

"Not too much, but I'll compile a list, and any extra hands would be wonderful. Oh, and we'll need a place to assemble all of this."

Brenda pointed toward the hallway. "Everything will be moved into the empty conference room, first door on the left. I have a notepad and pen on the counter at the front desk."

"Excellent. Give me twenty minutes to go to my room and then I'll get started."

Brenda nodded. "For helping me out of a pinch, I'm comping your stay. Welcome to Destiny."

"I appreciate that very much," Ram said as she walked past the woman and toward the front desk to write down her list and get her room key.

Ram traded the completed supply list for her room key with the front desk clerk. "Hey, is Brenda the catering manager or something?"

"No, she's one of the owners of the hotel, but she wears all the hats," the clerk responded.

Ram tucked that nugget away for another time as she headed toward the bay of elevators, giddy with how her day was going. She was using her artistic talents. Her stay had been paid for, allowing her to save more money. She had made a good first impression with the owner of the hotel, who had to be well-connected in this small town. A total win-win, for sure.

She texted Laney to let her know she'd arrived. So far, this decision to come here seemed to be off to a good start. Just maybe, all the bad juju she'd experienced in Knoxville would stay there permanently.

Chapter Two

A FRESH FLORAL SCENT permeated the air as Brock Pierson stood in the ballroom with two Sapphire Hotel employees, taking in the shit ton of flower buckets all over the room. When he stopped by to alert the front desk of the dead tree just off the main road that bordered their property, Brenda had stopped him in a slight panic. Her head groundsman had left early, making him unable to help with floral arrangements for the night's event.

Helping with floral arrangements wasn't on his to-do list today, but he couldn't refuse jumping in to help. He wanted people to know he could be depended upon when the need arose and, more importantly, that he wouldn't let them down. Especially when it was for people he respected, like Brenda and her husband. The two of them, alongside the owners of The Tipsy Pelican, Beth and Rick, had welcomed and given him a chance when he first arrived in Destiny when others had been hesitant.

Brenda handed him a thick piece of linen and Sapphire Hotel stationery, and asked if he could gather the tools and supplies listed for a woman named Ram, who needed these items to make centerpieces.

"Dude, are we supposed to do something with these?" The youngest of the two valets whined as his thumb swiped through whatever app held his attention on his phone.

The other shrugged his shoulders. "All I know is that I was called in to park cars for some event, not play with flowers. Oh, and move some hunk of junk that's piled high with crap."

A female voice radiated from the back of the room, causing everyone to turn their heads to see who it belonged to. "The truck is far from junk, and it doesn't hold one spec of crap. That was rude for a guest to hear. Please find suitable parking so my stuff will be safe and accessible while I'm here for the week."

A blush stained the valet's cheeks. "Uh...sorry. I'll get it moved."

"Great. Hurry back because today's your lucky day. You're going to help us with all these flowers."

Neither valet looked happy with her declaration, but they were smart enough to keep their comments to themselves. It seemed Brock had found Ram.

She advised the two valets about how she wanted the tables to be organized by type of flowers, glass bowls, and vases to establish a production line. That task at hand was no small job, while the clock ticked down. Now Brock understood why Brenda had seemed so stressed.

Ram hustled by Brock, picking up a pair of clippers and going to work on a flower bunch in her hand as she shared the last details of this assignment. She clipped off leaves and stems, working with skilled efficiency. She moved closer and paused to look up at him. "Okay, I think you can help with the vases, since you didn't shrivel up at the mere mention of flowers."

He liked this doe-eyed beauty and her energy.

"You must be Ram? I'm Brock Pierson."

"Oh yes, sorry. That's me," she answered, handing him the prepared flowers as she pulled more from the buckets. "I skipped over the introduction phase. That happens when I'm in the zone. I just arrived at the hotel—well, I'm moving to Destiny—when all this happened. And I volunteered because I love flowers. Geez, I'm rambling."

Another smile crossed his face. This woman fascinated him. She exhibited an intense mix of innocence, pride, and dedication, all while radiating happiness. She was cute when flustered. He was mesmerized by her.

He handed her back the trimmed beauties that he held and watched her arrange them in the glass bowl. "I work for the Town of Destiny as the Landscape Architect Manager. I had stopped by to let management know that I was removing the dead cypress that borders this property and the street, and figured I could lend a hand since that tree isn't going anywhere."

She flashed him a megawatt smile that hit him in the chest like a sucker punch, knowing he had caused her to smile.

"Thank you for your help. The more the merrier, as they say." She paused. "Hey, are you the person who designed the floral display beneath the Destiny sign as you enter town?"

He slanted his head and preened, like a peacock fanning its feathers. "Yup, that's my handiwork."

"You did a fantastic job. I love the design and the colors you incorporated. It seems the universe brought two floral artists together to save the day," Ram said with a giggle before dividing out the tasks between the four of them. They worked in relative silence except for questions and some complaining from the two valets, who didn't like working with roses.

Ram's approach was methodical. He watched her slender fingers manipulate the flowers and greenery until she was satisfied with the result, enjoying how she spoke to herself at times. A pretty woman whose hair reminded him of roasted chestnuts, while her curves were a work of art a man could appreciate.

Together, they had made significant progress in a little over three hours. When the last vase was completed, pride and happiness radiated across Ram's face right down to her round full lips. She pushed back from her chair and high-fived each person in the room. "Thank you for pitching in to knock these out."

He helped with the cleanup while she walked out of the room. Moments later, she reappeared with Brenda in tow.

"Oh, Ram, you did it! Seriously, you all did a magnificent job," Brenda said. She spoke into her walkie-talkie while she checked out each arrangement. In short order, several employees entered the room with carts, bustling with activity as they followed her directions and vision.

"Thank you for stepping up and helping me out. I have to say, you could have a career in floral design," Brenda said to Ram.

Ram beamed with pleasure from Brenda's praise. "Oh, I like that idea, but that's only a dream. But, if you know of anyone needing an accountant, please let me know."

"I'll keep that in mind," Brenda answered Ram, before her focus shifted to the two valets. "Go, take a break before you head back outside to finish your shifts," she said to them.

The two valets scurried from the room, leaving Brock in unfamiliar territory. He wanted more time with Ram. There was something about her that captivated him, that made him feel alive. The last time he felt that kind of warmth in his system was before he lost his sister to that damn disease. He thought of scenarios where he could prolong their time together, but each one seemed lame.

"Brock, you're a lifesaver, too," Brenda said, breaking into his thoughts. "Neither of you had to help me out, and for that I'm truly grateful. For a job well done, I'm buying dinner tonight, so please head on down to the restaurant when you're ready."

At the end of the announcement, Brenda disappeared from the room. Brock sent a silent thank you to her for giving him an idea that would sound natural. He'd invite her to sit with him, answer all her Destiny questions, and find out more about this woman with the big, brown eyes and heart of gold. The need to know more about her pushed him out of his comfort zone.

"That's so nice of her," Ram said, sweeping up the last of the wayward leaves and stems into the trash.

"Nice? It's the least Brenda can do since I have sore fingertips working with all those roses. Those thorns hurt." Brock groaned, giving her his best pouty face.

Ram sauntered over to him and patted his arm. "Oh, poor baby. I hope we won't have to amputate any of those digits."

"Me too. That would make my day job trickier," he said. "Hey, are you up for some company at dinner? I'm normally not this social, but I could offer to answer all your Destiny questions and anything else you can come up with," Brock said, hoping she'd agree.

"I'd like that. You lead the way," Ram said, motioning for him to take the lead.

Brock exited the oversized room, stepping off to the side. When Ram stepped alongside him, he lightly placed his hand on her lower back to lead her down a hallway toward the distant sound of chatter and music. He'd only eaten at the hotel restaurant a few times. Fine dining wasn't his go-to choice at night as a solo eater; nor did it fit into his current budget. Achieving his goal of paying off his debt took precedence over everything else.

At the hostess stand, he gave her their names, and they followed her back to a set table covered in white linen and matching napkins. He pulled out her chair, waiting until she sat before taking his own seat. The soft flicker of the candle in the center of the table gave Ram's skin an alluring golden tone. Even though this dinner was far from a date, it still held a romantic ambiance that he enjoyed.

He dropped his napkin across his lap and reviewed the menu and specials. When the waiter arrived, he ordered a beer while she ordered red wine. They opted to share an appetizer of shrimp and lump crab-meat cocktail and when they both ordered steaks, they also decided to share the steamed asparagus and scalloped potatoes. He appreciated the fact that she ordered what she had wanted. He always lived by the theory that if you're hungry, eat.

"What brings you to Destiny?" he asked.

The second the last word left his lips, he saw her visibly shrink back from the table. Great, he'd stepped in it on the first question, and here he thought that was an easy question. That bothered him, though, because he didn't like the thought that something bad might have happened to bring her here.

"I guess, I, uh, should get used to sharing that tidbit since most people will be asking me that question. The short version of the story is that I just broke up with my boyfriend, and we didn't part ways on the best of terms. He stayed behind while I decided that a change of location was best. It's just a situation I'd rather forget."

"I'm sorry. So, what are your plans now?"

Ram snorted. "The basic needs, you know, finding a job and a place to live."

He cocked his head to the side. "You are the adventurous type. So, why here?

She giggled at his question. "Well, my best friend, Laney, helped me pick Destiny. You could say I nailed it. I threw a dart at the map of the United States, and it landed on Destiny. So, here I am."

Brock took a sip of his beer and leaned back, watching her. "What does 'you nailed it' mean? because I know you're not referencing an interview, unless you're meaning the floral arrangements." Most people would not take a leap of faith like that without having a job or place to live mapped out."

She shrugged her shoulders. "You could call it that, or incredibly stupid. The jury is still out on my decision."

Brock leaned forward. "Have you always been this spontaneous?"

"Growing up with my mother, I've had some practice with figuring out how to make ends meet without a ton of planning. I guess you could say, it's a forced form of spontaneity."

He nodded, wanting to know more about her childhood. However, the waiter delivered a shiny silver, tiered dish frothing over with icy fog from the dry ice used to keep their seafood appetizer chilled. Delicate fingers snagged a shrimp, then scooped a portion of the red sauce onto her plate. He followed her actions and took a sampling of each item.

She chewed her bite and swallowed. "This is so good. I'm going to love eating all this fresh seafood."

"If you're looking for a place to live, there is a newer apartment unit that just opened earlier this year, the High Tide Apartments. The owners hired me to do the topiaries and floral gardens all around the common areas in the complex. The location is great; it's close to the marina and within walking distance to several shops and restaurants."

She took a sip of her wine before answering. "I appreciate the recommendation. I'll check it out along with your creations. How long have you been here?"

He wiped his fingers on his napkin. "I moved here two years ago. I started by picking up odd jobs at the hotel but was fortunate to land the job at the Township of Destiny. I've built my life from there."

Ram tucked a piece of hair behind her ear. "I like that idea of building a life, finding a place that you love and it becomes your forever home."

A lump formed in Brock's chest, catching him off guard, a bitter-sweet reminder of his life. "This place is magical. I wasn't sure about the small-town aspect for the long term, but now I couldn't imagine leaving. The locals are, for the most part, wonderful. Trust me, I've seen that firsthand. It's certainly a community that grows stronger together."

What he left unspoken was that this community had become his family. The guilt over what happened to his biological family still weighed on him, but not wanting to delve further into that topic, he steered the conversation back to Ram.

"So, how does a person love number crunching *and* flowers?"

Her eyes twinkled with mirth. "I happen to excel at math, but again, I acquired that skill thanks to my mother's inability to balance our finances. My natural tendencies lean toward the creative arts."

Man, everything she shared intrigued him. He found himself jumping feet first into this rabbit hole of Ram's life. "So, why flowers over painting or something else?"

She picked at that wayward strand of hair again. "Truthfully, my mom dated around a lot, and all the men would bring her flowers. They would smell so pretty, but if I didn't do anything with them, they just sat on the counter to die. So, I started arranging them for her and researching all the different varieties on my own."

"I bet your mom liked that you took care of them for her," he said.

Once again, he got the impression he'd asked one question too many when her shoulders slumped slightly. "No, she didn't care, but I did. They were too beautiful to waste. And, in a twisted way, it started my love of flowers."

They finished their tower and ordered another round of drinks while they waited on dinner. A comfortable silence settled between them as they watched the activity in the room unfold around them.

"How did you find your passion for becoming a landscape artist?" How long have you been doing this gig?"

Brock leaned back and studied Ram for a moment. He didn't know how to answer that question because he hadn't really thought about it. How do you explain that you fell into it when your luck had been down? No, scratch that, when you bottomed out.

"In the beginning, I worked for a large corporation, motivated to move up the ranks. Success at that point meant driving ridiculously expensive cars and living a lifestyle that I couldn't fully comprehend but I knew I wanted to achieve. When that dream exploded, I found this job. I guess you could call my early thirties my enlightened period. I realized this type of work appeals to me. It's rewarding when it's finished."

"Ah, it's a labor of love. So, you had all this talent and didn't know it, but something about working with your hands gave you satisfaction?"

"Not exactly. I had no idea that I liked doing it until now. My mom loved to garden. She could grow anything. In our neighborhood when I was growing up, we had the most attractive grounds. In the backyard, she grew all kinds of vegetables, berries, and fruits. She canned everything and shared the bounty, as she called it, with our neighbors. I learned all of this from her, and it just flourished from there...pun intended," Brock said, cracking himself up at how silly he sounded.

"I love that story. I bet she's proud of you. Where are your parents now?"

He picked at the label on his beer. His mood shifted to the darker side of his memories, the part he wouldn't share. "They both passed away several years ago."

Her hand flew across the table and covered his hand. She gave him a small squeeze. The warmth from her touch penetrated the queasiness in his stomach when he thought about his selfishness. "Oh my gosh, I'm so sorry."

The waiters appeared with their entreés and side dishes, breaking up the moment and her touch, which he missed the second she withdrew her hand. He appreciated the reprieve from having to relive the painful memories and the reminder that he was alone in this world. Once the plates were on the table, they both ate in companionable silence.

Over dessert, they shared some stories and discussed the town a bit further. When those plates were cleared, the waiter confirmed that their bill had been settled. Before he retreated, the server checked one last time to ensure they didn't need anything more. Brock reached into his pocket and tossed down several bills to cover the gratuity. He probably overpaid, but the last thing he wanted to do was short the server. It would leave him short on cash for the remainder of the week. She followed suit and added a few more bills to the stack.

"Thanks for making my first experience in Destiny memorable. Have a good night," she said while standing, so he stood too.

"You too, Ram," he echoed, returning to his seat when she turned to walk toward the front of the restaurant.

How long he sat there watching her form fade, he wasn't sure, but what he knew as an absolute was that he didn't like saying goodbye. They had interacted like they'd known each other for months, as opposed to hours. Well, except for the getting-to-know-you questions. He took a drink from his water glass, reflecting on everything until he realized his brain was conjuring up ways *to run into her* again. What the hell was he supposed to do with that knowledge? The last thing he deserved was the hope of a future when he'd cost everyone he had loved their own. His stomach soured from the truth of his accusation.

Chapter Three

RAM SPENT THE WEEKEND relaxing and touring Destiny. A restlessness motivated her to get up earlier than she wanted to on Monday morning. She had to get a jump on a few to-dos before she could relax on her mini-vacation. The first item on her list was to fill up her truck. She stood at the counter at the local gas station, paying for her fuel, a bottle of water and, feeling a bit lucky, she purchased a lottery ticket. As she strolled back to her truck, her phone trilled with Laney's infamous ring of "Girls Just Wanna Have Fun."

"Ram, you better have a good story for not calling me back last night. Not that I was worried, but it's always fun to bust your chops when I get the chance."

"Does sex count?"

"Holy hell! What did you just say?" Laney spat out, likely her morning cup of coffee. "Who are you and what did you do with my sweet Ram? Now spill, and don't skip any detail."

Okay, so maybe that misdirect was wrong, but her friend's reaction was still priceless. "April fools, but I did have dinner with the guy I texted you about, the one who helped me finish all those arrangements, Brock."

"Uh, it's June, babe, and it's not funny to tease about such vital events. So, tell me all the details about this man. Is he cute? Potential revenge sex candidate? If yes, does he have friends for when I visit?"

She shook her head at her friend's line of questioning. This was the exact reason she hadn't called last night after dinner, because she knew the probing would be endless, and she had been exhausted. She opened the door to her truck and hopped into the driver's seat. Leaning across the seat, she shoved the lottery ticket into the glove box, then slipped the transmission into drive before she started towards her next stop.

"Good grief. The dinner had been provided by the hotel as a gesture of thanks for our help. Might I mention, a completely friendly dinner, with most of the discussions being about life in Destiny and the weather."

"And..." The line went quiet for several long minutes as Laney waited for her to give in and answer the questions Ram was avoiding.

"Fine, he's a looker with his lean and fit body, tanned skin, and light brownish hair that has this cool, messy, but maintained look. He's tall too, but I didn't measure him. You satisfied now? God, Laney, you should have gone to work for the CIA."

"Anyone next to you is tall." Laughter rumbled across the line. "So, is he worth getting to know? Maybe forge a little fun-roll-in-the-sheets between the two--"

"Stop. I'm not ready for that anytime soon. He was nice and that was it."

"Don't get your skirt in a bunch, Ram. I'm always going to remind you that you're young and attractive. Life has ups and downs, but don't stop looking for that special person because you were bitten by the last douche. If those circumstances held true for everyone, there would be no happily-ever-after for anyone, and I, for one, refuse that notion. Now, I'm not telling you to run to the altar, but finding someone who interests you is not wrong."

"I know, but can we change the subject. I'm on my way to check out this apartment complex Brock told me about, and if it checks out, to see if there are any vacancies."

"That's good. Let me know how it goes. I'll give them a glowing review if you proceed. Talk to you later! Love you, Ram."

"Love you, too. And, Laney, don't ever stop supporting the fairy tale movement."

Ram turned into the parking lot and took in the view of the High Tide Apartments. The complex looked new and polished, but the floral gardens in front were exquisite. She loved the blend of tropical bushes like birds of paradise, ruellia white showers, hibiscus mixed with the blooming flowers like blanket flowers, daisies, and coreopsis. She even loved the school of fish topiaries, which provided dimension. Brock had really brought the fish to life with his choice of flowers and plants. The entire scene was colorful and breathtaking. The next time she saw him, she'd have to tell him how much she loved his work.

She walked toward the office and opened the door to a spacious and inviting area. Inside, there were two wooden desks with ornate carvings and a mailbox unit along one wall. On the other side of the room sat a small sitting area with a beautiful blue upholstered sofa, two wingback chairs in matching hues of bluish tones, and a huge television attached to the wall. She liked the simple elegance.

"Howdy," a man with a head full of graying hair greeted her from behind one of the desks. "How can I assist you?"

"I wanted to see if you have any vacancies for either a studio or a one-bedroom."

The older man turned to retrieve a set of keys from the credenza behind him. "You're in luck—I have three units available. I'm Earl, the owner and co-manager of this place. The real boss, though, is my wife, Elma."

"I'm Ramona. It's nice to meet you."

Earl moved to the door, holding it open for her. "Come this way, Ramona. I'll start with the one on the first floor. It's the studio. The other two units are upstairs."

As she followed him toward the first unit, she couldn't help but notice how well-maintained the buildings and property were. Earl and Elma obviously took pride in their place.

Ram pointed to the front planter area. "I can't help but admire your topiaries out front."

"Aren't they spectacular? Mr. Pierson did the work for us. He's a nice fella and did a good job. As my Elma says, those are our conversation pieces, so we featured them in our brochures."

Ram smiled at how he used the term *my* when he spoke about his wife. She followed Earl to the first floor to check out the studio, which was tiny. She inhaled sharply to stop the swarm of emotion threatening to peak. *Why did I give George access to my accounts? Oh, right, because I wanted to show him that I trusted him because I thought he loved me.*

"Okay, are you ready to look at the one-bedroom?"

She nodded and followed him up the staircase. The studio unit was too small, but she wasn't sure if she could afford the one-bed-room. She hated to go backwards, but she had to rebuild her funds. Mentally, she calculated her reserves, which consisted of her last paycheck and what Laney had given her. She knew Laney would help her out again, if necessary, but she would find another way.

This whole town, located along the shore, worried her too with its high cost of living. She figured if she had to work two jobs for a while to make ends meet, she could do that. It wasn't like she hadn't had to do that before. It was just that it upset her because she'd sworn to herself that she never wanted to be in that situation again.

The studio was located on the back side facing a street. The one-bedroom, however, faced the marina. When she entered, she looked out the kitchen window to see the tops of the sails and masts of the docked boats. The wooden flooring, quartz countertop, and stainless appliances were so beautiful. She loved this space. In her mind, she had already decorated the entire unit. The price had to be outside of her limit, but she swallowed extra hard, maybe hoping that act would drop the price.

Earl told her all about the amenities. He and Elma had chosen to build a smaller property with only fifty units because they wanted to create a community within their walls, a place to call home with a sense of pride. She really liked that idea, along with the one-bedroom. *I want to call this place home.*

"Well, this unit is amazing, but I'm sure the price is outside of my budget."

Earl tugged his shorts up and motioned for her to follow him outside. "Come back to the office so we can sit, have a glass of iced tea, then we'll discuss all the particulars."

When they returned, Earl disappeared behind a door, so she took a seat on the sofa. In a matter of minutes, he returned with a tray loaded with a plate of shortbread cookies and three glasses of iced tea. Then a woman joined them, holding a folder and a notepad in her hand.

"Hi, I'm Elma. Earl told me that you loved the one-bedroom. What's bringing you to Destiny, Ramona?"

"You can call me Ram. I'm moving here, and I'm hoping it will be permanent."

The woman's face brightened. "That's lovely. We love it here and have called Destiny home for over twenty-five years. Where are you staying now?"

"The Sapphire Hotel, until the end of the week, which is why I'm out looking now."

"Oh, that's such an amazing property. Brenda and Brad's properties are spectacular. So, where are you working?"

Ram grabbed her glass of tea and took another long gulp. It was a reasonable question, but she also knew that saying she didn't have a job wasn't a proper answer. She really hadn't thought through all the particulars when she jumped into the truck this morning. She would work around this question to the best of her ability. She knew the type of person she was, but these two sitting here assessing her had no clue.

"That's also on my list of to-dos, but thank goodness for savings," she replied, sending a silent thank-you out to Laney for her generosity.

"The unit you love is fifteen hundred a month. However, Brock did call in advance to let us know that you *might* be stopping by. He's a remarkable young man and also proof that you can never judge a book by its cover. Do you know what I mean?"

"Uhm, I just met him. I mean, I know what the phrase means, but not if you're asking about how it relates to Brock...should I?"

Ram shifted her eyes downward. Was she supposed to know something?

Elma took a sip of her beverage and patted her husband's knee. "Oh, never mind, you just got here. All I'm saying is he's a good one, and I'm sorry if I made you uncomfortable. Anyway, Earl and I have decided to offer you a friends-and-family discount. How does twelve hundred a month sound? If that's agreeable, then I'll leave this folder for you to complete."

"Wow, that's very nice. I'm grateful, but don't you need to do a credit check? Or call my past residence for a recommendation?"

"Oh, yes, we are thorough for everyone's protection. However, I've also spoken to Brenda, who vouched for you. Recommendations are always a bonus, but if something concerning comes up, we'll let you know. Please take your time and read the agreement. We want you to be comfortable too. There is a conditional thirty-day clause that allows both parties to terminate this agreement if it doesn't seem to be working out. The details are in there, and if you have any other questions, please let us know," Elma said, tossing her a wink.

Her emotions were off-kilter today. She felt tears pooling in the corner of her eyes, not from sadness, but a happiness that radiated from deep inside. It felt strange for people she barely knew to believe in her, to be willing to lend a helping hand simply because they valued others' input.

Her own mother chose to keep her distance because having a daughter crimped her lifestyle. She always seemed to be going on a date, and the men she liked were the ones who spent money on her. The problem was that the moment those guys found out she had a child at home, they left too, just like her father, who'd left her mother while she was pregnant. Her mom never hid those facts from her, and as Ram grew older, finding a man who had zero integrity didn't appeal to her. She had had a mom to raise when she was younger, and now, she got to focus on her life. *My life, my rules--a mantra I could live by.*

Decision made, she leaned forward to shake both their hands. "I'll take the unit. If I'm approved, can I move in a week from today?"

Elma checked the calendar and nodded. "That's fine. Here's a pen to complete the forms. This is our business card, with our cell phone number on the back. Please call with any questions or concerns."

Ram accepted the card. Then, she went to work listing her life's accomplishments and every identification number she had. When she finished, she gave the forms to Earl and headed toward her truck.

Her stomach rumbled, reminding her that she had skipped breakfast. When she flipped her wrist to check the time, she mentally picked the Conch Shell Café to try, maybe to serve as a tiny celebration because she'd found a place to live. Now the most significant task left was to find a job. If it took too long, she'd get some part-time jobs if necessary.

When she entered the restaurant, she immediately fell in love with the décor—a nice balance of ocean, sailboats, and seashells that perfectly completed the vibe. Yacht rock played in the background among the sounds of a busy restaurant during a crowded lunch hour. When it was her turn to approach the hostess stand, a waitress held up her index finger and pointed to an empty table in the back. She opened the menu and decided to try the daily special: conch chowder accompanied by a fresh salad of tuna, avocado, cilantro, and roasted corn.

The waitress dropped off her soda along with fresh, warm slices of sourdough bread. When her soup arrived a short time later, she slathered butter on a piece of bread. The soup smelled divine, and the first taste matched her initial observation. When the salad followed, it too was delicious. A foodie's delight that delivered on the promise of fresh local ingredients.

"Visitor or new in town?" her waitress asked while she picked up her empty plates.

Ram tossed her paper napkin into her empty bowl. "New. I'll be back here to work my way through the rest of the menu. The food is amazing."

"Glad you liked it. We have the best homemade cinnamon rolls in the morning, but get here early or they'll be gone. Where are you working?"

"I'm working on that one. Do you know anyone looking for an accountant?" The waitress scrunched up her nose and then hollered over her shoulder. "Helen, do you know anyone needing a numbers cruncher?"

"Nope, but have her drop off her resumé at the town's recruiting office inside the Destiny Township building, just down the street," Helen hollered before she disappeared into the kitchen.

Ram's waitress's face held satisfaction, like she had solved world hunger. "You can't miss the red brick building. They are open Monday through Friday and the first Saturday of every month. Mary knows all the connections. And if you also want the latest gossip, she's got it."

Ram nodded and thanked her for the information before plucking the bill off the table to review and pay it. It seemed she had one more stop to make before returning to the hotel.

What an excellent service for a small town to have a recruiting center. She wondered if all cities had such a service. With fingers crossed, maybe she would land a job sooner rather than later and be able to begin building her life again.

She only had to wait a few minutes before meeting with the woman in charge of the program. Ram had a slew of questions for the woman before she handed over the polished resumé she and Laney had updated before she left town. It wasn't that she had landed a job, but excitement flowed through her system. Progress made her giddy. Today had been a great day.

As she drove back to the hotel, she braked at the stop sign where she had to turn to take the long, winding road to the hotel. Parked off to the side on the shoulder was a work truck pulling a trailer. She also noticed the shirtless man, whose tanned back glistened from his labor, and the way his lean, powerful muscles bunched and contracted when he lifted a large branch into the chipper. She was held captive by the beauty of this man's body—a chiseled work of art that she was unaware of when she sat across from him while they ate dinner. Held captive by this view, she sat there watching until the harsh honk of a vehicle behind her jarred her from her daydreams.

The warmth from her embarrassment burned her insides. As fast as she could, she checked traffic as she lurched her truck forward, noticing that Brock had turned to see the commotion her ogling had caused. Great, she had zero doubt he knew who sat behind the wheel of her truck, piled high with all her worldly possessions. Now she was committed, so she had to pull over. Plus, she owed him a thanks for the apartment recommendation.

She lowered her window on the passenger side, waiting for him to approach. God, she hoped her cheeks weren't bright red from her embarrassment. "Hey, Brock, how's it going? I wanted to say thanks for putting in a good word for me with Earl and Elma. I found a place to stay."

Brock rested his forearm on the window frame and leaned forward. "I'm glad to hear it. I'm good, just getting caught up from Friday's ordeal."

An earthy scent mixed with fresh wood swirled inside her truck. "That's my fault. I hope you didn't get in trouble or anything since you're doing this today."

Brock flashed her a warm smile. "All is good."

"Can I help you out with any of this? I mean, fair is fair," Ram said before her brain had a chance to process what had just popped out of her mouth. Why the hell couldn't she just keep her thoughts to herself? It's not like helping everyone would make her mother see her value. However, offering to help Brock was the right thing to do.

"Nah, I'm about an hour away from finishing, but I appreciate the offer. I just have to collect all the smaller branches, which takes time."

Nope, she was doing this. She threw her transmission into park and killed her motor before opening her door and walking around the truck to face him. "Spoiler alert: I'm stubborn and I feel it's only right that I help. So give me an assignment because two hands equal lighter work, or whatever that saying is."

Brock straightened to his full height, making her feel so tiny in his presence. His gaze traveled her body, which had her skin reacting as if he'd touched her. When he finished, he tugged on the T-shirt that had been tucked into his back pocket. He slid it over his head and down his torso, which made her almost cry out in disappointment. This entire scene would not be shared with Laney or she'd never, ever hear the end of it. Oh no, this would be a memory she'd tuck away for herself to enjoy again later.

"I like your determination. There are a few safety things we need to cover first, if you'll follow me, please."

Determined steps moved him toward this truck, where he opened the door and scrounged around inside until he turned to her with gloves, vest, and hard hat. He motioned for her to put on the safety garb and then proceeded to the chipper.

"Now, have you ever worked a chipper?"

"No, but I know what they do," she answered while she tightened the headband inside the hat to fit her smaller head.

He waited until she was finished before he continued. "This button here is the emergency kill switch. I'll have you pile them here, off to my right. I'll be wearing earplugs, so if you need me, make this motion with your arm and I'll stop."

Ram listened to the rest of his safety debrief, nodding her head when necessary, a little amazed at how he looked so damn hot wearing his jeans, boots, and a hard hat. He nestled his bright orange earplugs into his ears and handed her a pair of her own in a sealed package from his pocket. Accepting the offering, she inserted the soft, moldable plastic and went to work gathering branches. About thirty minutes later, she had to stop to catch her breath and get a drink of water. The humidity and hot temperatures made this work extra hard. *Welcome to Florida,* she thought to herself.

She made the hand signal to Brock and, true to his word, he shut everything down in an instant to give her his complete attention. "Sorry, but I need a quick break."

"I've got cold water in my cooler," he said, walking toward the extended tailgate and hopping up on the lip so he could sit.

She did the same, accepting the cold bottle he produced from the cooler. It felt so good in her hand that she rolled it across the back of her neck, practically moaning in relief. He watched her the entire time. "Whew, it's hot. How do you do this work outside all the time?"

"Trust me, June is way better than mid-July to August. You condition your body to it. Don't make yourself too hot; I appreciate the help, but stop anytime you want."

She gulped down the rest of her water, tossing him the bottle. "Let's get moving. We're almost finished. I'm sure you have other things you need to accomplish today."

"Yes, ma'am," he said with a wink.

They finished the last of the work and packed his truck with all the supplies. The last thing he did was double-check the chipper, ensuring the hitch was secured. The partnership between them was easy and low-key, as if they had done this for years rather than mere hours. She figured that when people clicked, they clicked, and it didn't require a ton of practice.

"You're a taskmaster, Brock, but we did it! I'm off to the hotel for a dip in the pool. Have a good afternoon," she said on the way to her truck, feeling sticky from her own perspiration.

"Thanks again. Do a cannonball for me!" Brock hollered out.

She didn't trust herself to look backward, or she might have invited him to join her, although that would be senseless since he was still on the job. The tires of her truck crunched over rocks and dirt until they met the pavement.

When she glanced in the rearview mirror, her heart skittered at seeing him standing there, watching her drive away. Romantic entanglements were a no-no, but flirting with Brock came naturally. Friendship was a good place to focus. A person needed friends, and she wouldn't have to worry about losing the last shred of her dignity if things with him went south too.

She liked Destiny and didn't want to even think about leaving again.

Chapter Four

I T HAD BEEN A week since Brock had met Ram and only four days since he had last seen her, which felt like an eternity. He had been forced to savor the image of her wearing his hard hat. She had looked sexy as hell. The inside of it still held the faint scent of her almond-cherry shampoo. It was pathetic for sure, but he'd never had such a visceral reaction to another person before.

If he were being honest, it freaked him out. He craved her presence. That could be problematic because developing a relationship, whether friendship or more, meant sharing information. And his story wasn't the kind that people celebrated. It was the kind of stuff that made people avoid him, and he couldn't blame those who judged. A familiar ache that had plagued him for years had reared its ugly head.

The last thing he'd expected the other day was for her to pull over and help him, to repay his kindness in kind, but she did. She had impressed him with her work ethic; that type of loyalty, in his experience, was rare.

Man, he wished he'd taken a picture of her working. She had looked so adorable, yet competent as she snapped branches with her foot, arranging them in neat piles for him to send through the chipper. He appreciated that she didn't have to mindlessly chatter the entire time. She just worked alongside him in mutual silence.

He had waged war in his head over this need to see her. What would it hurt to invite her to lunch? This friendly gesture didn't need to mean anything beyond literally checking in on her. He could separate his desire from the equation. He knew the score, and he'd lost the right to anything deeper when he had destroyed his family. Now his head hurt from all this thinking, and he wanted that damn ache to recede. He had led a simple life before he had met the sexy, sweet, and amazing Ramona Fritz.

On autopilot from the hardware store, he made a U-turn on the road and headed toward the Sapphire Hotel instead of back to his job for the day. He pulled into the circular drive and signaled to the valet he'd only be a minute.

"Hi, Brock," the front desk worker said as he approached.

"Will you call Ramona Fritz's room for me?"

The clerk picked up the phone, pointing toward the house phone. "I'll dial her room."

He moved to the phone and lifted the receiver. The line rang twice before her voice came across the line, making him smile. "It's Brock. You up for a little lunch today?"

There was no hesitation, which caused his chest to puff up from his excitement. "Yes, where should I meet you?"

"I'm in the lobby. Come on down and I'll drive."

The moment she entered the lobby, the rest of the world melted away. An odd sensation, but nonetheless true, as he watched her walk toward him, a radiant woman wearing a bright blue-colored sun dress with white sandals that showed off bright pink toenails. He looked down to see his dirty work boots, jeans, and long-sleeved T-shirt branded with the Destiny township logo. He was relieved that she didn't appear to be concerned that he had just come from working outside.

"You made my day. Where are we going?" she asked, her voice matching her enthusiasm, which did crazy things inside his body.

He extended his arm in front of himself to allow her to lead. When she passed, he placed his hand at the small of her back as he followed her to his truck. "I thought I'd take you to a favorite place of mine. I'll warn you up front, it's not fine dining."

When they reached his truck, he hesitated. Indecision wracked his brain. If this were a date, he'd open the door, but it wasn't a date, right? More like two people who were friendly, eating lunch. Why was he making this so hard?

The clunk of the passenger door had his head turning to see her jumping up and onto the seat. Relief swamped his system. Her action saved him from his internal debate. Still, this whole scenario left him on edge. Why? They were becoming friends; Wasn't that good enough? Didn't she deserve to be treated like the lady she was?

He blew out a frustrated breath to clear his head. When he slid behind the wheel, he forced himself to look forward. He needed a few moments to pull his head out of his ass and get this lunch back on track. Two friends eating lunch at one of his favorite places. Done.

"You okay?" she asked with a bit of concern lacing her words.

He turned left on the main road, leaving the hotel to take them to the pier. "Yup. I had a flash that I was missing a meeting, but realized it was tomorrow. Work has been busy."

The rest of the short ride was spent talking about trivial things as storm clouds formed. When he turned into the pier, he parked and escorted her down the docks towards the boats until he turned to the right and followed the pier out to the end. In front of them were crystal blue waters, with a light breeze whipping through his hair, bringing with it the salty brine from the sea. It was a beautiful day, even with the mix of white and gray puffy clouds.

"May I introduce you to Flip Flops, a fish taco stand that catches its own fish? Everything they serve is fresh and delicious," Brock explained.

"Wow...is all I can say. This view is splendid, and the food smells delicious," Ram said and pulled at a strand of hair stuck to her glossed lips to tuck it behind her ear. "What do you recommend?"

"All of it. Order when you're ready," he urged, pointing to the free-standing daily specials chalkboard. He waited to place his order until she was ready.

She studied the board and then turned to place her order. "I'll have the Taco Tuesday special."

"Great choice." He winked at her, pulling out his wallet, before turning to place his own order. "Make it two and two large iced teas."

"I'll buy mine," she said.

"Nope, I've got it. It's my turn to thank you with food," he replied, enjoying the look on her face. "It's my treat. Your help the other day went above and beyond, and I enjoy your company. I mean, who else is going to get you acclimated to all that Destiny has to offer?"

"Good point, and the fastest way to my heart is through food," she elbowed him lightly in the side as she moved toward the counter to pull out some napkins from the holder.

"That will be thirty-five dollars," the cashier said before turning back to shout out their order to the man working in the back.

Brock pulled his credit card from his wallet when the lady informed him it was cash only today because their card readers weren't working. He winced when he pulled the bill section open to see it was empty. He had used the last of his cash the other night when they were together. He closed his eyes for a moment as his body temperature rose. *Damn it.*

Ram nudged his arm, handing him some cash. "Here, this covers the tab and tip. I'm going to find us a place to sit. You get our food."

He appreciated that she'd just glossed over the fact that he didn't have any money. Embarrassment had to be staining his face. He hated the debt he owed and that his wages were garnished. The sooner he had that paid off, the better, because it seemed like his discretionary funds were always low. It was a topic he did not like to speak about. Ever.

Turning his head, he saw her facing the ocean with her hair blowing behind her. She radiated beauty and compassion, looking like a siren perched on the bench. When he heard their number called, he grabbed additional napkins, straws, and the tray containing their lunch.

He slid the tray across the table. "Thanks for the save back there. I haven't had time to hit the bank since our dinner."

"Don't worry about it. It's not like you knew it was cash only today. I'm starving, let's see how this place stacks up against the Conch Café. My lunch the other day was amazing."

Pleased that she didn't seem upset and more than happy to let the topic go, he asked her about the café. "I think you'll be happy, but it might be hard to pick a winner since both are damn good. I'm glad you're getting out and discovering Destiny."

She squeezed fresh lime juice on her tacos and took a bite before she answered. A moan of satisfaction tore from her lips, which had him staring right at her as she chewed. "These are heaven."

"Indeed, they are. Wait until you try the chicken-fried lobster platter. It's a special that they don't have too often, but it's out of this world," Brock said around a bite.

"Okay, you had me at chicken fried to be honest."

Brock took a sip of his drink. "Any updates on the job search?"

She wiped her mouth with a napkin. "No, not yet, which isn't ideal. There was one interview I was so excited about, but I didn't get it. I also got a call from one of the local car dealers looking to hire a finance person. I declined that one because I really don't want to work in that industry or those hours. I hope that decision doesn't bite me in the ass."

"I can't blame you there. Well, that just means the right job is coming," Brock said before he inhaled his last taco.

"I love your enthusiasm. I hope you're right. I move into my apartment on Monday, and I had hoped to have a job by then. I mean, I know it all takes time, but I'm an overachiever," she said with a giggle.

"Do you need any help with moving? I could stop by after work, to help carry things or whatever else is needed?"

Ram wiped her hands on her napkin, her shoulders relaxed. "That would be great. It's on the second floor, but everything I have is in the back of my pickup, so I don't think it will take too long. What time were you thinking?"

"How about three-thirty? I'll meet you at the complex."

"Thanks, Brock. I'm so excited to move in," she said, picking up the tray and dumping the trash into the receptacle.

They strolled back to the truck so he could return her to the hotel. On the drive back to the hotel, a brief rain shower pelted his truck. He had an irrigation replacement he had to finish, so this afternoon's storm would delay him a little. The township had finally approved his proposal and found the budget needed to replace all the old and cracked polyline with PVC piping in the common areas. Mentally, he went through all the things he needed to accomplish between now and Monday, so he could be at her place on time. He typically didn't like to work on the weekends, but in this case, he'd make an exception.

He guided his truck around the circular drive and slid the gearshift into park.

"You want to wait until the rain stops?" he asked.

"No, I like the rain. It's so beautiful, but this high humidity is brutal."

He nodded his head. "Thanks for joining me. I'll see you Monday."

"I loved lunch—thanks for including me. I'll see you then," she said, disappearing inside the main doors.

B ROCK'S EYES THREATENED TO close while he stood under the hot stream of water. He was beat. He had worked extra-long hours over the weekend wrapping up his project so he could be at Ram's place on time today. Of course, the remainder of his week exploded with additional urgent needs, but he would deal with those tomorrow.

He turned off the tap when his fingers started to shrivel. After he toweled himself dry, he brushed his teeth, shaved, and finished getting dressed. Since her unit had a staircase, he decided to wear a pair of cargo shorts, a T-shirt, and sneakers. He grabbed his ice chest that he'd stuffed with water and soda and ran down the mental list of items he'd composed during his shower. Satisfied he had everything, he stowed the cooler on the passenger's floorboard of his blue F-150 truck.

When he turned into the driveway of High Tide Apartments, he drove towards the marina and parked right next to Ram's vehicle. He saw her waving from the walkway as she descended the stairs toward him. He could get used to this sight and the warmth that suffused his body that followed.

"You're here right on time," she greeted with a huge smile on her face. His tired muscles, refueled by adrenaline, bounced to life.

His hand covered his heart as he plastered his best sorrowful expression on his face. "You doubted me?"

"Nah, never you, Brock. Come on, I have a surprise for you first. Then I'm working you to exhaustion."

His cooler was forgotten as he followed her upstairs, intrigued by the idea of her surprising him. He couldn't remember the last time he had been surprised. Well, clarifying that in his mind, a pleasant surprise.

She paused outside her front door before turning back to him to stand off to the side.

"Open the door and tell me what you smell?" She practically hopped from one foot to the other.

Okay, not the kind of surprise he thought he was getting. Although he still had no idea what she had in store for him. "Uh, is this the whole 'this smells bad, so you smell it' kind of thing?"

"Go on, scaredy cat," she taunted.

When he opened the door, he prepared for the worst. When he inhaled the mouth-watering savory smell of garlic, butter, and Italian herbs, it was far from what he expected. He turned back to her, his eyebrows scrunched as he tried to process how she'd managed to cook all of this. "Yum, but how did you find the time to do this?"

She practically floated on air as she passed him to enter the kitchen. "I love to cook and decided what better way to break in my new kitchen on the first day in my apartment than to make homemade lasagna and garlic bread? I wanted to reward all your hard work with a proper home-cooked meal. So, I stocked the refrigerator earlier and went to work on this so it can bake while we unload. I bought a few supplies at the store to accomplish this task, along with the food. But don't get too excited, because we're going to eat this on paper plates."

His mouth dropped open. She had rendered him speechless with her gesture. He didn't even know where to begin. A home-cooked meal hadn't happened for him in years, and the fact that she wanted to surprise him made all of it even better.

"You're spoiling me. I'd better earn my dinner, so let's get started. Lead the way, Ram."

He followed her out the door, and for the next two hours, they unloaded her truck and arranged the small amount of furniture she had brought with her. When they finished, she brought him a beer and then worked in the kitchen to finish dinner. The one thing he noticed that she didn't have was a bed and a mattress.

"Where are you going to sleep?" he asked. The tab of the beer she had offered him hissed when he popped it back.

"I left mine behind. I didn't want to bring that one with me. There are a few pieces of furniture I need to purchase, so I'll get a new one at some point. Tonight's dinner will be served on the coffee table. You can choose to sit on the floor or sofa according to your preference."

He nodded and took a seat on the sofa. A part of him liked the idea that she hadn't brought along the bed that she'd shared with her boyfriend. He closed his eyes while he waited for dinner to be ready. A nudge at his shoulder had him popping his eyes open.

"Sorry to startle you. You dozed off, but dinner is served."

He wiped his hand over his eyes and stood. She had set up their dinner spread across the bar top buffet-style. Everything looked delicious as he grabbed a plate, loaded it with lasagna, salad, and garlic bread.

"You want another beer or red wine?" she asked, pulling the cork out of a wine bottle she was opening.

"The wise answer is water or a soda, if you have it. I'm so tired that another beer wouldn't be good with driving."

She shooed him from the kitchen. "Go sit and eat. I'll bring your soda."

Once she handed him his drink, she sat cross-legged on the floor. "Isn't this place great?"

"It really is. I really appreciate you doing this for me. Your lasagna is the best I've had in years."

"You've never dated a woman who knew how to cook before? You'll have to work on closing that gap since you like to eat." She laughed, scooping another bite into her mouth. "Was your mom a good cook?"

He paused, going back in time to think about the question. He found himself being forced to open the door to the past that he had tried to bury, all because of Ram's innocent question.

"I would say a decent cook, but Mom dedicated her menu items to finding ways to use everything without much waste. My family lived paycheck to paycheck. We ate a lot of canned fruits and vegetables from her gardens when we were growing up. But because my parents were frugal, they built a modest savings account that they used for vacations and presents. They were good parents, and for that, I'm grateful."

"I get it. My mom never had a lot of money either. She didn't really want to be a mom, thought I cramped her style. You know, aged her because guys didn't want a woman whose title also included mother. She stayed until I was an adult. Then, when I turned eighteen," Ram made air quotes. "It was time to move out so she could get her life back on track. So, that's what I did."

Brock watched her tell the story like it wasn't as horrible as it sounded. "Do you even talk today? What about your father?"

"Oh, we talk—twice a year on her birthday and Christmas Day. You know, the basics, like what she's been doing, who she's dating, or the wrongs she's been forced to survive. I haven't seen her since my eighteenth birthday. My father, I was told, loved the process of making a baby, but the actual raising of a baby part had him running in the opposite direction."

A sudden surge of anger and disappointment coursed through Brock's body. Unprepared for the mix of feelings, he remained silent. How could anyone treat this marvelous woman that way? She was so full of life and radiated happiness. Man, if he were lucky enough to have her by his side, he'd cherish her. He'd vow to always be there for her, to never let her down, because he'd learned that lesson the hard way and had paid the price every day since.

He sighed. "Um...I ah...don't really know what to say. That's bullshit, and I'm sorry they let you down. It's not right, Ram."

She stood, adding his empty plate to hers. "You sound like my best friend, Laney. She gets her panties all twisted about it, too. I think it's because she has the ideal storybook parents."

He nodded, thinking about his mom and dad. He had had great parents, but he'd wasted valuable time when they were alive, staying away from home to focus on achieving a lifestyle that was the complete opposite of theirs. His heart ached. Now, he'd give anything to tell them he was wrong.

It was late, and he needed to go before he did something to remove that look on her face and show her she meant something to him, like pull her into his arms and hug her.

"Can I help with the dishes or anything before I leave?"

"No, I've got it. Besides, you moved all this stuff for me. Go home and get some sleep. Exhaustion isn't a good look on you," she replied, heading to the front door.

At least she was smiling again. "Hey, I've got a contract over at the Burn Sand Estate tomorrow to design an over-the-top garden display in the backyard. I'd love to get your thoughts on my idea. Afterward, we can head to their private beach and enjoy the afternoon."

She rested her head against the door frame, her right toes balanced on the top of her left foot. "I'd like that. What the heck is the Burn Sand Estate?"

"You'll have to wait and see."

"Okay, I like a good mystery, but don't you work tomorrow?"

He smiled, liking that she just went straight to the point. "I took tomorrow off for this project. It's a big one that I run through my side business. I occasionally do contract work. So can I pick you up at eleven?"

At her acceptance, he turned to head down the stairs to his truck. When the door behind him clicked closed, he exhaled. Exhaustion must have been affecting his emotions. Being with her was easy, and when it came time to leave it always felt wrong, because the moment he left, he missed her. Damn, he had to figure this whole thing out because it didn't matter what they did, they always had fun together. He needed to compose himself and stop with all these...whatever they were...because the bottom line was that they were friends. Right?

Chapter Five

RAM WENT THROUGH THE motions of doing the dishes while her brain spun out of control. Even her body ached, and not from the physical exertion of the move. Nope, she ached in all the right places. She used the back of her hand to rub her nose and sighed. She dried the last pan, staring out the kitchen window. Brock confused her. Being with him was easy, and everything wasn't all about him.

She wanted him.

Wait, what?

Scratch that, she can't want him.

I never want to feel used again. What George did to me hurt. It's that simple.

Laney's distinct ringtone ripped through her musings, and she cringed. There was no way she could talk to her tonight. If she did, she'd cave and tell her about Brock, along with her traitorous desires. When it involved men, Laney would always side with romance. Her friend fiercely believed that everyone deserved their own happily-ever-after.

The problem Ram had now with that philosophy was the fact that her ex had killed that notion, obliterating her heart in the process. She needed time tonight to build up her defenses so she could make good decisions where Brock was concerned. No, she'd call her tomorrow.

After spending the day with Brock, because I like him. Holy smokes, what the hell is wrong with me? Oh, right, ding, ding, ding...I like him.

Padding toward the hall closet, she grabbed her pillow and blanket. The sofa would be her bed until she got around to buying a new mattress. She snatched her cellphone off the counter. On its display, she noticed she had two voicemails. Pressing the button, she listened to words that made her chest pump with excitement. The Tipsy Pelican needed an accountant. She scrambled back to the counter to scribble down the number to call back to confirm the interview for Wednesday. Giddiness overtook her body, making her clap her hands while she twirled around in circles until she plopped down on her sofa.

She set her alarm on her phone as happiness bubbled out of her pores. If she landed this job, she would be on her way to rebuilding her life. And maybe, fingers crossed, this would be the last time she had to completely start over again. She liked Destiny and could see herself having a future here. She nestled down and closed her eyes.

Tomorrow, she would get to see Brock and watch him in action. He truly had talent, but the fact that he had asked for her opinion flattered her.

T UESDAY MORNING, BROCK ARRIVED right on time. Ram had chosen to wait for him on the balcony to avoid any delays since he was meeting with a client. The moment she saw him, she waved and headed toward his truck. He had barely stopped before she had the door open, handing him her bag. He looked good in his board shorts, tank top, and flip-flops. His tanned and toned arms were on full display, and she enjoyed watching his muscles bunch and flex with every move.

"Morning, Ram. How was the first night in your place?"

She secured her seat belt. "Amazing. It's such a cool apartment, with all those upgrades. Now, a bed would be better, but no complaints. I must say, you look refreshed."

He flicked on the turn signal. "A great meal and sleep can do that for a man."

His comment soaked her brain. *A super-hot and handsome man.* She liked that her meal had meant something to him.

She pulled the visor down to block some of the sun from piercing her eyes while she stared out the passenger window, taking in the views of the marina. When he turned down another road that bordered the ocean, she had a feeling that whoever owned this place had uninhibited views of the ocean.

"Hey, what do you know about The Tipsy Pelican?" she asked without taking her eyes off the gorgeous view of white sand and crystal blue waves in the distance.

"It's a dive bar in town, but I should say, it's *the bar.* The locals love it, but so do the tourists. It's got live music, great food, and a fun beach vibe. Why?"

She turned to face him. "Is it sketchy? Like, I shouldn't go to the interview on Wednesday?"

"No, not at all. It's one of the busiest bars in town. In fact, the owners, Rick and Beth, are great people."

He rolled down his window to access a gate code box standing to the side of an enormous iron gate. After he punched in a code, she heard the grind of a motor while the elegant barrier parted. When the space was large enough for his truck, he drove onto the property until they reached a circular driveway in front of an enormous, garish mansion and stopped.

"This is Burn Sand," he said, sweeping his hand across the front windshield. "It's a hard one to describe. The owners, Bernadette and Sanderson, are on a yearlong cruise."

"Wow, it's...large and...so bright with all the teal and orange accent colors. They must have lots of money." Ram ducked down in her seat to crane her neck upward to see the top of the house. "Uh, where do you sail for that long?"

The faint sound of his laughter had her turning her head in his direction. "All of those statements are accurate. The name of the cruise is The World, so I'm guessing every damn place on earth."

She nodded, tilting her head toward her shoulder. "So, you have free rein on design, or did they give some parameters?"

"I'll answer that in a minute. Grab your stuff. I'll take care of the business part, and then we can head down to their beach. You may meet Drew. He's their caretaker who lives in a boat on their dock. He also performs at the Pelican."

She grabbed her bag, sliding from the truck and walking around to the driver's side. He reached into the bed, grabbing two bags himself. She followed him through another ornate gate into the backyard. There was a pool, gazebo, eating area, and U-shaped covered patio just off the house, along with several marble statues of various Greek Gods. If she stood with her back to the home, facing the center of the yard, toward the cliff edge, a large grassy area overlooked the ocean—a breathtaking view. Both sides of the yard were adorned with beautifully maintained mini hedge pathways, complete with fountains in the centers of each.

"Oh my gosh, this is spectacular." She pointed to the ocean, then pulled her phone out of her shorts to snap a few pictures. "You can see for miles."

He set his bags down and pulled out a tape measure and a notepad with a binder clip on it. "Bernie shared her vision but stressed for way longer than it took to share the details of it. Her tastes are eclectic. She wants this middle area transformed into something magical, something that produces a lot of oohs and aahs.

She dropped her bag next to Brock's stuff. "Brock, you're so talented. I love all of this. Okay, so with zero pressure, knowing that you knocked it out of the park the last time, dazzle me with your creative genius. Let's hear the plan."

He took several big steps, counting to some measurement in his head. When he finished walking in an oval pattern, he explained that this area would mimic a coral reef. He then stood in several other spots to demonstrate where he wanted to place the pod of topiary dolphins jumping out of the water over the reef at various heights. His main goal was not to block the spectacular view of the ocean. He bent to retrieve his pad to show her his drawing, and on the following pages were the various plants and flowers. He'd selected colorful plants and flowers that provided texture, bringing the reef to life right down to the sprinkler system he would install to keep everything lush and vibrant.

"So, what do you think?" he asked.

She accepted the proffered pad, flipping through the pages. "Holy crap, I love it. Oh, I love Bird of Paradise. You could create additional depth and texture by adding some lobster claw plants. Have you considered incorporating plumerias, given their long blooming season? Or even adding a few agave plants around the perimeter to create the outline?"

"I like your ideas for creating more depth. I think I'll add some coral honeysuckle too. Thanks, Ram."

"Those are pretty. Promise me that you'll bring me back when you're finished."

"It's a date," he winked.

"Do you build your topiary frames?" she asked.

"Yes, I do. I find the work cathartic," he said. He bent down, giving her a nice view of his ass while he dug out a tape measure. "Will you write down some measurements?"

"Sure," she answered.

The tape made its wobbly metal sound as he extended and retracted it. Between measuring, he called out the numbers. She wrote everything down, and once he finished, she smiled at him, handing him back the pad and pencil.

"Thanks for your help. You ready for some sand and waves?"

He stuffed his supplies back into one of his bags and grabbed the rest. He walked toward the far edge of the property, where she saw the start of a wooden staircase. After traversing down two flights of stairs, they stood on the private beach. Off to the left, she saw the dock and boat he'd mentioned earlier. She wondered if the owners even appreciated all this beauty, or was it just an expectation?

When she turned to ask him a question, every word she knew flew right out of her head. Brock had stripped off his tank top and stood there barefoot wearing his trunks low on his hips. She took in his muscular and sculpted abdomen, along with those sexy v-lines that disappeared underneath his waistband. Every part of her body roared to life, and all she could do was stare.

"What? You started to say something," Brock said.

Please don't let him realize I'm drooling from the sight of him. That would just make the day awkward. What was she going to say? She had to say something, but all rational thoughts had dried up. She blinked, but he just stood there watching her. Not trusting what would come out of her mouth, so she tugged her shirt over her head, peeled off her shorts to reveal the bathing suit she wore underneath, and dashed for the water.

The moment the cold water penetrated her warm skin, her brain cleared, making her feel more in control. Another splash had her looking over her shoulder just as his body disappeared into the waves. It wasn't more than a few seconds before he popped up right in front of her, bobbing in the water.

Thankfully, he didn't ask her again about what she'd left unsaid. Instead, he flashed a huge grin and splashed a big wall of water in her direction. She retaliated, and before long, the moment ebbed into a loud ruckus of water and laughter. When a large wave smacked her in the face, catching her off guard, she coughed and choked on a mouthful of salty water.

Strong arms encircled her midsection, dragging her against a solid chest. "Hey, I've got you. You, okay?"

"I-I..." she sputtered, followed by some other guttural noise.

She gripped his shoulders while she tried to clear her throat and slow her breathing. The shore moved closer as he moved toward it. The easy pleasure of being in his arms and under his care while she recovered hit her square in the chest. There was no spectacle, no "who's-watching-me?" moment, like something her ex would orchestrate. Instead, there was only a man who jumped into action and expected nothing. He just reacted to protect her because he cared.

"Thank you," she said, pushing out of his hold. "I think I'm good, although I taste the briny ocean water."

He grabbed her hand, tugging her out of the wake and onto the firm sand. In these moments, it felt natural, as if they were a tight-knit unit who anticipated each other's needs and wants thanks to years of experience. There was no doubt in her mind that he would protect her. Had she ever felt that way before with Jerko-ex? *An easy answer: not even a tiny bit.*

"You could be picking sand out of your teeth," he teased, his face distorted with mock detest. "I've got a little something that might help."

He strode toward his bags and squatted. His large hand disappeared inside a bag until he pulled out an oversized towel and spread it across the sand. Next, he retrieved a small cooler along with a big thermos. Her heart fluttered against her chest like a schoolgirl enjoying her first crush. He did this for her, and it made her happy––like giddy happy. There were no grand, expensive gestures or promises. Just simple actions that mattered.

"Oh, I love surprises! What did you bring?" she asked, knowing her voice had risen an octave.

The side of his mouth ticked upward as he gave her a sexy look of all-knowing male satisfaction. She wasn't going to lie—that did something to her insides.

"I'm no chef, but I've been told my tuna salad is legendary. I think it's the fresh dill, but we'll have to see what you think. I also made homemade lemonade."

She clapped her hands before she realized what she was doing and decided she didn't care how she looked. This would be one of the best lunches she would ever have, and she would lock this memory away in her brain's lifetime bucket. Again, he did this for her, because it made him happy. The stark differences between Brock and George overwhelmed her senses in the best way.

"Ooh, I love picnics. You are so thoughtful. I can't believe you did this for us."

"You're worth it." He opened the box and handed her a bag with a sandwich and another with red grapes. His face morphed into something like worry. "Shoot, I forgot the plastic cups. You okay with sharing?"

"Fine with me," she said. She pulled her sandwich free from the plastic bag. The first bite tasted amazing. Flavors of lemon, fresh dill, pickle, and mustard burst to life in her mouth as she chewed. Moaning her satisfaction, she flashed him a big grin. "Yup, Brock's tuna is a masterpiece."

His eyes danced at her compliment. "I can live with that."

They ate in silence, admiring the view of crystal blue waters and the melodic sounds of the waves rolling against the white sandy beach. When they finished eating and cleaned up their trash, she kicked her legs out, leaned back, and propped her body up with her hands. The warmth from the sand soaked into her flesh, but when he mimicked her actions and his hand connected with her own, fireworks danced in her stomach.

She rolled her head toward him and bit her bottom lip. Just maybe she would be able to hold herself together by doing that. The intensity of his gaze had her heart pounding against her chest. How, after only a handful of encounters, could this man unravel her carefully crafted shield? Could life be that unfair? Could this be the real deal after such a disastrous one?

After several long moments, he leaned forward, framing her face with one hand, and pressed a kiss to her lips. The tender moment flowed into a toe-curling kiss that caused her belly to flip with anticipation. When he pulled back, he smiled before returning his attention back to the ocean, allowing her a reprieve from her emotions and thoughts. She didn't know how long they sat there with their fingers entwined, but the one thing she did know, it would never be long enough.

The clouds started to roll closer to the shoreline, and the waves intensified.

"Looks like Mother Nature is giving us a signal that a storm is coming," she said, sitting upright and breaking the connection.

He nodded in agreement. Bags in hand, he followed as she headed toward the stairs leading them back to his truck. The moment he shifted into reverse, the first giant plops of rain pelted his truck, creating a symphony of natural forces. The sun's rays streaked through dark gray clouds, and the air was salty and fresh. God, she loved Florida. Maybe not the bugs, but everything else made her happy, including the storms.

"Thanks for coming and sharing your thoughts on Burn Sand. I'm sorry you didn't get to meet anyone, but you will at some point."

She leaned toward him, pointing out his side window. "Look, that store next to the Sun-Sand-Books is for lease. Wow, that just happened."

He glanced sideways. "Yup, I think they are closing down after the Fourth of July weekend. They were from the East Coast, and they only had the tourist shop for a few years, but I heard something about the husband needing to move to a drier climate in the Southwest or something like that. They'd only been here for a few years, but that tourist shop was always busy.

She sat back in her seat and exhaled. Brenda's words came back to the forefront of her mind, that Destiny didn't have a local florist. That spot would be outstanding for a flower shop, right between the Conch Shell and Sun-Sand-Books, the local book nook. She could fill a void in the town by doing something she loved. Instead of feeling overwhelmed by the possibility of starting her own business someday, she found herself diving into the minutia of making it happen. She hadn't even realized the truck had stopped until Brock shifted in his seat.

"Someone zoned out on me. Do you want to share what's put that look of joy on your face?"

Energy and excitement vibrated through her body. "Not yet, but I will. I promise."

"I'm going to hold you to that. Whatever it is, it has you all worked up. I like that look on you."

She reached over and wrapped her arms around him. He didn't hesitate, wrapping her up tight in return. This day had been perfect. She enjoyed the easy camaraderie and how he made her feel, like she was precious, but that he didn't need to smother or set boundaries.

When she pulled back to look at him, she bit her lip for a moment. "You've got yourself a deal."

His gaze penetrated deep into her eyes, and if she wasn't mistaken, the beat of his heart sped up. His head dipped a moment before the soft warmth of his lips fluttered against hers. She trailed her hand up his neck and held him tight. What had started out as a sweet, tender kiss morphed into a deep melding of lips and tongue. She gave herself freely to the passion of the moment and what was yet to come. His kiss sang through her heart, and nothing up to this point in her life had felt this natural.

When he stopped, he pressed a kiss to the tip of her nose. "You're exquisite, Ram."

"You're not bad yourself. Thanks for another amazing day," she whispered against his lips.

She sat upright and grabbed her bag before she exited the cab. Dashing up the steps to her apartment, she knew he'd wait until she was safely inside her unit before he left. She locked her door and stowed her stuff on the counter. Butterflies had taken flight in her system and her lips still tingled from his touch.

Oh, man, she had to call Laney. She had so much to share, right down to the fact that she wanted Brock, which worried her because could he be another mistake? She sat down on the sofa and curled her legs underneath her.

Ram's bestie was the only caller listed in her favorites list, and she answered on the first ring. "I guess I'll call off the wellness check with the Destiny Police Department. Geez, Ram, I was getting worried."

She cringed at the concern in her friend's voice. "I'm sorry. I'm fine. In fact, I'm better than fine because I just had a marvelous day."

"OMG, did you sleep with Brock? Details, Ram, I need details."

She couldn't help but laugh. "No, I didn't sleep with him, but we kissed. Like the best kiss I've ever had. It literally made all my body parts excited." She ignored Laney's catcalls on the other end. "I thought things with jerk-o were good, but his kisses sucked compared to Brock's."

"I love a good panty-melting kiss. It's an indescribable pleasure. I'm jealous, Ram. Just another reason in the growing list that George wasn't the one. What else happened today, aside from smooching?"

"He's a landscape architect and he's brilliant. I'm going to text you some pictures of his work. Today, he showed me his latest project and then, we had a picnic lunch on the beach that he made for me."

"Ah, how romantic! That's wonderful. I'm happy for you."

Ram twirled her hair around her finger. "I'm confused, Laney. I'm not the best judge of character. What if he hurts me?"

"Ram, stop it. You dated an asshole. Every person who dates has been hurt in one way or the other, but that doesn't mean everyone is bad. You learn from it and move forward. And you don't let them have access to your money, honey."

"I know. I still can't believe I was that gullible. You think I would have learned to be more sensible after watching my mother all those years. I just...you know, I wanted to believe he was the one, but in the end, he used me. I'm tired of being used," Ram's voice wobbled.

"I love you, Ram. You know I'm not pushing you to jump into another relationship until you are ready. But you are not your mom, and her fucked up life isn't because she didn't love you. Your mom is a selfish woman who puts herself first. Just like George, who was a gigantic dickwad who didn't deserve you. I, for one, cherish every day with you and consider myself lucky our paths crossed."

"Thanks, Laney, I love you too. I just need you to keep my head on straight."

"Easy peasy, my friend. You are a beautiful soul who will find a forever match worthy of you. I believe that with every fiber of my being. You can't control the how or when, but you must be open to the possibility when it presents itself. Now, tell me everything so I can live vicariously through you."

Ram spent the next thirty minutes telling Laney all about Brock and how they'd spent their time together. It didn't go unnoticed that just telling her about him made her happy. "I like him, Laney," she said.

"I can tell. That's awesome. Don't listen to your head—especially about the past--unless it's a good concern. Listen to your heart and enjoy yourself. I miss you."

"I miss you, too. You need to move here."

"Well, moving isn't an option, at least at this point. How about a visit over the Fourth of July weekend? Then you can introduce me to Mr. Sexy Kisses in person."

Ram groaned. "Why did I tell you that? I swear I forget who I'm talking to at times. You can only come if you promise not to embarrass me—and never, ever, call him that. Please."

"I make no promises," Laney replied.

"Oh, I almost forgot, I have an interview on Wednesday for an accounting position."

"That's great news. See, everything is working out. Good luck and call me after your interview," Laney said.

When the line went silent, she rested her chin on the phone, thinking. Laney had been right, comparing Brock to George was wrong. He didn't deserve to be labeled the same way. She couldn't remember the last time her ex had acted like a gentleman or did something for someone else. Sure, he'd made her the center of his world, but looking back, that just meant she did everything for him.

She wasn't going to waste one more second on the past. Instead, she wanted to focus on her future and Brock. And if things went sideways, she could cut him loose before she risked another failure.

Chapter Six

RAM WALKED INTO THE Tipsy Pelican bright and early on Wednesday morning. She knew she'd be early, but that gave her an excuse to look around the famous dive bar. The smell of hops mixed with a subtle cleaning agent filled the air. The darkened interior matched the nautical vibe, including the nautical décor. She smiled at the wood-carved, paint-chipped pelicans and then at the fish netting and buoys hanging from the ceiling. The wooden tables were scarred from years of patrons and drinking adventures. There was a small stage off to one side, and a long bar sat on the opposite wall.

"Morning. You must be Ram?" a cheery female voice asked from behind the well. When Ram nodded, the other woman continued. "I'm Beth."

"Nice to meet you. I'm excited to be here. I've read most of the posts and reviews. This place is a special institution to the community."

"It is. I think the live music helps to keep it going. Drew Slater is our resident act, but we also bring in talent from all over the world. Plus, the T-shirts and tanks are quite popular. It always makes me smile when my husband and I travel and see someone wearing one." Beth motioned for her to come to the bar. "Grab a seat. My day bartender is coming in late today, so I must prep the bar for her."

Ram knew the importance of dressing for success, but suddenly felt she had overdone it today with the beige pantsuit and red sleeveless blouse underneath the blazer she had chosen. She peeled the blazer off and slung it over the back of the seat.

"Is there anything I can do to assist you while we talk?" Ram asked, looking around at all the chairs sitting upside down atop the tables.

"I like an all-in girl. We've gotta stick together, especially with my husband, Rick, and his brother always causing trouble."

"Are you bad-mouthing me to our potential new accountant?" a deep baritone voice asked from the doorway. The sunlight shining brightly behind him blacked out the man's face and body. He made his way to the bar, extending his hand to Ram. "I'm Rick, the luckiest man in the world because I can claim her as my better half."

"See, Ram, you train them early. That's the key," Beth said, before leaning further over the counter and shielding the side of her mouth with one hand. "He's a keeper."

She loved their banter. They made a handsome couple. There was zero doubt that they were in love. Working here would be fun, and she had the impression that it would be a tight-knit community, which appealed to her. Her only concern was whether this bar was big enough to afford her salary. If not, perhaps she could find employment at a few places to earn a comparable income to her past earnings. She pulled out her notepad and retrieved her pen from her purse, anxious to get down to it.

She listened while Beth and Rick gave her a rundown of their operation—from the liquor to the food, employees, insurance, merchandise, entertainment, and advertising. While they tag teamed their overview, Ram asked clarifying questions on a few points and jotted down some notes. When they shared their income statement, she sat back, impressed. She had no idea this place generated that much business.

"We read your resumé and performed our due diligence, which included Brenda's glowing review. So tell us about you."

"I'm starting over in Destiny, and my goal is to make this place my home. There's something special about this place. I've never experienced anything like it, so it's hard to pinpoint without sounding a little flaky—which I'm not. I have a dream that has recently materialized that I want to pursue. I found the perfect place, but I need time to build my capital. So, I'm laying down roots and hope to be a part of this community for a long time."

Rick gripped Ram's shoulder. "I've always told my wife that there's a reason why we call it Destiny. I think you've found yours."

Beth swiped a white cloth down the center of the bar, leaving a streak of moisture in its wake. "We can offer you eighty-five thousand a year to start, plus benefits. Although you look magnificent, the dress code is casual, and hours can be flexible, with remote options available. I'll show you where your office is located, if you accept."

Ram tried hard not to bounce in her seat. The salary was higher than she'd anticipated. The flexible hours were a bonus, which made her even happier. "You've got a new accountant."

"Excellent. Now my husband needs to work the counter so I can take our new employee back to her office to complete the paperwork and give her the tour of the best bar in Destiny."

Ram pushed back her chair and stood so she could shake Rick's hand. After she scooped up her jacket and notepad, she followed Beth behind a door to a set of offices in the back. She sucked down a deep breath, taking in the surroundings. When Beth opened the door, Ram looked at the large space, which held a standing desk and a comfortable-looking ergonomic chair, as well as multiple windows that gave her a lovely view of the pier.

She snapped her gaze to Beth. "This is my office or yours?"

Beth twirled and pointed at Ram with a smile plastered across her face. "I'm glad you like it; it's all yours. Before I forget, here's the key to the door and the file cabinets. We are having a new safe delivered and installed tomorrow. Fair warning: Rick picked it out, so it's huge. Now we need to get your laptop ordered."

"Wow, I'm speechless. This is amazing. Thank you," Ram sputtered, trying to hold back the surge of emotions threatening to overwhelm her.

Beth walked up to her and wrapped her in a hug. "Forgive me if I'm overstepping, but it seemed like you needed one of these."

Ram hugged her back just as tightly before stepping back. "I did, I don't know what came over me, but I'm incredibly grateful for this opportunity and...and all of this. I'm just happy. I know I keep saying that, but I truly am."

"Good. Now, on your desk is a corporate card and all the paperwork. Take your time going through it all and head up front when you're finished. I'll finish the tour of the bar."

When the door closed, Ram just stood staring at the view out her window. Holy hell, she pinched herself to make sure this wasn't a dream. Her life couldn't be more sublime. All of this, combined with Laney's visit around the Fourth of July holiday, had her soaring higher than a kite. She tossed her jacket on one of the two chairs facing her desk before taking a seat behind her work surface.

Unable to contain herself, she had to share her news. She called Laney, who didn't answer. Ram left her a voicemail.

Then, she called Brock.

"Hey, Ram, tell me the good news," he asked in his deep voice that she could feel all the way to her toes.

"I got the job."

"I had no doubt you'd nail it. You're amazing," he said. An intermittent high-pitched beeping echoed in the background. "Sorry, supplies are being delivered, and the forklifts are in use. Let's celebrate tonight. Dinner?"

Brock had taken her day from wonderful to over the moon, all with one question. "It's a date."

"I'll pick you up at six."

She pressed the red button on her cell, wishing she could bottle these euphoric feelings to savor whenever she wanted. Now she had to force her mind back to the pile of paperwork before her so she could complete her orientation. Forty minutes later, she compiled the stack, taping it on the glass to align all the pages. Leaving her blazer behind, she headed toward the bar where Rick was now stocking the beer coolers.

"Hey, Ram," he looked up to greet her as she approached. "Will you take these to Beth? She's in her office," he said, pointing off to the side of the stage.

She was about to respond when the front door opened. A uniformed man pushed a hand truck loaded with boxes through the doorway and greeted the owner. She nodded at Rick, not wanting to interrupt and followed his directions. At the closed door, she knocked, only entering when she had the green light.

"Here you go, Beth." Ram handed her the stack.

Beth flipped through the pages. "Any questions?"

"Not really. I've ordered my laptop, which will arrive tomorrow with the rest of the office supplies," she answered, taking a seat opposite Beth.

Beth tucked the documents into a folder labeled *"Fritz, Ramona."* Then she shifted her gaze to Ram's. "Now, I've got to ask. What did you mean earlier when you said you didn't want to sound flaky? Did you mean your dream or something else?"

Ram sat upright biting her bottom lip. "I, uh--"

"Wait. There's no obligation to answer, and I didn't mean to make you uncomfortable." Beth held up her hand. "I'm being nosy. In this business, you learn to listen because everyone talks while they're drinking."

Ram let her shoulders relax, blowing out a breath. This was normal chit-chat, and speaking about her past had to happen. When would she learn to stop making this topic awkward? Maybe when she forgave herself for trusting that jerk. It wasn't as if he had given her an itinerary detailing his intentions.

"You'll have to forgive me. The unpleasant part is that I had a loser for a boyfriend who drained my accounts right under my nose. I've moved here to start over, because I wanted a place where I wouldn't have a chance of running into him. The hard part, which I think is the tension that you sensed, is that I'm embarrassed for being so naïve. The flaky reference was more to me because moving here seems to be my destiny."

Beth giggled. "You know, you're not the first to have found your destiny in Destiny."

Ram couldn't help but laugh too. "Yes, which is why the word flaky came to mind."

Beth took a sip from her tumbler. "And the dream?"

"To open a florist shop. I have a lot of saving to do before that happens, but flowers are my love language."

"Oh, good idea, Ram. We don't have a local florist."

"Yup, I heard that from Brenda, too."

Beth wiggled her fingers, tips touching in front of her face. "I need to introduce you to Brock. He works for the township as our landscape architect. He's super talented. Let me tell you, that man is hot. Not as good-looking as my husband, but damn close. There isn't a better way to get over an asshole than to find a man worthy of your time."

Ram's hand flew to cover her mouth, trying to cover a knowing smile, but Beth beat her to the punch. "Busted. You've met Brock, haven't you?"

She lowered her hand, nodding her head. "Yup, we met the day I arrived. He helped me complete all the floral arrangements for Sapphire."

"Well, there's that. If I didn't stress it enough before, he's a good one; he might know a thing or two about starting over, too." Beth gave her a pointed look. "Okay, let's get back to discussing all things Pelican."

Ram followed Beth out of her office toward the kitchen. Earl and Elma's words about Brock floated through her thoughts. Maybe the starting over had to do with the death of both his parents. She tucked that information away. The measured *whack-whack-whack* from the knife-wielding chef let everyone know meal prep was in full chop. Her mouth watered at the whiff of buttery garlic and toasted bread, reminding her that she'd skipped lunch. Beth whisked her around the kitchen area, food storage, and coolers until they landed inside the locked liquor and wine storage room. One side contained a wall of boxed glassware, and the rest had racks from floor to ceiling full of bottles.

"I affectionately call this room my torture chamber because auditing all of this makes me crossed-eyed."

Ram made a circle in the large space, eyeing everything until she stood next to Beth again and patted her shoulder. "Yup, glad that's not my task."

"See I knew you were smart," Beth winked at her. "That's okay, between you and me, I always manage to guilt Rick into doing it for a foot and shoulder massage."

"Nice one," Ram said.

"Well, that concludes the inner workings tour of the Pelican. I figured you've heard enough from me today, and I've got to make some calls. I'll see you tomorrow, Ram. Hopefully, your laptop will come early so you can start reviewing the software for payroll and our books."

Ram parted ways with Beth heading toward her office. She had to admit she liked the sound of that, but she loved the view even more. Plopping down in her chair, she swiveled so she could watch the action happening at the pier.

Excitement bubbled in her stomach when she thought about her date. All she had to figure out was what to wear. She'd planned on curling her hair and wearing a little extra makeup. Her goal was to get a *wow* reaction from him tonight. As she thought about the shoes she wanted to wear, her phone blurted out Laney's song. Good, she could help her with wardrobe choices.

"Laney, I just landed the best job. I'm sitting at my desk, which has two windows that face the pier."

"That's cool. I'm so proud of you," Laney said, her voice wobbled through the last part.

"Oh my God, what's wrong?"

"Nothing, I don't want to ruin your moment."

"Seriously, what the hell is up? You're worrying me," Ram implored while her mind conjured up at least ten horrible ideas.

"You know the husband and wife who own the two apartment complexes that I manage? Well, she died this morning in a horrible car accident."

"Oh, Laney, I'm so sorry. They were both always so nice. Is there anything I can do for you?"

"Other than twinkling your nose like a genie so you can just appear to hug me, there's nothing. I'm so sad. They had a wonderful marriage and were connected at the hip. I mean...I don't know what he's going to do now."

Laney's voice cracked before the sobs came across the line. Ram felt terrible that she couldn't do more than listen to her friend cry.

After a few minutes, Laney blew her nose and let out a deep breath. "Life is so unfair. I've got to go and pull myself together. I have a tour in thirty minutes for two newlyweds. The last thing I want to do is freak them out with my raccoon eyes."

It made her feel better when her bestie sounded a little more like herself. "I'm having dinner with Brock, but call if you need me. I'm here if you need to talk."

Laney cleared her throat. "I'm good, I promise. And Ram, just enjoy yourself and let the night unfold organically. Don't overthink it, because life is too short."

Chapter Seven

THE MINUTE THE LAST shrink-wrapped pallet touched the ground, Brock signed the bill and headed toward his truck. He had been driven to make this night memorable. An idea had taken root in his brain from the moment she had accepted his invitation. He had already made reservations at the local Italian restaurant for six-fifteen, so that part was finished. Now he had to shower and shave before dinner, but more importantly, he wanted to pick up a gift for Ram that exemplified her in every way.

When he reached his place, he glanced at his wristwatch and grimaced. Tonight was different because it was their first official date. This woman had him tied up in knots, the very best kind, but that worried him. Ever since she'd crossed his path, he'd become addicted to her. He never believed in words like fate and soulmate, but he found himself becoming a disciple. He had to get moving so he wouldn't be late. In his closet, he selected a pair of black slacks, a white button-down shirt, and a pair of socks and boxers. He located his dress shoes after he showered.

Denying his attraction to her felt wrong, but it also meant he had to conclude his penance.

Logically, his family wouldn't want him to punish himself, but being able to enjoy life when theirs had ended stung like betrayal. Something he could have prevented if he hadn't been selfish and blown off his father to fix the old furnace. When he'd heard his mom and dad had died in their sleep from carbon monoxide poisoning, his heart had been ripped from his chest. His sister's support and unwavering love got him through the loss of their parents, but when she died, her loss stung the most.

Ram made him want things he didn't deserve, but damn it, she broke right through his icy center and tempted him. She made him feel alive. All the numbness he'd endured melted away. A beauty with milky white flesh and those pouty, kissable lips. That kiss made an indelible impression on him right down to his core. He'd never thought about gifts for anyone other than his mother and sister until Ram.

Now, he wanted more.

When he pulled into the parking spot in front of Ram's unit, he glanced up and moaned. Ram looked stunning in her dress. She'd curled her hair and had even put on makeup, not that she needed any. A zing of awareness radiated through his body when it dawned on him that she'd done all this for him.

He'd scrambled out of his truck, barely reaching the passenger door before she arrived. "All eyes will be on you tonight, sweetheart."

"You don't look too shabby yourself. I might need you to wrap your arm around my shoulders to ward off all the single ladies."

He could smell the subtle scent from her perfume, a mix of vanilla and cherry, as she moved past him to slide into the seat. "Maybe I'll just kiss you silly when they're watching."

"Promises, promises," she taunted, and pulled the seatbelt across her body.

Oh, he planned to deliver on that one. He closed her door and got back behind the wheel.

Once the truck was rolling down the road, she turned to him. "I'm starving. I didn't get lunch today. Where are we headed?"

"Gravy—it's a great Italian restaurant run by a couple from Brooklyn."

"Mmm, sounds delicious." She licked her lips, then she asked, "Do they make their own pasta too?"

Brock took a long breath to calm his desire. The sight of her licking her lips was going to be the death of him. "I'm pretty sure everything is homemade, right down to the desserts," he replied.

She rested her hand on his forearm. "I want your word. We won't desert dessert."

He erupted in laughter. This woman, before him, lived life and spoke her mind—a stark difference from all the women he'd previously dated. Looking back, he'd pick Ram every day of the week. "You'll get dessert, sweetheart. That's an easy one."

After they arrived, he pulled a gift bag from behind his seat and presented it to her when he opened her door.

"What's this?" Her big brown eyes widened alongside the smile that bloomed across her face. She eagerly accepted the gift and his hand. "I love surprises."

"You can find out inside," he replied.

The restaurant was bright and cheery. He'd always liked places that had outdoor lighting. The inside was much darker, giving off a romantic atmosphere as the instrumental version of Sinatra songs played through the speakers. Moving his hand to the small of her back, he guided her inside to announce their arrival. A few moments later, they were led by the hostess to their table. He pulled out her chair before taking his own seat.

"This place," she said with a whimsical quality to her voice as she looked all around. "Beautiful, just beautiful."

His chest puffed up a little from her approval. It mattered to him that he'd made her happy. The waiter stopped by to introduce himself and take their drink orders.

Brock looked directly at Ram. "You good with me ordering?"

"Dazzle me, Mr. Pierson," she cooed, her eyes twinkling with delight.

Returning his attention to the waiter, he ordered a bottle of Pinot Noir along with two appetizers. He didn't want her to wait any longer than necessary to get something to eat. He could only assume that her day had been hectic, but knowing she'd gone hungry didn't sit well with him. He would have found a way to bring her something if he'd known.

Big brown eyes were fixed on him. When she knew she had his attention, they skimmed to the side where she'd placed the gift bag. He should make her wait just because he loved her excitement, but he wanted to see her reaction more. He tilted his head, giving her the green light, and faster than a snake could strike, she had the gift bag on the table.

She snapped the tape holding the middle together and pulled the piece of tissue hiding the top of his gift.

She sucked in a rush of air, gushing. "Oh, my gosh, it's stunning. I've never had a bonsai tree."

He was overwhelmed by the joy of her response to his gift. It made his chest swell with more than pride--a feeling that warmed him from the tips of his toes upward. A pleasure that had become an addiction, just like that.

She snapped a picture of the plant with her phone moments before her fingers went to work, typing something out. "I love it, Brock. I'm sending this to Laney. You know, my friend who is coming to visit me at the end of the month. She also wants to meet you."

"I thought it might look good on your desk or somewhere. Congratulations, Ram."

Ram reached across the table and grabbed his hand. A sizzle of heat spread up his arm. "It will look spectacular. Did I tell you I have windows? You'll have to come and see for yourself."

He squeezed her hand. "I'd like that, and then we can have lunch."

She released his hand when the waiter appeared with their wine. While he went to work presenting the wine and uncorking it, she tucked her present away to make room for the food that would be coming soon.

When the wine had been poured, Brock lifted his glass to Ram. "To many more great moments."

The distinctive tinkling from the delicate glass followed his toast. She took a sip of her red. "This bonsai symbolizes a variety of things like harmony, balance, patience, or luck. What made you choose this for me?"

That was his Ram. Asking the question on her mind instead of sidestepping or hinting. "They require commitment to care. These beauties can last for many years and hold sentimental meaning, representing friendship, loyalty, and love as well. I like the overall message; it marks the start of"—he pointed between them—"us, however, we choose that to be."

He took a drink of his wine, needing a moment to compose himself. He'd just laid his heart down on the table. Until that exact moment, he hadn't known he planned to confess all of that tonight. Now, he was committed because he wouldn't back down on this. Even if guilt rotted his gut because he got to live instead of his family, at some point, he'd have to share the story with Ram, but not tonight.

"Brock," she spoke softly, dabbing the corner of her eye. "I-I don't know what to say. In the best possible way, you're right. And Laney was right but I'm not telling her that. It would go straight to her head."

The waiter delivered the appetizers, and before he retreated, they ordered their main meals. The distinct sound of forks and knives tapping against the porcelain filled the room as they ate the first course. He liked that they could just enjoy the meal without the need to fill every second.

After a bit, Ram lifted her head and wiped her mouth on the linen napkin. "Since Laney's coming, I need to get a bed. Do you have any time this week that I could use your muscles and truck for delivery?"

He raised an eyebrow at her question. "What do I get out of it?"

She sat back and crossed her arms across her chest. "So, we're negotiating?"

He mimicked her actions. "Yup."

"Okay," she watched him for several seconds, letting her gaze work over him. "Dinner, movie, and second base, if you impress me."

Thankfully, he hadn't taken a drink right before she answered, or it would have been spewed across the table, creating an embarrassing moment. His bark of laughter had her laughing. Never in his wildest dreams did he think she'd respond as she had. And he loved it.

He sat forward, trying his best to school his features so he could respond with a look of seriousness. "I accept," he sputtered on another laugh. "I surrender, because my thoughts are rending me speechless."

She shrugged. "I would have accepted a counter to include third base."

His groan had her waggling her eyebrows at him. "You are a vixen."

She leaned forward to take a sip of wine. "You have no idea."

Oh, he hoped to find out when the time was right.

They chatted about their jobs and the projects they were working on. The simple pleasure of sharing a day's work with her was a new joy, her animated gestures showing how happy she seemed about everything.

He shared the details on his two large orders, one for the township and the other for Burn Sand. When he finished that contract, it would be another chunk of money he could apply toward his debt. That project had grown in cost when Bernie wanted to add even more topiaries to his plan, but the payoff at the end would be worth it. Making a mental note, he'd call Bernie to see if they would pay a bit more of the supply cost upfront to help balance his finances. If not, it would be a long month since he'd fronted all that cost so far. He couldn't wait for the day when he didn't have the government on his back.

He was looking forward to planning their next outing. "How does Friday sound for the bed? I'm not sure what you're planning, but there is a warehouse store that has furniture and mattresses."

"That works for me," she said and tugged a wayward strand of hair away from her eye. "I have really appreciated all your help in getting me settled here. It can be super lonely when you don't have any family or friends around in times like these. Do you have any other family?"

His stomach dropped liked a boulder on a rocky pass during a rainstorm. Her question caught him off guard. It's not that he didn't want to talk about his parents or his amazing sister, but sharing those stories kept his heart in tatters. All the pain rushed back, filling every void in his body.

He forced down his emotions. Ruining the night wasn't his plan. All he had to do was answer the innocent question. It was just a simple answer, but soon enough, she would learn the ugly truth.

"I'm not an only child--"

"Wait, let me guess," her gaze snapped to meet his. "You're protective. You got your manners from Mom, but you developed the other because you were her big brother."

He watched her for a moment, processing what she'd said. When they were younger, all the boys wanted to date his sister. He'd threatened each one to mind their manners or face him.

"Yes, but--"

The waiter arrived, ending his reply, to deliver their entrées. Relief flooded his system. The server attended to their meals by adding freshly grated Parmesan cheese, then refilling their wine glasses. Once they were alone, he tossed out a question of his own. Call him a coward, but he didn't want to return to that topic.

He picked up his fork and paused. "Did you hear the news? The winner of that huge lottery is from somewhere around here. I don't think they've released the place that sold the winning ticket yet."

"No. How much did they win?"

"It was close to fifty million," he said between bites of his branzino.

Her eyes went big. "Wow, that's unthinkable. Could you even imagine? What would you do if you won?"

"Aside from the obvious...paying bills and investing, I'd travel and start a charity. You?"

She scrunched her eyes and pursed her lips. "The charity part is noble, but I'm not that honorable. Savings, travel, for sure, but I would follow my dream. Oh, and I'd add finding a reasonably priced home close to the ocean. I didn't realize I loved the ocean so much."

He stopped eating to direct all his attention to her. "What's your dream?"

A look of sheer bliss radiated across her face. "I'd open Spiny Jewel Box, a florist shop in Destiny. I've heard from several folks that the town needs one."

"I like it and the name. I hope that becomes a reality someday."

She forked a piece of pasta. "That's my plan. I even told Beth about it. There, now it's out in the universe that I'm going to be a small business owner at some point or die trying."

"Something tells me you'll succeed. Okay, what's for dessert?"

"Uh, tiramisu, it's the only logical choice after this scrumptious dinner."

When they consumed the last bites, Brock leaned across the table to grab her hand. "You ready?"

She nodded, a dreamy look on her face. "We just need our bill."

He could see her confusion when she realized a bill wouldn't arrive. He had prepaid the bill with cash he had set aside for tonight's dinner. He had no way of knowing what dinner would cost, but he appreciated that the owners allowed him to do this, given his tight finances. He would settle with the restaurant tomorrow to get back the overpayment.

"It's been handled," he said and stood with his hand extended to her.

It looked like she had a follow-up question, but instead, she stood accepting his hand. He escorted her out to his truck and back home. The moment he pulled into a parking space in front of her unit, he slid the gearshift into park and turned in his seat. Before he could make his move, Ram launched herself into his body and wrapped her arms around his neck. Her lips were mere millimeters from his own. When she spoke, he felt the warmth from her breath.

"You, Brock, are dangerous because you make me happy. Tonight was magical and I love my bonsai, but please don't hurt me."

He moved his hand upward until he cupped her cheek. "I can't promise that because I'm human. What I can promise is always to be honest and that I'd never hurt you intentionally."

A wayward tear ran down her face that he wiped away with his thumb. She inhaled sharply. "I didn't date a lot, so when George paid attention to me, I fell hook, line, and sinker. Everything seemed perfect, but when he moved in, he just took over. He used my vulnerability, and I allowed it. Then, he said he found his soulmate, leaving my life in shambles. It was embarrassing and stupid. I didn't think I was that type of person, especially after watching all the men who came in and out of my mother's life."

He pressed a kiss to her forehead. "That's horrible, Ram. He's an asshole, but I bet you weren't the first person he did that to."

Her brows knitted. "I hadn't thought of that. I bet you're right."

A possessiveness surged through his body. Knowing that a person had treated Ram that way, or any woman for that matter, irritated him. It made him want to find the bastard and have a discussion.

"I'm sorry you went through that, but it did bring you here to Destiny."

He angled her head right as his mouth found hers. He kissed her deep and long, trying to convey to her how he felt about her. She rocked his world. He nipped her chin, fueled by desire. He worked down the sensitive skin of her neck until he kissed the pulsing hollow at the base of her neck. Her whimpers of delight pleased him.

Raising his mouth from hers, he gazed into her eyes. "I like the taste of your lips, Ram. I could spend hours devouring you, but I need to walk you to the door for both our sakes."

She pressed her lips against his, kissing him once more before she rested her head against his forehead. "That's a terrible idea, but you're probably right. It's a workday tomorrow," she murmured, sliding back into her seat.

The interior of the cab lit up as he opened the door to the truck to escort her to her apartment. "Here, give me a minute––"

She held up her hand. "Not needed. You stay here and watch."

"You got it. Goodnight, Ram," he said, shutting his door.

He watched the sway of her hips as she took the steps up to her door. There was no doubt in his mind that those sexy moves were for his benefit. When she disappeared into her unit, he put his truck in gear to begin the drive home. Tonight had been great. He smiled, knowing he'd hit a home run with his gift. Now the only thing bothering him was whether he could keep his promise when he told her the truth. Or would she despise him?

Chapter Eight

R AM COULDN'T BELIEVE IT was already Thursday, which meant Laney would arrive later today. An adrenaline rush zipped through her body, knowing that in mere hours they'd be together. Thankfully, the bedroom furniture she had to order arrived on time. After Brock left the night before, she'd stayed up extra late making her new bed and organizing her dresser and bedside tables. With the directions to the airport already loaded in her phone, the only thing left to do was watch the clock.

A rapid knock at her office door had her lifting her head to see Rick entering with a box.

"Nice little tree," he said as he plopped down in the chair opposite the desk. "I forgot to tell you. I need the checks for the liquor deliveries today since I moved them up a day early to accommodate the Pelican's Flock Festival."

"No worries," she said, turning to her laptop and grabbing her mouse. A few clicks and keystrokes later, she turned back to him. "I have them here. Have the amounts changed, or are these invoices correct?"

"They're correct."

"Okay, I'll get them prepared and place them under the register drawer."

Rick stood and placed the box he had carried in on the edge of her desk. "Cool. Beth said I was a turd for forgetting. So, I brought gifts just in case." He dug into the box and tossed her two T-shirts. "For you and your friend."

She unfolded the shirts and giggled. "*Rocking and Flocking and I Don't Flocking Care, I'm Rocking* was printed on the front of each, and the backs had the usual Tipsy Pelican branding.

"Thanks! Laney will love it," she said, refolding the shirts to place them beside her purse. I really appreciate the time off tomorrow."

"No problem. See ya later," Rick replied, gathering his box again and turning toward the door.

She returned her attention to her work, entering the required information to print each check. The last one had just been sent to the printer when another knock had her lifting her head.

"Come in," she hollered.

The moment the door opened and she spied Brock, her body warmed.

"Hey, sweetheart," he said, sending her another wave of tingling in all the right places. "Do you have time to grab a quick lunch?"

She checked the time on her computer. Not only did his kindness touch her heart, but his impromptu visit sped up her heart rate. Oh, she'd fallen for this man who was the exact opposite of her ex in all the best ways. "I do. I need to drop these checks off on our way out."

Ram pulled the papers from the printer and checked each one before she gathered her purse and walked toward Brock. She gave him a hug and a kiss before opening her door, leading him back to the bar.

Brock waved to Beth and Rick, who were sitting at the bar with another man. "Hey, Beth, Rick, Kurt, it's good to see you," Brock said as he approached them.

Ram scooted behind the bar to place the checks at the bottom of the till drawer, alerting the bartender on duty that they were there for the deliveries.

"Ram, this is Kurt, Rick's brother. He also owns Thibodeaux Security," Beth announced. "His company will be our security for the holiday weekend. When you get back, will you wire his payment?"

"It's nice to meet you," she replied, accepting the contract and invoice from Beth and placing them in her purse. "Will do."

Brock grabbed her hand to leave. Once they were outside, he put his arm around her shoulders. She dug her sunglasses out of her bag to protect her eyes, and the moment she put them on they fogged over from the high humidity. "Does the Conch Shell sound okay?" he asked.

The moment she agreed, he maneuvered them in the opposite direction, towards the restaurant. She noticed that the vacant store still had the available sign in the window as they entered the café. Why she cared, she wasn't sure. She didn't have the money to do anything about it.

They grabbed a window seat, beating the lunchtime rush. Ram and Brock ordered, both taking the daily special—a salad and conch fritters.

"What time does Laney arrive again?" Brock asked.

"At five-thirty, so I have to leave here by four, right?"

"Yup, that'll put you in the middle of rush hour."

A new waitress came to their table to take their orders. Ram unrolled her napkin, placing it in her lap. "I figured, which is why I have her favorite dinner ready at home. She loves my chicken stuffing casserole."

Brock waggled his brows. "Save any leftovers, because that sounds delicious."

They swapped updates and discussed local news until the waitress returned with their lunch and a pitcher to refill their iced teas. When she left, Ram asked, "What time do you want to come over to head to the Flock Festival?"

"Is five too late? I'm planning on spending tomorrow working on Burn Sand."

She took a bite of the fritter. Her eyes went wide as she reached for her tea. After several long sips, she finally found her voice. "Holy smokes, they are super-hot."

She took one bigger gulp before responding to his question. "That's fine with me. How are you progressing?"

"Good, actually," he answered. "I've got half of the trenches dug for the PVC piping, and I've finished making the topiary frames."

She cut open another fritter, allowing the steam to escape. "Don't forget, I get to see the finished job."

"I haven't," he replied. Then, he caught the server's attention, giving her the universal scribbling hand gesture to ready the bill.

When the waitress returned, she had the bill and two to-go cups for their iced teas. Brock handed her his credit card and then went to work on transferring his beverage. The woman swiped his card on a handheld device she had carried to the table.

"Uh, your card declined," the waitress said, placing it on the table. "Want to pay with a different card or cash?"

Brock's gaze moved from the server to Ram's for a brief second before trailing off to the side. He let out a deep breath before he spoke. "Ram, I'm cashless. Do you mind picking up the tab for me?"

Not wanting to make an uncomfortable situation worse, Ram nodded, digging into her purse until she had a credit card between her fingers. Her mind whirled with how to respond when she handed the server her card.

"No problem. We've all experienced that before, right?"

Her comment fell flat when the server and Brock didn't respond. It stirred a niggle of apprehension in the back of her mind. She dismissed that thought as fast as she could. He didn't deserve to be judged. Right? She watched the machine spit out two receipts. She filled out both, leaving one on the table and tucking the other into her wallet along with her card.

"Thanks. I'll pay you back, Ram."

Again, she wasn't sure what to say, so she just nodded and smiled, trying her best to get them past this moment. The walk back to the Pelican happened in the blink of an eye. Brock said his goodbyes at the front door, leaning down and kissing her before telling her to drive safely.

She stuffed her sunglasses back inside her purse and entered the bar. The scent of stale beer hit her nose while she stopped to let her eyes adjust to the darkened interior.

"How'd lunch go?" Beth asked in a whimsical voice from the bar, her laptop and paperwork sitting in front of her.

"Good. We grabbed a bite over at the Conch," she answered. "I'll get that money wired. Let me know if you need anything else before I head to the airport."

Beth swiveled in her chair, following her retreating form. "I'm glad you two are dipping your toes in the dating pool. I think you make a handsome couple."

Ram couldn't help the grin that spread across her face. She liked him. Her concern over his lack of funds was rising, however.

Checking her watch, she had three hours to complete her to-do list before leaving for the airport.

T HE MINUTE SHE SAW Laney emerge from the double glass door, she exited her vehicle and practically tackled her. Together, they made a scene with all their chatter and commotion, but she didn't care.

"You look happy, Ram. Like a totally different person than the last time I saw you."

Ram hugged her harder. "That's a good thing, right? Let's get this gigantic suitcase in the back. You do realize you are only here for three nights."

Laney stood with her hand perched on her hip, giving her a raised eyebrow. "Uhm, I'm on vacation. You never know what outfit, heel, shoe, purse, or accessories will be necessary to dazzle. Besides, I haven't had sex in like *forever*. Did I mention I need to get laid?"

A woman who seemed to be watching their interaction from the onset frowned at Laney's remarks.

"We need to move this inside my truck." Ram dropped the tailgate, and once they had Laney's bag in the back, she closed it. Laney stowed her carry-on inside the cab as Ram climbed back behind the driver's seat. In no time, she had maneuvered her truck away from the passenger pickup zone and had merged into the exit lane.

"First, you are not having sex in my new bed or apartment."

Her bestie adjusted the vents and turned the air conditioning dial to full blast. "Prude. I guess I'll have to live vicariously through you. How's *your* sex life?"

"We're not discussing that in detail, but what Brock and I have done has been amazing—like toe curling, shooting star, body in flames, off the charts amazing."

Laney gave her a side eye glance, "Yeah, no details then, but I do love picking on you. I'm so happy for you, but also jealous. I want a prince charming, too, but I won't settle until I find one worth my time and energy."

"You'll find the right man when you're not looking for him. I'm convinced of that philosophy now. When I moved here, I said no more men. Then I met Brock and he knocked my socks off."

"Uhm, you sound ancient when you use the term 'knocked my socks off,'" Laney teased.

"I can't wait for you to meet him, but something happened today that's got me a little worried," Ram explained the whole lunch scenario to Laney, who sat in her seat, not saying a word.

Finally, Laney twisted in her seat to face Ram. "That's it? His card declined, something practically everyone's experienced in life, and you're worried he might morph into your ex dickhead?"

Well, when her friend put it like that, it sounded terrible, but she had a right to be concerned.

"Come on, Laney. I don't want to be blind when the evidence is slapping me in the face," Ram groaned.

"We've got to work on your idioms. Anyway, I don't want to sound crass, because you went through hell with George. You have a right to be cautious, but don't look for problems that aren't there. People can have money issues, and it doesn't mean they're going to drain your accounts, cheat, and lie. Has Brock lied to you? Cheated on you? Have you told him about what George did to you?"

"No. I don't think he would. But I also haven't told him everything about George." Ram admitted, glancing at her friend.

"If you think he's worth it, tell him about George and just ask the man about his money issues. If his answer is reasonable, then let the relationship happen. There are so many other reasons that aren't dastardly to make a relationship end."

Ram didn't respond for a while. She let what her friend said absorb into her soul. A wave of guilt washed over her because she had been unfair to Brock. She could have asked, but instead she lumped him in the George bucket.

Instead of responding to Laney, she pointed out a few attractions as they neared Destiny, including Brock's handiwork on Main Street, where she would open her floral shop if all the moons and stars aligned, and where she worked at the Tipsy Pelican. She even took her out to The Sapphire Hotel, where the views of the ocean were magnificent.

"Are you hungry?" Ram asked. "I've got your favorite ready to pop in the oven for dinner."

Laney clapped her hands like an enthusiastic small child. "Yes, I'm starving. It's rough now because I don't have you to cook for me."

"No, you're lazy. I've shown you how to make your favorites."

Laney threw her head back and laughed. "Busted, but in truth, it's more the dishes that I despise."

"Spoiler alert, that's what everyone dislikes. Oh, and figuring out what to make every damn night," Ram said, flipping on her turn signal as she pointed off to the left. "See the pier? My apartment building is right over there."

"Holy shit, Ram, that's awesome! Did you ever think you'd live that close to the ocean? This town is super cute. I can see why you're loving it."

Ram guided her truck into the parking lot of her complex, stopping right in front of her unit. "Yeah, this move has been the best decision, except for you living in another state. Now, getting your bag up those stairs is going to be a workout."

Laney flexed her arm and shook her head in mock distress. "I guess that's why you're doing the heavy lifting."

"Ha, ha, I've got ya, but I'm glad it's only a weekend. If not, I'd have to borrow Brock's forklift."

"Sweet, I'm glad to know that's an option for my next trip," Laney tossed out, unfazed by her friend's sarcasm.

Ram hefted her big roller bag to the ground with a *thunk*. "Hey, thank you for having my back. It's only been a little while since George wrecked my world. But you've got a point, judging Brock isn't right either."

"No, but if he does manage to hurt you, he'll have to answer to me," Laney said in her no-nonsense way, complete with a perfectly lacquered nail pointing at herself.

Chapter Nine

B ROCK STOOD INSIDE THE Tipsy Pelican drinking a glass of water after spending the morning helping Rick and his employees set up for the Flocking Festival, a favorite of Destiny locals to celebrate the Fourth of July, featuring different bands and singers, and a portion of the proceeds from ticket sales went to local charities. He had stopped by after work last night to see if Rick needed help again this year, since it seemed to always grow in size. It had become one of his recurring events that he worked on the side to earn extra money.

This time, instead of putting it toward his debt, he wanted the cash to pay Ram back for yesterday. The rest he planned on depositing at the ATM machine later so he could transfer that amount to his secured credit card, freeing up room to charge. *I can't wait until that debt is paid in full because yesterday was embarrassing.* It seemed Bernie and Sandy weren't in a spot on their cruise to receive phone calls, so he could not get that advance. The last thing he wanted was to endure another card decline.

"Hey man," Rick said, handing him an envelope. "Thank you for helping again. It's always nice to have an extra set of muscles. This event has grown so much over the years."

Brock slid the envelope in his back pocket. "It's a town favorite. Plus, the tourists flock here for the entertainment and fireworks."

Rick shook his head at his friend. "You're horrible at pun humor."

"Don't pick on him. It's taken him forever to come out of his shell. We must nurture his tender heart, Rick," Beth admonished while setting two plates on the counter full of eggs, bacon, hashbrowns, and toast.

"Yes, our little boy." Rick's sarcasm had Brock rolling his eyes.

Beth yanked at a T-shirt she had tossed over her shoulder, snapping Rick with it before she tossed it at Brock. He caught it midair, opening it to read the slogan: *Flocking it all night long.*

"Thanks, Beth. As you know, free is always for me," he said.

Beth waggled her brows at him. "I know, but your shirt has a special meaning. So, go make that happen."

Rick made a big show of smacking his cheek. "Good Lord, woman, are you meddling again? Come here so we can talk."

Brock didn't need to look in a mirror to know that his cheeks had brightened from Beth's comment. He pulled his plate toward him and finished his breakfast while he listened to Beth and Rick going over the final plans for the two-day festival, which started at eleven that day.

"TGIF, my flocking bitches," one of the bartenders announced as she walked toward the counter. She had her specially designed event shirt knotted in the back, paired with her signature jean cutoffs––not exactly Daisy Duke style, but close. She'd worked there for as long as Brock had been coming to this place.

"Thanks for the wardrobe. I'm off to Burn Sand, but I'll see you later," Brock said. He wiped his mouth before drinking the rest of his water. Just as he got to the door, it burst open, displaying a hulk of a man.

"Hey, Kurt," Brock greeted.

"Morning, dude. My team is ready and in place. Beth, Rick, do you want to run through the logistics once more?"

You had to appreciate Kurt for his directness. The man could be intense, but his military training was still sharp, making him one of the best in the security business.

Once outside, Brock slid his sunglasses over his eyes and headed to his truck. The rest of his morning was simple. He would hit the ATM, then head off to work on his contract. When that job was completed, he could apply another chunk of money toward his debt. He checked his watch; He had about four hours before he had to head home to shower and then pick up Ram and Laney.

B ROCK SAT IN HIS truck in front of Ram's apartment, sucking down a big breath. A strange thought hit him square in the chest––meeting Laney would be like meeting Ram's family. A twinge of nerves revolted in his stomach. He pulled the envelope from the beverage holder and opened his door. He ascended the stairs until he stood outside her door. He heard the distinct sound of female laughter from inside her unit. His knock on her door was followed with a commotion that sounded like a stampede.

When the door popped open, two women stood there with big grins covering their faces. Laney's gaze assessed him from north to south. Her black hair was knotted on top of her head. She wore her festival T-shirt and jean miniskirt with flat sneakers and no socks. Ram wore her shirt too, but with a pair of jean shorts and sandals.

"You must be Ram's man," she giggled, turning back to Ram, who rolled her eyes at her.

She playfully pushed Laney aside and walked up to hug him. "Ignore her. She's been sassy all day. If you hadn't guessed, that's Laney."

He nodded at her friend as he walked into her apartment with Ram still in his embrace.

"It's nice to meet you finally," he said. Releasing his woman, he retrieved the envelope from his back pocket. "This is for you. I told you I'd pay you back for lunch."

Ram's eyebrows scrunched together as she took the envelope. She opened it, and her gaze snapped back to him. "This isn't necessary, but I appreciate that you did."

"It is because I always pay back my debts," he said, making his way over to where Laney sat on the sofa. "What did you two do today?"

Laney crossed a slender knee over her leg. "We spent the morning at the beach. Then we had lunch at Flip Flops and did a little shopping."

"We had the special fried lobster roll with browned butter. Oh, Brock, they were delicious. Have you had those yet?"

He watched Ram lick her lips, and his mind went haywire. She had that effect on him. "I haven't, but I'll have to try it."

Laney interjected. "Oh, and she showed me the available space for her 'when-miracles-happen' florist shop.

"And Brock, look, we found those on the beach. Aren't they beautiful? They're called sand dollars. I never realized they were sea urchins," Ram said, pointing to the coffee table.

"They're super cool. Maybe they'll bring good luck to the finder," he said. He reached over and picked one up.

"Maybe. Laney googled it earlier. They stand for peace, unity, and friendship. If you break them open, you'll release the little teeth inside, which represent releasing doves to promote peace, goodwill, or perhaps good luck. So, we've made a pact ––we're part of the Sand Dollar Club."

He loved the satisfied looks on their faces, like they had found a buried treasure. It meant a lot to him that Ram had one set aside for him. That he belonged with them. "What did you do, Brock?" Ram asked, plopping down between him and Laney.

"I helped Beth and Rick with setup for the festival and then worked out at Burn Sand."

"Oh, the mansion where you're designing the dolphin plant spectacular?" Laney asked.

"Yes, I'll send you pictures when it's finished," Ram said, nodding. "Hey, do you want me to heat up leftovers for dinner, or do you want to eat there?"

Laney laid her arm over her flat stomach. "I'm not hungry since we just had lunch. Can we nosh later?"

Ram turned her attention to Brock. "You okay with waiting?"

"I'm a go with the flow kind of guy. Are you two ready to head out?"

"Give me a second," Laney said, standing. "Let me grab my sunglasses, cellphone, and purse."

Ram followed her to the bedroom, and after several minutes, they returned ready to walk over to The Pelican. On the way there, Brock held Ram's hand while she and Laney talked almost nonstop and, at times, over each other. Their energy made him tired, but he could see how happy Laney's visit made Ram.

The moment they entered the dive bar, the band playing had the crowd dancing and swaying to the music's beat. The back patio was filled almost to capacity, and the big garage doors that separate the space were raised. He spied a small table in the back and squeezed Ram's hand. When she looked up at him, he pointed to the open table. They weaved their way through the crowd until he could claim the chair that backed up to the wall. It gave him a good view of the entire bar. Laney and Ram sat on either side of him.

When the song ended, the band announced they were taking a fifteen-minute break. The open space where everyone danced emptied, and the noise level disbanded from a central point.

Ram squeezed Brock's knee. "Hey, I want to show Laney my office. We'll be right back."

Brock nodded and pointed to the bar menu on the table. "What do you two want to drink?"

"I'll take a Piña Colada," Laney answered.

Ram stood and kissed Brock on the lips. "Surprise me."

A silly grin morphed across his face as the waitress appeared. He placed their drink orders and got a pelican platter to share. He was hungry again. He nodded at Rick as he hustled by on his way to the back patio. It looked like another good year of record-breaking crowds. The waitress stopped by and dropped off the drinks and rolled silverware before she flew to another table.

"Nice touch on the plant. Ram loves it. So, since we have a few minutes, what are your intentions with my girl?" Laney asked, giving him a serious look.

Brock sat back and crossed his arms over his chest, giving Laney his full attention. "To make her smile. I enjoy every moment that I get to spend with her. She's amazing."

Laney's smile overtook her face. "That answer works for me. But if you hurt her, I'll have to go all cavewoman on you. It won't be pretty, Brock."

Brock took a drink of his beer. "That's fair. I hope to never provoke that side of you. I'm also glad she has you in her life. She talks about you all the time."

"Did you miss me?" Ram asked as she approached their table and gripped Brock's shoulders. "Ooh, a strawberry daiquiri, right on."

The band started to warm up to resume their play. He and Ram nibbled on their plate of goodies while Laney told them a funny story about a newlywed couple who moved into her complex.

Ram wiped her hands on the napkin. "Do you think the owner will sell since his wife died in that accident?"

Laney's eyes glossed over. "I hope not. I love working for them--er, him. God, that accident wrecked his world. They were the sweetest couple."

Ram reached out to grab Laney's hand and squeezed it. "I'm so sorry. Life is unfair at times."

When the next song started, it brought everyone out of their seats to dance. Ram tugged Laney toward the dance floor, and when she looked back at Brock, he shook his head. Dancing was not his thing in a group setting. He could do a slow dance here and there, but gyrating to a tune wasn't his thing. Now, watching Ram dance was an entirely different topic altogether and he could spend hours watching her. As the night progressed, he enjoyed the live music and getting to know Ram's best friend. In many ways, it made him feel even closer to Ram because he'd made it inside her inner circle.

Finally, the band started a slow song. He pushed his chair back and stood. When Ram and Laney returned, he winked at her and gripped Ram's hand, tugging her back toward the floor.

"Now it's my turn," he whispered against her ear. He tucked her tight against his body. He loved how they fit together. The beat of her heart thudded against his chest while her soft, curvy flesh molded to his body. Finally, when the song ended, he lifted her chin with his finger and kissed her. Her lips had the subtle taste of berries from her drink. A tender kiss to begin with, until he devoured her. Desire burned hot inside of him. Reluctantly, he ended the kiss because they were in public. He escorted Ram back to the table, where Laney fanned herself.

"Holy moly, that was hot. You two burned a hole in the floor. I may or may not have snapped a few pictures, if you two are interested," Laney said.

"Hell yeah, I'll take any pictures of the beauty that you want to share," Brock said.

Laney grabbed her phone. "Number, then I'll text you some."

The three of them laughed and shared stories between dances for the remainder of the night, until it was time to go outside to see the fireworks show. The lead singer announced that after the next song, it was time to take this party to the pier.

Ram turned toward Brock, flashing a devilish grin. "Oh, we have to cap off this night with shots."

"Order them," Brock replied to her, wondering what concoction she'd choose.

When the cocktail waitress approached, Ram and Laney announced at the same time, giggling, "Three slippery nipples."

He asked her to bring the check as well. Well, shit, he liked the sound of that order, and the images that raced through his mind regarding his Ram. When the server returned, she dropped off three shots and the plastic tray with a sheet of white paper.

Ram had opened her wallet to retrieve her card until he covered her hand with his own. "I've got it."

Her eyes narrowed and she leaned close to him. "Are you sure?"

He hated that she questioned him, but he understood why she had. Before his sister's illness, he had plenty of money. Now, almost every cent he earned went toward his epic failure. At some point soon, the debt would be paid, but his sister would still be gone. Ram deserved an explanation, as his financial situation would remain strained for a while longer.

"Yes, I took care of that this morning. I had to reload the balance on my secured credit card. My creditworthiness isn't the best at this moment, but I'm working on it."

Ram squeezed his hand. "Thank you for trusting me enough to share that. Later, when we have more privacy, we can talk about this more, if you'd like."

Interrupting Ram and Brock's discussion, Laney handed out the shots. She raised her glass. "I love you, Ram. To the Sand Dollar Club, may our adventures continue while our friendship grows."

A loud clink followed the slam of empty shot glasses in rapid succession. The shot had a corny name, but the butterscotch always tasted good. He would have loved to take Ram home tonight and taste it on her lips, but he didn't want to intrude on her time with her best friend. After all, Laney was heading home Sunday morning, then he would have Ram all to himself.

"Okay, ladies, let's head toward the pier so we can watch the show. Rick and Beth go all out for the fourth."

Brock held Ram's hand and Laney grabbed his other as they navigated the crowd to find the perfect spot against one of the railings lining the pier. Laney hopped up to perch on the top rail while he leaned against the barrier, tugging Ram against his body. This night had been one of the best he could remember in a long time.

It also made him realize that he needed to tell Ram about his past if he wanted to have any type of future with her.

Chapter Ten

R AM HATED GOODBYES. SHE missed Laney and their daily connection. She and Laney had so much fun together this weekend. They spent most of Saturday lazing around the pool, recovering from Friday night and discussing anything and everything in between. Laney adored Brock. Not that Ram needed Laney's blessing, but it still felt good, having her endorsement.

Horns honked at the airport as drivers maneuvered their cars into tight spots to drop off their passengers. When her friend looked backward, Ram waved one last time before Laney disappeared behind the big glass doors of the departure terminal. A pang of sadness smacked her straight in the chest.

The measured ticking sound from her turn signal filled the cab of her truck until she merged into the flow of exiting vehicles. Once she made it to the freeway, she moved to the center lane. Not two minutes later, a *boom* followed by a vibration in her steering wheel let her know her tire had a problem. She slowed until she got to the shoulder, stopping on a nice, wide, level spot. She jabbed the hazard button.

She blew out a frustrated breath, resting her forehead on her steering wheel. Calling the tow company crossed her mind, but she was more than capable of changing a tire. The moment she opened her door, the humid heat clung to her body. The sun shone bright. *Well, shit, at least it wasn't dark outside*, she told herself. She opened the tailgate, hopping into the back to reach her toolbox that ran the width of her bed. She rummaged around until she found what she needed and went to work.

She dropped the jack on the ground by the front passenger tire and checked the rear passenger tire in front, then got low on the dirt until she could see the lift points. The front of her shirt had a nice strip of dirt across her boobs. She dropped the spare tire and then began loosening the lug nuts. A trickle of sweat traveled down her spine. She moved to her passenger door to retrieve the water bottle sitting in the cupholder.

Perhaps it would have been better to call in a tow company to the flat. She shook away that thought, determined to finish the job. She lifted the front end with the jack, removed the lug nuts, swapped out the tire, and when she finished, she tossed everything into the back. She'd organize it later. Right now, she wanted to feel the air conditioner blasting on her overheated skin.

She sat still while her skin cooled, but exhaustion had staked its claim on her. Almost an hour had passed, but she was proud of herself. Now her priorities had changed. She wanted to get home to shower and take a nap.

Once again, about fifteen miles down the road, her truck started pulling to the right, accompanied by a predominant hissing sound. *What the fuck?* She pulled off onto the side of the freeway and jumped out of her truck, her anger fueling her speed. When she rounded the truck, she saw that the passenger's front tire was losing pressure as it hissed at her.

A car pulled up behind her. When the door opened, she was greeted by a middle-aged man. "Hey, miss, do you need help?"

She ran a hand over the top of her head, trying to remove the wayward strands of hair plastered to her forehead.

"No, thanks. My boyfriend is on his way," she said.

He nodded, "Do you want me to wait with you until he arrives?"

The entire time she'd changed the last tire, not a soul stopped. This time, she gets the nicest man. "No, I'm good, but thanks. I appreciate your kindness."

Her good Samaritan returned his vehicle and left. She got back into her truck and decided to make good on her falsehood. When the tow truck came, she'd be stuck because she didn't have another spare. If she called Brock, her truck could be towed to a shop and he could take her home.

He answered on the first ring. "Hey, sweetheart. Is Laney gone?"

"Yes, I dropped her off earlier. Hey, are you busy? I've got another flat and need a ride."

The line was silent for a minute. "What do you mean by another? Are you okay?"

"Yes, I'm fine, although I'm not sure what I did wrong. Anyway, will you come and get me? I'm going to call a tow truck to take my truck to a shop, but I don't know a good one. Do you?"

He gave her the name and address of a shop close to Destiny. "Where are you?"

She gave him her location, then ended the call to contact her roadside assistance company. Who endured two flats in one day? When the second call ended, she figured Brock would arrive in about twenty minutes, which gave her time to put everything away that she had previously stored in the back of her truck.

She tugged the tailgate down and used the bumper to help her up and into the back of the vehicle. She wiped down her tools with a spare towel before she organized them. The crunching of gravel had her looking behind her. And just like that, her irritation faded with Brock's arrival.

When he stepped out of his truck, he wore a ball cap, cargo shorts, and a T-shirt. Her body pulsed in all the right spots, but it was the day's growth of stubble covering his jaw that gave him that rugged yet handsome look.

"You are beet red," he said as he approached. "Let me help."

"I'm almost finished. I planned to put all this away at home, but my second flat tire had other plans."

Brock rubbed the back of his neck and then walked toward the front of her vehicle. "I'm not seeing the valve stem, which means the tire was mounted backward. That's most likely the source of the leak."

"Super," she said flatly. "I never thought to check for that during my last service before I drove here from Tennessee."

"Hell, Ram, that shouldn't have happened." Brock rested his arms on the side of the bed. "It's hot as hell out here."

She pulled her shirt upward and used the bottom to wipe the perspiration coating her forehead. If she flashed Brock her bra, she didn't care. "In hindsight, I should have called the tow truck in the first place."

Brock stared downward, not meeting her eyes. "Or me, I would have dropped everything to assist. You know that, right?"

The distinctive knocking and low rumble from the diesel motor caught her attention, and the spinning yellow lights confirmed her suspicion that the tow truck had arrived. She walked toward the end of the bed, where Brock stood with his hand extended to help her down. Once she hit the ground, he pulled her into a giant hug before letting her greet the tow truck driver. The moment seemed heavier than it should have been, which confused her.

She waited until the driver got closer, so she didn't have to yell over the freeway noise. With the driver, she reviewed what had happened and what she wanted to do next. The driver's fingers jabbed the screen of his handheld device until he turned it around for her signature. She gave him the keys, and in under ten minutes, she was sitting next to Brock as he drove her home, the cab silent while he gripped the steering wheel with both hands. He drove like they had entered a storm, but the skies were far from it.

She reached over to rest her hand on his leg. "Are you upset with me?"

Seconds ticked past while she waited for him to respond. He inhaled a deep breath. "Not, you. Just with myself..."

"I don't understand, Brock," she asked. She removed her hand, twisted her body, and faced him as best she could.

"I would have changed the first flat. Or any, for that matter. You know that, right, sweetheart?" he asked, his voice deeper than usual.

"I do, but this can't be about a tire. What's up?"

He flexed his fingers on the steering wheel. "It's hard to talk about, but my selfishness contributed to my parents' death. I was supposed to come home the weekend they passed to help Dad fix the furnace. He was a frugal man who didn't want to spend the money *in season* to have a repair person come out. Instead of showing up, I made up an excuse with the promise of coming another weekend. That weekend never happened because they died from carbon monoxide poisoning. When I found out you needed help and didn't call me right away, it made my mind whirl with horrible thoughts. Like I'd let you down, or maybe you thought I wouldn't show? I don't know..."

Her hand returned to his leg. "I didn't call because I'm stubborn. I thought I could fix it myself, just as I did with any problem as a child.

It's hard to spend your life without a lifeline. You just wing it until you figure it out."

He dropped one hand onto hers, entwining their fingers. "You are stunning and capable, but I just don't want you to *feel* like you must do it all alone. I'm here for you."

"You're right. Next time, you'll be my first call. Together we'll figure it out. I'm truly sorry about your mom and dad. I can't imagine what you went through, but you didn't cause your parents' deaths. You're not the only child who has chosen not to spend time with their parents."

"Did your sister blame you?"

She felt the muscle in his leg contract under her hand. "No, she didn't."

She turned back toward the front of the cab. "I'm glad you weren't alone to deal with it. It's horrible."

The remainder of the drive happened in silence. Her heart hurt for him. All that guilt had to be unbearable. It didn't feel right to say goodbye, and she also didn't feel like being alone. He had confided in her and shared something so personal, and she felt the sudden need to soothe his battered soul. It meant a great deal to her that their connection had deepened. As they approached her complex, she turned her head in his direction.

"Stay for dinner as a thank-you for picking me up. Or stay because I want to make you smile. Or just because I want you here. You decide the reason, but please stay."

He simply nodded, grabbing her arm before she could slide to the ground. "Thank you, Ram, for everything."

"I need to shower first," she said. "Then, we can figure out what I'll cook."

"Just so you know, I happen to like you hot and grimy."

She chuckled at his comment before rolling her eyes at him. All she wanted was to feel clean and refreshed. She made a beeline for her front door and then straight to the bathroom. She turned on the tap and peeled off her clothing. Right before she stepped under the spray of water, she cracked the door and hollered out to Brock, "Make yourself at home. I'll be out in a few."

After washing the grime off her body, she slathered on lotion, applied deodorant, and twisted her hair up into a messy bun. Realizing she didn't bring a change of clothing in her haste, she wrapped the towel around her body and strode toward her bedroom. She pulled out what she needed from the dresser and chose a loose-fitting sundress. Taking one last glance in the mirror, she opted for a spritz of her favorite perfume before heading toward the front room. The crack of a bat, followed by rowdy cheers, told her that Brock was watching baseball on television. The sense of this being a typical Sunday routine scene appealed to her.

"Ready for dinner? I've got ground beef and chicken, but let me check to see what else I have on hand for those options," she said, walking to the refrigerator.

She grasped the handle and swung it wide. A cool blast from the fridge washed over her body while she inventoried ingredients. A slight shuffling caught her attention right before a warm arm snaked across her middle to draw her back against a solid chest. The intimate act caused a stir low in her belly.

His mouth nestled beneath her ear. "My hunger isn't for food," he murmured, just beneath her ear. A wave of goosebumps dotted her skin from his carnal statement.

When his teeth nipped the delicate skin beneath her earlobe, she trembled. His lips trailed upward and across her jawline, enticing her to turn her head to give him enough room to claim her mouth. His kiss was urgent and commanding as he devoured her. He shoved the refrigerator door closed. In one fluid motion, he tugged her body around until his body pinned hers against the door. His hard edges melted against her softer flesh.

She remembered his masterful fingers and lips from their previous explorations, but this moment held the promise of ecstasy. She fisted a handful of his hair, tugging him even closer. Her body quivered with desire and longing. Molten heat radiated from her core. Every nerve ending in her body danced.

She wanted him.

She wanted everything.

In her deepest dreams, the ones you never whisper out loud for fear they won't materialize, she wanted all the things she didn't have while growing up. She wanted to belong, to be unconditionally loved, and to be part of something greater than herself. Did she dare to believe that her dream could finally come true?

Chapter Eleven

B ROCK PULLED HER UP hard against him, devouring her again. Their kiss exploded in a torrent of emotions and desires, flooding every recess of his body. A need, like a wildfire in search of dried grass, tore at his restraint, demanding more. She curled her leg around his, anchoring him to her. Damn if he didn't like the idea of her trying to mount him.

She emitted a deep moan at the base of her throat. The sexiest noise he had ever heard. The only one that counted. He tore his mouth away to rest his forehead on hers. Her face was flushed, lips red and swollen from his kisses. He swelled with pride knowing that he had caused that beautiful reaction in her. One he could witness every day.

"Why'd you stop?" she demanded. A small pout formed at her mouth.

He liked that she sounded displeased. "Because you matter, and what comes next is your decision."

Her eyes glazed with desire. She tilted her head forward, narrowing her eyes. "Yes, a total yes. To be even clearer, if sex doesn't happen, I'm going to be *really* mad at you."

He dropped one arm under her knees and wrapped the other around her chest to lift her into his arms. "Your wish is my command, Ram."

A satisfied smile crossed her beautiful mouth.

He strode toward her bedroom. At the foot of her bed, he let her legs swing downward while he kept her body pressed against him. His body was rigid and primed. His hands trailed slowly down her body, feeling and touching everywhere. He palmed the globes of her breast through her thin cotton dress. Taking his time, he used his thumbs to torment the taut peaks of her nipples. Continued moans of pleasure told him all he needed to know. He moved lower until he gripped the hem of her dress, tugging it up and over her head until it fluttered to the ground.

Standing back, he savored the goddess who stood before him in only her lacey white panties. She was a jewel that he wanted to treasure. Her arms moved to cover her breasts. The thought that she might be uncomfortable bothered him.

"Please don't hide this gorgeous body from me. Ever."

Her eyes moved upward until their gazes locked. After a few seconds, she lowered her arms, letting him see all of her.

"You are the best gift," he crooned.

Her womanly curves and smooth skin glowed, but with those pouty lips and her impish brown eyes, a man could lose his soul. This woman would be his undoing, and God help him, he wanted to possess every inch of her inside and out. Not because of what he took but because of what she gave to him freely.

She prowled toward him. Her hands gripped his T-shirt, yanking it up his body. When she couldn't reach any higher, he took over, removing it for her. Her eagerness matched his as she explored. Her cool hands touched his heated flesh, running over his abdomen and pecs. Small bare feet padded around him as she slowly circled him. A mix of lips and delicate fingers traveled along his skin, over his sides, and down his spine. Her leisurely pace had him vibrating with anticipation of where she'd touch him next.

When she completed her circle and faced him again, she reached up on her tiptoes and pressed kisses on the delicate skin on his pectoral muscles. When she finished her ministration of care, she caught her bottom lip between her teeth, making her look sinful. Carnal desire, raw and powerful, coursed through his body.

"Your body is a work of art," she said admiringly. "Muscles and hardness, even a few scars that I want to know about. I want to know every square inch of you, Brock."

He retrieved a condom from his wallet, tossing it onto the bed. While her fingers went to work on his pants button and zipper, he dragged in a deep breath. His erection strained against the zipper of his pants. Moments later, his shorts dropped to his feet, and without haste, he slid his boxers down until he could step out of both, leaving him fully naked. His erection strained toward her. Hot and heavy, but the need to reconnect had him tugging her back into his arms to feel the velvet sensation of skin-to-skin contact.

He backed them toward the bed until she lay on the surface. She inched toward the headboard, and the scent of vanilla and cherries from her perfume filled the air. He knelt on the edge of the bed and skimmed his hands up her legs. When he reached the delicate lace she wore, he trailed a finger across the length of the elastic band before he worked it down her legs and off her body.

"I've wanted this since the moment you wore my hard hat. I've had fantasies about that day."

She leaned up on her elbows so she could look him in the eyes. "Hmm, that's good to know. It gives me a lot of ideas on how to torment you. Now, no more small talk. I need you, Brock."

He loved that she didn't mince words and spoke her mind. That also flipped his switch because he needed her with the same desperation. It had been a long, long time since he'd enjoyed a woman's body. He licked and laved his way up her body until he reached her depths and tormented her bundle of nerves. Intense ripples of pleasure had her calling out his name.

"Brock," she moaned out.

Hearing his name fall from her lips drove him insane. The sweetest sound that he had to hear again.

"Again, Ram. Say it again, sweetheart," he commanded, his voice low and intense.

"Brock, Brock," she moaned. Her body quivered in release.

He reached to grab the foil condom packet. Fully erect, he sheathed himself and crawled up her body until he aligned himself at her entrance. Hard and hot, wicked and sinful, love and devotion were all words that swirled in his mind. Passion drove his body, creating fissures of erotic excitement.

"I want to be patient," he grumbled.

Her hand gripped his cock. "Take me, now," she gasped.

He needed no further instruction. He thrust and paused, then thrust again and again, repeating the action until he filled her completely. Taking a moment to regain his composure from all the emotions swirling deep inside him, he found his rhythm fueled by her hums of satisfaction as he pumped his hips with a determined cadence. The gentle touch of her inner thighs, paired with her body's warmth, felt like heaven. He'd found home. The moment she soared, clenching him with her inner muscles, he lost his control. His measured strokes became more urgent. A coil of tension at the base of his spine had him on the edge. She writhed under him. When he plunged once more, his world erupted into a colorful array of hope and happiness. In one deep roar, her name echoed throughout the bedroom.

He rolled to his side, tucking her against his body. Sublime pleasure hummed throughout his body. His heart hammered against his chest while his breath sawed in and out. He had no doubt in his mind that every second with Ram made his life better. The question he had was whether he was worthy of that happiness. The simple answer should be no, but it might be time to move forward. He closed his eyes to stop the truths from rising to the surface. A principled, man he was not.

"What's wrong?"

Brock leaned over to press a kiss to her lips. Then he rolled from the bed to head to the bathroom.

"Not a thing, sweetheart. Everything is fine."

She deserved to know everything, but now wasn't the time for explanations.

When he returned to her bed, he slid beside her, pulling her back into his arms and kissing the crown of her head. Ram snuggled deeper into his side and sighed. She was content, and it wasn't long before her breathing evened out into a deep sleep. He tightened his grip, hoping she'd never slip through his arms and disappear.

THE RAYS OF THE morning sun brightened the room, rousing him from sleep. Ram hadn't moved all night long, but the space next to him was now vacant. He would have preferred to have awakened with her snuggled next to him, but the scent of coffee and bacon had his stomach growling. He twisted off the bed and moved to the pile of clothing. He had just slid on his shorts when Ram appeared, wearing his T-shirt. Her hair was brushed back into a ponytail.

"Morning, sexy. I thought a hearty breakfast would be good considering we burned quite a few calories last night," she said, waving him toward the kitchen.

He followed his curvy vixen. When he reached the kitchen, his eyes went wide. "Holy shit, Ram. How long have you been up?"

On the counter, she had served up orange juice, coffee, pancakes, scrambled eggs, potatoes, bacon, sausage, biscuits, and gravy.

She waggled her eyes. "We haven't shared a sleepover breakfast, so I wanted to make sure I covered the major food groups so you'd have your favorites."

His fingers snagged a piece of crisp bacon and took a bite. "This could be the greatest breakfast feast I've ever been served."

She lifted a shoulder. "That's a shame, but we have time to correct all your wrongs."

God, if she only knew. That would be a herculean task that would never happen. But since her comment referenced the food, he piled his plate high.

He had no plans but to eat as much of this food as he could. She too loaded her plate and took the seat next to him. In the background, the local news cut to a local field reporter who stood inside the local gas station in Destiny.

"This was where the winning lottery ticket was purchased, and so far, no one has come forward to claim the prize of over fifty million dollars. So check your drawers, purses, and wallets. Someone's life is about to change in a huge way. The winning numbers will be posted on our website."

Brock looked at Ram. "Wow, can you believe that someone we know could be the winner. That blows my mind."

"Maybe it's you," she teased as she refilled his juice and coffee.

"Absolutely, not. That's not where I spend my money these days."

She wanted to dig into that comment but let the moment pass. After they finished eating, he helped her put the leftovers in the refrigerator and started washing and drying the pans while she showered. He loaded the remaining dishes into the dishwasher. A feeling of peace washed over him as he stopped to look around the room.

Did he dare to grab hold of what he wanted, a future with Ram? He knew he didn't deserve it, but damn it, he also couldn't let go. While her truck was at the repair shop, he planned on being her chauffeur for the next few days. This gave him the opportunity to see her again tonight so that he could tell her everything. It was time. She deserved to know about his past, to see if she would be willing to accept his flaws and live with the consequences of his sins.

Chapter Twelve

RAM'S BODY HUMMED IN all the right places. Oh, she knew Brock would have talents, but last night exceeded her expectations. Brock had infiltrated her armor and made his way into her heart. He was nothing like George, but she still had to admit that a very small part of her waited for the other shoe to drop. Not that she looked for problems, as things had been going pretty well since she moved here.

She thought it would be better to call Laney back since she had left about ten messages on her phone the previous night. Ram had quite a bit to tell her, but it seemed that all those updates would have to wait. She glanced at what she had to accomplish for Monday. Payroll was the top priority on her to-do list. Then she would finish the invoice reviews and payments for the various vendors after lunch. There was quite a stack due to the Flock Festival.

Her fingers flew across the keyboard as Ram went line by line for each employee in the payroll program. The melodic clacking of keys lulled her into a groove until the buzzing of her office phone interrupted her rhythm.

"Hey, Ram. Lunch has arrived." Beth had mentioned something about a celebratory lunch today to thank everyone for their hard work at the festival. Ram's chest tightened, knowing she had taken the weekend off while most of the rest of the staff worked.

Ram drew a line on her piece of paper so that she wouldn't lose her place. "On my way."

She made her way up front to see everyone gathered, even those who were not working today. Laughter and chatter flowed throughout the room.

The daytime bartender pointed her fork her way. "Tell me, how did you wrangle Brock? God, he's hot, and I have tried many times to get him myself because he's hot."

Ram clenched her teeth. The thought of her trying to get Brock's attention made her a little jealous. "He is that, but you'd have to ask him."

Beth placed her hand on Ram's shoulder, causing her to jump. "Watch it, Melody. She may not know you're a 'love them and leave them' type of girl."

Melody shrugged her shoulders. "Hey, men shouldn't get all the fun. And for the record, I don't poach. I'm just stating facts."

Ram grabbed a paper plate and filled it with a few items. She took a seat next to Beth, who had the television remote in her hand.

"Anyone following that storm in the Atlantic? I want to know if it's got hurricane potential," Beth said. "You've gotta love Florida's summer weather."

One of the bouncers mumbled something that she couldn't understand about storms. Beth keyed in the digits for the local news station on the remote. The anchor teased the weather report and then cut back to the lottery story, now reporting that they had the date the ticket was purchased. Man, was this town obsessed with this story.

"If I won that money, I'd be traveling the world," another bartender said.

The other bouncer stood up and flexed his arm. "I'd open my gym and work out all the time."

Beth waved her hand. "Shh, everyone, I want to hear the meteorologist. It appears that the storm may form towards the end of the week or possibly the start of the following week. We'll need to keep an eye on it."

While everyone went back to eating and talking, Beth pulled out her cell and called Rick to report what she'd heard about the weather. Ram had never really had to worry about a hurricane's path in Tennessee. It was more geared toward dealing with the remnant impacts of storm systems, so all of this fascinated her.

While Ram finished lunch, her thoughts drifted back to the lotto story, and she remembered that she had purchased a ticket when she had first arrived in town. Mentally, she worked backward until she determined the date she had bought the ticket. She realized that the day the ticket was purchased, she was at *that* gas station. *Holy shit, could I be the owner of the winning ticket? And where did I stash it?*

There was no way she had won the lottery. That stuff didn't happen to her.

Ram jittered her foot against the floor. If she hadn't lost it, that ticket was inside her truck, which sat at the repair shop. She needed to retrieve the stupid ticket and verify that she hadn't won. Maybe then her palms could stop sweating, and she could focus on something else.

She stood and headed straight for her office, then closed the door. When she sat down, her phone rang, so she answered it. "Hello?"

"Is this Miss Fritz?" a male voice asked.

"Yes."

"It's Bill from the repair shop. Long story short, we ordered the two tires you needed, and they won't be here until tomorrow afternoon. So, it will probably be a few more days before your vehicle is ready."

"Oh, uhm, alright. I need to get something out of it. I'll be there before you close."

The next call went to Brock, who thankfully answered on the second ring. "Are you busy? I need your help. Like right now."

"I'm finishing a clean-up job at the library. Is everything okay?"

"Kind of, but I need a huge favor. Can you pick me up and take me to my truck? When I'm wrong, I'll buy you dinner. I know this makes no sense, but I'll explain it all when you get here."

"Okay. Is an hour too long, or is this immediate?"

That would give her enough time to finish payroll, which was important. Afterward, she could start on the invoices and finish those tomorrow.

"Ram, you still there?" Brock asked.

"Yeah, sorry. I was going through what I had left to accomplish at work. An hour is good."

Ram pressed her palms into her forehead and forced a deep breath into her system. It was time to focus. She worked for the next hour, and when it was time, she gathered her things and stopped by Beth's office to let her know she had to leave a bit early. She could work from home later.

True to his word, Brock sat in the parking lot, waiting for her to exit the bar.

"What's going on, Ram?" Brock asked the second she buckled her seatbelt.

"Today at lunch, the news provided a new detail about the day the lottery ticket was purchased. I had forgotten until that moment that I bought a ticket. We need to get to the repair shop. The ticket is in my truck, Brock. It could be the winner. I mean, I doubt it, but I don't know."

"Got it," he said, and then turned to look at her. "Is your truck ready, or are they still working on it?"

"No, they had to order tires, so maybe in a few days," she answered.

Brock stomped on the pedal, and they were off. It didn't take very long to get there, which made her happy. Her nerves were on high alert. Brock killed the ignition and followed her inside.

"Is Bill here?" she asked one of the workers, who looked annoyed that he had to stop to respond to her.

"He's in back. Can I help you?"

"I just need to retrieve something from my truck. Bill knows I was coming."

She provided the necessary information to verify she was the owner and then accepted the proffered keys from the employee.

She headed to the back lot with Brock on her heels. She opened the passenger's side door, then popped open the glove box. Right on top of everything sat the white paper with black lines and numbers. Holy moly, she could be holding fifty million plus in her hands! The pit in the bottom of her stomach faded into butterflies. Tucking the ticket away in her pants pocket, she grabbed Brock's hand and yanked him back toward the building to drop off the keys.

Once they were back in his truck, she turned to him with her phone in hand. "You ready for this?"

He raised his finger. "Give me a sec to pull across the street into that shopping complex."

"Good idea. We wouldn't want people to see me laughing hysterically when it's not the winning ticket," she said.

When his truck lurched to a stop at the back of the open space, he turned to face her.

"Don't forget that I should get a fee for my participation," he winked.

He is joking, right? A sudden pang of insecurity hit her. She shook her head, thinking that this whole notion of her winning millions had her brain scrambled. So instead of answering, she pulled up the news station's webpage to find the winning numbers.

"Here, you read the numbers to me," she said, passing her phone to him so she could view the ticket in her hands when he read the digits out loud.

Brock pinched the screen to enlarge the image. "17-21-39-2-27 and the Powerball is 11."

Ram's hands trembled, a mixture of hot and cold flooding her system. "Uhm, I-I think I won. Switch with me, I-I must be mistaken," she stammered. They swapped the phone and paper, and she repeated the numbers.

Brock's eyes went wide. "Here, let's verify the date to make sure we're looking at the right numbers for the right drawing. Perhaps we should also verify this information on the lottery's official website. The station could be wrong."

"Good idea." Her fingers swept across the screen, then she repeated the same sequence of numbers.

When his head nodded and he cast her a side glance, she squealed. "Holy fucking shit, what the hell do I do now?"

Brock made a mangled noise that was part exhale and a laugh. "Aside from the obvious of claiming your reward, I'd say you might want to find a financial advisor."

Ram's smile dissolved into tears. "I don't know why I'm crying. This is good news. Oh God, Brock, what's wrong with me? I- I think I'm in shock."

"Understandable," he said, reaching over and tugging her into his arms. "That's quite a large sum of money."

She gripped him tightly. His embrace was the lifeline keeping her grounded. "My head's spinning. There are so many things I could do."

"Yup, and I've got some ideas too," he mumbled against the top of her head.

Her inner warning light flickered, but she chalked it up to the emotions of the situation. After all, this was Brock, and he had no access to her finances. Laney's advice came to mind. She figured it would be better to claim the ticket with him having her back. Plus, she didn't want to risk losing the ticket, so it made sense to turn it in now. She'd get her ducks in a row after being declared the winner.

She retreated from his hold and lifted her head to press a kiss to his lips. "Will you take me to the lottery office? I figure they'll need to do their authentication process of person and ticket, and I'd rather turn it in now."

"You bet, give me the address."

After she googled the address, he plugged it into his navigation system.

At the lottery office, the process took much longer than she had thought, even after they confirmed she held the winning ticket. However, she understood the scrutiny, but the whole photography session wasn't her favorite. Not once had Brock grumbled about the long wait. Instead, he supported her the entire time. By the time the lottery office had completed all its steps, she was zapped.

She appreciated Brock's understanding when he agreed to reschedule their dinner that night. He drove her home, promising to pick her up the next morning. She needed to process this unexpected luck and update Laney. Plus, she had to finish the work she hadn't completed earlier that day.

She changed into a pair of boxers and her favorite worn T-shirt, heated up a plate of leftovers, and grabbed her phone. She took a few bites while balancing her phone in one hand and somehow managed to press Laney's number.

"Sorry, I got busy at work," Laney stated instead of a greeting. Then she heard the slight wobble in her voice.

"What's wrong?" Ram asked, placing her plate down on the coffee table. Her appetite faded when she heard the distress in Laney's voice.

"I miss you, for starters. The owner of the complex is going to sell the properties. He sat me down today to tell me he's going to go live with his daughter and enjoy retirement as best he can without his wife. I don't blame him one bit, but I'm going to miss working for him."

"Oh, Laney, I'm so sorry. I know you loved working for them."

"I do. And I feel like a bitch because I'm here wallowing in self-pity, when that man's wife was killed. You're in another state. This past weekend reminded me how much I miss you. I'm just down."

Now Ram wasn't sure about sharing her updates. She didn't want to rub her good news in her friend's face. "What can I do?"

"Nothing, but thanks for asking. What's been happening in your neck of the woods? Tell me something to take my mind off my pity party."

"Well, Brock and I tested out the bed. And it's super comfy." Ram didn't mean to chuckle, but this whole situation was funny.

"Wait, what? You finally did the deed, Ramona Fritz?"

At least her friend sounded a little happier. "We did, and no, I'm not giving you any details. But it was spectacular—like mind-blowingly amazing."

"No details wanted, but I'm happy for you both. I'm sorry, I'm bummed by everything happening here."

"Fair enough, but I do have some other news, and I'm pretty sure it will put a smile on your face. When your boss sells his properties, you can move out here and take some time off to relax for a bit before you have to find a new job. I'll take care of you."

Laney chirped out a clipped laugh. "Well, it better start with you having won the lottery, because I can be expensive. It's not like I have a deep savings account."

"Well, I do. I won the lottery. Fifty million, two hundred and fifteen thousand, and nine hundred dollars, to be exact. So, I'm pretty sure I can take care of you for a limited period."

There was dead silence on the other end of the line. "Did you say fifty million? Are you bullshitting me?"

"I'm still trying to process this myself. I'll send you the picture they took of me standing in front of the check."

"Holy guacamole, Ram. You're that Amazon guy now. Do you get it all now? How does this work?"

"I think he's more in the 'B' for billions category, but I did opt to take the full amount."

"Wow. You're a multimillionaire, Ram. So, what now?"

"I need to find a good investment banker. It can take several weeks to get the money, but for now, I'm just going to work, and I'm thinking I may open my floral shop. I was going to name it Spiny Jewel Box, but I think Sand Dollar Floral Boutique is more fitting now. It holds special meaning to me."

"I love it, Ram. Do you see yourself staying in Destiny?"

"Hell yes! I love it here, and you will too. Think about it, Laney. And if you moved here, your parents would come for a lot more visits."

"That's a true statement. Do it, Ram, open your shop and buy a house. I'll send you my thread count requirements for the sheets in my new guest room."

Ram burst out laughing. "Only you, Laney, only you would have requirements."

They talked for another hour, making to-do lists while discussing every dream scenario. The good thing about Laney was that most of it was talk, because they were both levelheaded. A girl can dream. It wasn't as if her win was going to make national news. When she finished her call, she crawled into bed and crashed. The adrenaline from the day had ebbed, and the last thing she remembered doing was setting her alarm.

Chapter Thirteen

B ROCK STOOD AT THE counter as Rick vigorously wiped
down the bar top, his nose scrunching from the strong smell
of the chlorine-based chemicals he used.

"I heard from Drew that you're almost finished with the updates
to Burn Sand. He said it's looking good," Rick said with a grunt.

"Yeah, I'm happy with it. I think Bernie will love it. Do you want
to see some pictures?"

Rick walked toward Brock. "Hell yes, let's see the coral reef with
dolphins."

Brock unlocked his device and pressed the photo icon, holding
his phone so that Rick could see the screen. The last picture in his
roll was one of Ram standing in front of her oversized check at the
lottery office.

"Holy shit, Ram's the winner? Is this legit?" Rick asked, his
finger tapping on the small image until it filled the whole screen
on his phone. "I heard during the news broadcast last night that
a winner had come forward, but I didn't stay up to hear the full
story."

Brock's eyes snapped to Rick's. "Oh, yeah, but that stays between us. She's overwhelmed by her newfound wealth, along with
all the 'what now' scenarios."

"Man, Beth will be upset when she hears this news if Ram quits. She *really* likes her."

"I'm done with today. This sucks," Beth's voice roared from somewhere in the kitchen area.

Before his wife arrived, Rick rushed to bring Brock up to speed. "Beth's already had a rough morning because her favorite line cook gave his notice. So, we know nothing, because your news will cause me additional heartache, and it's only Tuesday. You know the saying—unhappy wife, unhappy life."

Brock fist pumped Rick and then slid his phone into his pocket. "Morning, Beth."

Beth stalked toward Brock, pointing her finger at him. "Did you know about this?"

"About what?" Brock asked, happy to know in that exact sentence that he had no idea what she meant. He glanced at Rick, who looked like he might bolt at any second. He whipped his gaze back to Beth, who looked like she was ready to either hit something or cry. Great, now he was in the middle of it.

"This," she said, slapping her phone down on the counter. "Why is the universe crapping on me today? God knows, I'm overjoyed for her, but what about me? I don't want to find another accountant or a cook. I happen to like them both."

Rick and Brock leaned toward her phone to see the image, which was a picture of Ram smiling like a shooting star on a moonless night, standing in front of a big check. This story ran on a national site. His stomach tightened because he hadn't expected this news to travel this fast or wide. He hoped Ram was preparing herself for this blast of notoriety and whatever it brought.

Brock placed his arm around Beth's shoulders. "Yes, I took her yesterday. I'm sorry, Beth."

Beth leaned into his embrace for a moment. "It's always the good ones that get chosen for greater things. What's she going to do now?"

Brock shrugged his shoulders. "I don't know. We were going to have dinner last night, but after all this happened, she wanted to go home to process it alone. I certainly hope leaving Destiny isn't part of her plan. That would make me unhappy."

"Rick, our Brock is in love," Beth replied. She pulled out a bar stool and took a seat.

"I didn't use that word, Beth, but she does mean something to me," Brock countered. He turned to lean his arms on the counter so he could see them both.

"Spoiler alert: those are the signs of love," Rick said as he tossed his cloth into a bucket on the bar.

Brock ran his hand through his hair. "Maybe, but I still question if I deserve that outcome. Once she learns about my past, will she still be interested?"

"If she cares about you, then she'll listen," Beth replied, covering his arm with her hand.

"We did, even after my brother uncovered every detail of your past," Rick said.

"Kurt is meticulous," Brock added. He put his arm around Beth, giving her a brief hug. "I'm sorry you're having a lousy day. Hey, has Kurt heard from Bernie or Sandy? I've tried to reach them multiple times, including this morning. I'm finishing their yard project today and wanted to see if he can send the payment."

"Kurt hasn't heard back from him either. Cruise ships can be spotty with cell reception, let alone the various destinations," Rick responded.

"Speaking of payments, here's your check," Beth added. She slid a piece of paper across the worn wooden surface of the bar.

"Thank you. If Kurt does hear from either of them, please have them call me," Brock said as he retrieved his keys from his pocket. "I've got to head out to pick up Ram. Her truck is still at the repair shop."

W HEN BROCK PULLED INTO Ram's complex, he noticed two news trucks parked in the parking lot inside the complex, and reporters standing outside on the ready. Wow, that was fast. He figured he'd give her a heads up that when she opened her door, she'd be pursued. He dialed her number, pleased that she hadn't made it outside yet.

"Morning, sunshine. Are you aware that reporters are standing outside of your unit waiting to talk to you?"

"Ugh, seriously? I just claimed the prize."

"Yes, but you're now a national news story."

"Super," she said. She split open the window blinds for a moment. "Well, I guess I'll answer their questions. Then they can move forward to more interesting stories and stop staking out my residence."

She opened her front door, and in an instant, the reporters leapt to life. When she reached the lower half of the staircase, she was met by two large black cameras, along with several microphones aimed directly at her. She smiled and spoke with them for about a minute before she retreated to his truck.

"Good job," he said.

"You don't even know what I told them," she huffed.

He rolled his head her way. "True, but you looked beautiful."

When the truck was on the main road, she looked over her shoulder. "I can't believe they were camped outside my home. Yesterday I was just a girl going about her routine, and today I'm on the news. This whole thing is beyond comprehension."

"Heads up, Rick and Beth know. It's my fault. I was going to show Rick a picture of Burn Sand and had forgotten that I had taken a picture of you from yesterday at the lottery office, in front of the giant check. He saw it, and then Beth heard us talking. I'm sorry, Ram."

"Great." Her irritation was evident in the tone of her voice. "Why were you even there?"

"Once a week, I spray down their entire patio and furniture," he said.

She turned toward him, placing her hand on his leg. "I'm sorry. That came across as bitchy. I'm just off kilter, I guess. I didn't realize you did so many odd jobs for them."

"I do. It brings in extra money, helps me pay back my debts, and fills in the downtime."

When he arrived at the Tipsy Pelican, he pulled up to the front and stopped. "Call me when you hear about your truck. My day is open aside from an errand and wrapping up Burn Sand."

"Will do. Hey, how about dinner tonight?"

"I'd like that," he replied.

Once she disappeared into the bar, he headed toward his next stop. Since Ram now had money, she could lease that place next to the café for her florist shop. He figured he'd meet with the building owner to get the lowdown. The idea came to him yesterday, and he went ahead and set up the appointment for today. He knew it was a prime location and might not last long on the market. This way, he could share the news with her tonight.

After he'd met with the owner, he breathed a sigh of relief that the storefront was still available. Another offer had fallen through, so he put a verbal offer down on the space, which would secure it for seventy-two hours. If she wanted to move forward, the owner was willing to defer the down payment until her funds came through from her winnings. That would give Ram enough time to decide if she wanted to jump on this opportunity or let it pass.

His phone vibrated in his pocket as he strode to his truck. "Hey, Beth, what's up?"

"Kurt is talking to Bernie now, so I thought I'd try to reach you. Bernie and Sandy didn't realize they'd missed so many calls. She tried calling you, but you didn't answer earlier."

"I was in a meeting. What's the message?" Brock asked.

You have two options for payment. If you want to run the money through your side business for garnishment, it'll take two weeks because their accountant is on vacation. Or she can wire you the funds now into your personal account."

"She can wire me personally. I'll email her my account and routing information, and I'll handle the rest."

"Great. I'll relay that to her when she's finished talking with Kurt.

"Thanks, Beth. I appreciate you getting that handled for me."

That news made him happy. This project had been expensive, but the payment from this side job would make a good-sized dent in the debt he owed. The government garnished his wages on every paycheck, but when he earned extra money on side jobs, he set up direct payment options so he could pay back his debt sooner.

This money he owed served as a reminder of his biggest regret in life. He respected the noose around his neck, but with every payment, that tension lessened. He worried that when he finished paying it off, when he was free and clear of his sins, he would still be left with the knowledge, memories, and consequences of his actions. His only question was whether peace and forgiveness would follow?

Chapter Fourteen

WHEN RAM ENTERED THE Tipsy Pelican and her eyes adjusted to the interior lighting, she saw Kurt and Rick engaged in a discussion. Her heart sank at the sight, because she had a pretty good idea of what they might be discussing.

Then she saw Beth crook a finger at her. She inhaled a deep breath, preparing herself for the discussion she knew was coming. She took a seat next to Beth, the chair screeching against the floor. What Beth said next caught her off guard.

"Don't leave us. It'll make me cry," Beth said in a flat tone. "Of course, if you do stay, I'll have to kick you out so you can chase your dreams. Destiny needs that florist shop."

Ram leaned her head on her hand. "Have I told you how awesome you are, Beth? I can't believe I won, but I have no plans to leave right now. When I do, I'll make sure you are covered until you find another accountant. I'll even train the new person. A little food for thought; do you remember my friend Laney?"

Beth sat up a little straighter. "Yes, she was lovely. Is she moving here?"

"She might be. It's still up in the air, but her employer is selling his business, which will leave her jobless," Ram replied, giving Beth a big smile. "She's a hard worker with accounting experience."

Beth reached over to pull Ram into a big hug. "That might work out nicely, and I bet getting her to move out here permanently would be nice for you. Is Destiny's newest business going to specialize in flowers?"

"I've thought about it, and it appears the universe does want flowers. I love it here, so it seems like a no-brainer."

Beth smiled. "I like the sound of that. Now, if you open your shop, you'll need to take Rick under your wing to educate him on how much I like flowers—roses, tulips, lilies, and the like. That man hasn't bought me flowers, in like, forever."

Ram patted Beth's arm, turning her lips downward. "That's horrible. He'll be my first convert. Maybe I'll even build a program around Rick to help educate other men on how to romance with flowers."

Beth raised her eyebrows and laughed. "Oh, I like how you think, Ram."

Ram stood up and slapped her forehead. "Oh gosh, I just remembered, I need to run back to my office to grab two renewal contracts for your signature. I also want to review the invoices from Flock Fest. I have a few suggestions on how we can save money."

"Sounds good, I'll be sitting here," Beth said.

Ram strode down the hallway toward her office. When she swung open the door to her office, Brock's bonsai tree and the view of the pier from the window made her smile. She would miss this office when she left, but that wouldn't be for a while. Only when Beth and Rick were covered would she even consider walking away. She had several things to figure out before that happened.

She rifled through the stack of papers on her desk until she found what she wanted. Then she grabbed a pen and updated her to-do list, since she'd finished a few tasks at home last night. Once she had everything gathered in her arms, she made a pitstop in the kitchen to get a glass of Coke. Last night's sleep had been restless, and she needed a jolt of caffeine. She had just entered the main part of the bar when she saw Beth on the phone and heard her say Brock's name.

Bernie offered you two payment options. If you want to run the money through your side business for garnishment, it'll take two weeks because his accountant is on vacation. Alternatively, he can wire the funds directly into your personal account now.

Her stomach dropped to the floor. The beat of her heart pounded against her skull. What she'd overheard almost caused her to drop everything she held in her arms, but somehow, she just barely managed to keep her composure. His wages were being seized. What else had he been hiding from her?

She pivoted on her heel and stomped to her office. She plopped down in her seat, twisting the chair until the pier came into focus. She wanted the truth from Brock. Her insides crumbled from her fear of being used. Snippets of past conversations and situations with Brock flooded her mind. A ringtone from her phone zapped her back to the present.

She fumbled to grab the device. "Hello," she answered, sitting upright and turning her chair back toward her desk.

"Miss Fritz, this is Mrs. Coventon. I forgot to tell Brock when we met that I'll need you to complete an application now to hold the space. All I need is your email address. Once the funds, clear, you can make the first and last month's payments."

The room spun, and Ram's heart threatened to explode in her chest. Brock was already spending her money. He had no right to do this. All the past warning signals slammed to the front of her mind. His needing money, his credit cards declining, his debt, and those weird and random comments that had bothered her.

No more, she was finished with him. She would not allow him to make her look like a fool––once had been more than enough for her.

"I'm sorry, Mrs. Coventon, but he didn't have any authorization to speak on my behalf."

The sound of papers being shuffled could be heard on the line. Then a voice that sounded a little strained. "I understand, Miss Fritz. I apologize, but I want to be clear, as there has been quite a bit of interest in the space. Are you saying you're not interested?"

Ram fought for control before she snapped at the woman. After all, she wasn't to blame for this situation, but she was confused. She pinched the bridge of her nose and counted to five before she responded. "What space, exactly?"

"The available storefront next to the Conch Shell Café."

Surprised again by the woman's answer, she wasn't sure what to say. She was interested in that space, but why did Brock do this without her? What was he up to? This feeling of uncertainty bothered her. Was he manipulating her?

"Miss Fritz, are you still there?" The woman's voice penetrated her manic thoughts.

"Sorry, yes, I'm here, I'm just thinking. Things have been a bit hectic since yesterday. I'll text you my email address for the application, but yes, I'm still interested."

"Oh, that's great, then. When you return the completed application, let's set up a meeting to discuss this opportunity and address any questions you may have."

"That sounds like a plan, thanks, Mrs. Coventon."

Ram rubbed her temples, trying to fend off the onset of a headache. She sent the woman her email address and decided that what she needed was some fresh air. Brock had betrayed her. He kept secrets from her. Now she had no other option but to end their relationship.

She refused to give him the opportunity to hurt her any further. It was time to move forward on her own.

She gathered more of her work along with her purse. She'd work from home the rest of the day. She dialed up a rideshare and headed toward the front. Thankfully, it was empty except for the bartender and a few customers. She waved as she passed through the door, pleased to see the car already waiting out front as she made her escape.

The moment she closed her front door, she peeled off her clothing, slipped on her favorite nightshirt, and curled up on the sofa. She sent Beth an email to let her know she planned to work from home the rest of the day. Beth had responded almost immediately to make sure she was okay.

Ram's head pounded, but she forced herself to work through the to-do list. If she kept her mind busy, then there wouldn't be room to think about Brock. She headed to the kitchen to get a glass of water to take two ibuprofen. The next few hours passed, and she accomplished a great deal of work. That alone made her feel better.

The call record on her phone showed several missed calls from Brock and one from the repair shop. Perhaps Beth or Rick could take her tomorrow to retrieve her truck. Well, that would be a tomorrow problem to solve. A loud thump at her door was followed by a voice she recognized. One that made her grimace.

"I know your home. I spoke to Beth," Brock hollered.

She contemplated ignoring him, but a wave of anger rolled through her system. She wanted answers. To tell him to his face that they were finished. She yanked the door open and crossed her arms over her chest. He had the audacity to look worried.

"Hey, Ram. So, I think I'm right, you are mad at me."

She gave him her best icy glare. "You're a genius."

"Why are you upset?"

She pinched her eyes together. Her anger simmered just below the surface. "Are you kidding me, Brock?"

His eyes widened. If she didn't know better, he appeared uncomfortable. "Should I leave, or do you want to talk?"

"Why didn't you tell me that your wages were being garnished?"

His face fell. "I should have. I wanted to last night, but we didn't get to it."

"Last night? You had so many opportunities before that, Brock. My ex stole my money. So you can imagine how I felt when I heard Beth talking about garnished wages earlier. I should never have stumbled upon that information. It should have come from you––upfront and honest."

Brock's face pinched tight, and his gaze locked on hers. "I didn't know that about your ex. You never shared that with me. But you're right, I should have told you. Can we discuss this inside?"

She hesitated for a moment before relenting. "Only for as long as it takes to have this conversation." She closed the door, keeping it against her back.

He shifted from one foot and then tucked his hands in his pockets. "I'm sorry he took your money. That makes sense now, as to why you had to start over, but I would never do that to you."

She tossed her hands in the air. "Really? You didn't have any problems spending my money today when you met with Mrs. Coventon."

Her hands balled into fists at her sides. She got some satisfaction from the look on his face. He seemed shocked that she knew that tidbit of information.

"It wasn't a secret. I met with her to get some information for you about the space. I had planned to tell you all this tonight. The verbal agreement I made with that woman was only for seventy-two hours, so you'd have time to think about it. I thought I was doing a good––"

That basically aligned with what Mrs. Coventon had said. The problem was that she didn't like that he'd gone behind her back. That he had made a financial commitment without her consent or knowledge. What else could he be doing?

Red warning lights flashed in her head, and she would be a fool to ignore them again. Her world tilted while gravity pulled her toward the black hole of her life. Rational thoughts fled, and what remained were her fears and failures.

"And the garnishment? That's a big deal. Did you conceal a divorce? A child? Or maybe both? That omission makes everything an outright lie, Brock."

If she wasn't staring at him like a mad woman, she would have missed the flash of anger, or maybe it was resentment, in his eyes. Maybe she didn't want to hear his explanation.

"I didn't lie, Ram," he roared, but his gaze dropped to the floor. When he spoke next, his voice sounded deep and hoarse. "The U.S. Government is garnishing my pay for tax evasion."

That wasn't what she expected to hear. "So why not tell me that in the beginning?"

Brock ran his hand through his hair and exhaled. "Great question, Ram. I did tell you I had debts. The truth is, I hadn't dated in years, and I didn't think all of this would happen with us. Then when it did, I wanted you to get to know me before I told you that I had spent a full year in federal prison for defrauding the government of over half a million dollars. I guess you could say hindsight is twenty-twenty, and if I could have a do-over, I would have told you up front."

She pressed her hand to her mouth. She had dated a criminal who had kept all these secrets from her. Worse, she had fallen in love with him. "I can't do this, Brock. We're finished."

His eyebrows knitted together. "That's it? You don't even want to hear me out, to hear my side of the story?"

"I just heard it. There's nothing you can say that will change my mind. You're a felon who kept secrets from me. You're no better than George. I want nothing to do with you either."

His mouth gaped open for a second before he closed it, nodding his head. "You're right about everything with one exception. I'm nothing like George."

He didn't say another word and left. The moment the door snicked closed, she ran toward it, twisting the deadbolt. She slid down the door until her butt landed on the floor and cried until she'd given herself hiccups.

Damn him for making her love him—for thinking they had a future together—a *criminal. I didn't see that one coming.*

When her tears had faded, she blew her nose and dragged herself back to the sofa. She needed to hear Laney's voice. She needed someone to tell her everything would be all right.

"Hey, millionaire, how's my rich lady of luck?" Laney asked, who was met with more sobs.

In a wobbly voice, Ram told her what had just transpired with Brock, including what he'd said in the truck yesterday. When she finished, she waited for Laney to tell her she'd done the right thing. That Brock didn't deserve her, and that someday she'd find someone who didn't want to use her.

"Why didn't you let him explain what happened? I mean, hasn't he earned that right?"

Ram exploded at her friend. "Are you serious? That's your response. He. Is. A. Criminal. Who. Kept. Secrets. From. Me. There are no answers he could provide that could make a difference. Geez, are you forgetting all the earlier signs that we discussed?"

"He's not your ex-boyfriend, Ram. You never told him the details of what your ex did. In a way, you kept secrets from him. I'm sorry, but I'm not sensing the same ick from Brock that I did from George. Did you even listen to why Brock met with that building owner? It was for you. All that said, if you're done with him, then I support your decision. I will always have your back, but I don't want you to regret that you didn't give him that opportunity."

"I'm done with this topic," Ram declared. Her body ached, and her face felt hot.

Knowing from experience not to push anymore, Laney changed the subject. "I saw that you made national headlines today. How does it feel to be a star?"

"I'm not a star. I'm just a shiny news story that will be pushed aside for something better soon. Oh, I almost forgot, if you decide to move here, The Tipsy Pelican will be looking for a new accountant. I planted that seed with Beth today."

"You're always thinking, Ram," Laney said with a chuckle. "I wish I were there to hug you."

Ram twirled a piece of hair through her fingers. "Yeah, me too. Today sucked."

"Get some rest and let's talk later when you're not as upset. I love you, Ram."

Chapter Fifteen

A WEEK LATER, BROCK'S alarm clock squawked. He swatted at the device, but the damn noise wouldn't stop. He grumbled and shifted to sit up in bed, realizing it was his mobile phone blaring Rick's ringtone. Where the hell was his phone? His gaze darted around the room until he zeroed in on his shorts sitting on the chair across from the bed. He lunged to retrieve his phone from his pocket.

"This better be good," Brock mumbled.

"Dude, you're still sleeping?" Rick asked.

Brock rubbed his eyes to remove the grit that had collected. "It's six in the morning. That's what people do."

"True, but when you're married, you don't. I'm in need of your assistance here at the Pelican. The slow-moving tropical depression is expected to make landfall by tomorrow or Thursday morning at the latest. My paranoid wife wants to board up the back sliders and lay a row of sandbags as a precaution. You know the whole, 'the last time' blah, blah, blah."

"Sure. Let me jump in the shower, and I'll be there in thirty minutes. Do you need me to bring anything?"

"Nope, I already hit the hardware store earlier in the week. That was also a honey-do item."

Brock groaned when he stood, his body stiff from another night of tossing and turning. When he reached the bathroom, he jumped in the shower and went about his routine. In no time, he was dressed and out the door. At least he could get coffee at the Pelican. He had a gut feeling that helping Rick wasn't the only topic on the agenda.

He had not heard from Ram since last Tuesday night. It was not like he thought he would, but he figured she would at least want to hear him out. Doing so wouldn't absolve his guilt or crime, but he felt she owed him that much. Her utter disdain when she spat the word "felon" at him rankled. It wasn't like he had murdered anyone. He thought she knew him better.

When he arrived, he pulled into an empty parking space. The sound of a hammer pounding guided him toward the back of the place.

Rick pointed to a paper cup sitting on an empty table. "Morning. There's your required coffee."

The aroma and flavor made him hum his appreciation. Beth liked her coffee as much as he did. They could spend hours talking about roasters and beans. When he finished a few sips, he moved toward the stack of boards leaning against the wall. He retrieved one and handed it to Rick, who directed Brock on how to hold it while he pounded in the nails. They chatted and laughed about baseball and some other topics while they finished securing the board against the sliders.

"Now we move to the tedious job of shoveling sand into the bags. I had a load delivered yesterday," Rick said. He walked around the building on the opposite side. Two shovels were already standing upright in the pile.

Brock squatted, opening the bag for Rick. "Holy crap, I think you got too much."

"Nah, that's by design. I figured some of the staff might want to make a few for their own homes."

That was Rick, always helping his family, friends, or the community. They worked in silence for almost another hour until they had filled enough bags to circle the perimeter of the back patio and along the bottom of the glass doors.

Perspiration clung to their bodies from exertion and humidity. Rick took a big gulp from one of the two water bottles that had appeared on the back patio.

Rick wiped his mouth with the back of his hand. "What happened with Ram sucks. She's made a mistake."

"It's hers to make. I'll always be a convict. I'd do it again if the outcome could be different," Brock replied as he looked Rick straight in the eyes.

Rick gripped his shoulder. "I know, man. Just remember, you're not alone. Beth and I are here for you. Now, here's the bitter pill you get to swallow. Beth has meddled. And by *meddle*, I mean, she ripped into Ram yesterday. So, when you come inside for breakfast, guess who will be there?"

Brock leaned his head back and groaned. "I had a feeling that this was leading up to something."

"When you're married, you'll get it. I don't mess with Hurricane Beth. Ever. She will defend those she loves to the end of the earth. And you, my friend, are part of her love circle."

Brock wanted to bolt, but running from this would only make Beth strike harder. When they entered the bar, Beth stood with Ram, who looked uncomfortable. A small part of him liked that idea because it might mean she still cared about him. Beth, on the other hand, looked like a warrior goddess bringing two rogue people together to right a wrong. God, he loved Rick's wife, but some things were outside her control. His gaze slid to Rick's, who gave him a thumbs up before he disappeared into the back.

Beth's hands went wide, pointing to them both. "I know I'm being a busybody, but I care about you both. It's been six days, you two. Ram, believe me when I say this, you need to hear his story. Brock, don't get wrapped up in your head. You both need to leave your egos at the door and communicate. Okay, I've said my peace. I'll leave you two alone to talk. If you need me, I'll be in my office."

Ram's gaze shifted to the floor. "Sorry. This is my fault. I asked Beth to take care of my bonsai tree. I didn't want to see it every day because it reminded me of you."

The heavy and awkward air between them made him sad. They had always shared great chemistry. It had been one of the reasons he'd gravitated toward her. He tugged out a chair and took a seat. This morning's work and not sleeping for the last two nights had caught up to him.

"You could have just thrown it out," he groused. So much for thinking she might still care.

She gawked at him. "Why would I do that? It's beautiful."

"You had no problem throwing me away," he griped back, annoyed that he could not control his rising anger or keep his mouth shut.

She winced at his comment. "I-I didn't throw you away. You did that yourself. But Beth and Laney both think I was wrong for not hearing you out."

"Beth is protective. She and Rick have been great friends to me, despite everything. Just answer one question for me. Do you want to hear what I have to say, or are you just doing this because Beth finagled this *chance* meeting?"

"The latter. Brock, you already told me you wanted to be successful and rich. You chose to break the law by manipulating your taxes and got caught. Right? I can't spend the rest of my life wondering what you're doing behind my back. I already survived that embarrassment once."

"Yeah, I'm living the high life now—rolling in all that cash."

His anger went from simmering to a full-blown boil. How dare she sit there and pass judgment on him? Her flippant remarks and poor assessment of his situation made him realize he didn't need her in his life. He wasn't proud of what he did. Yes, he was a criminal, but deep down, he was a good human being who had tried to save his sister.

He stood, raising his hand to stop Ram's reply so he could speak instead. "I think it's good we're done. I don't judge books by their cover. Your assumption couldn't be further from the truth. You don't deserve me."

He paused at the door and looked back at her. "The lesson I learned is that some people hear prison and just jump to the worst possible conclusions. That's you, Ram. I'm nothing like your ex-asshole."

He heard her sniffle before she wailed, "You promised you'd never hurt me."

The door slammed shut behind him, like the final chapter of a book. He refused to be around someone who thought so little of him. He hadn't broken his promise to her, but there was nothing he could do about his past. He understood she'd been burned, but he had never treated her with anything but respect. He couldn't say the same thing about her, so it was time for them to forge different paths forward.

Chapter Sixteen

A BURST OF LOUD clacks from the wooden blinds filled the quiet room when Ram pulled the cord to open her blinds. The local weather forecast predicted the storm would arrive sometime today. The strong winds had arrived, but the rain had yet to come. The array of grayish, blue, and black clouds fascinated her. Mother Nature could produce some beautiful skies.

She'd chosen to finish up the work week at home. Her stomach had been knotted for days. It's not that she was sick, but she didn't feel well either. Her mood hadn't improved either in the days following her second discussion with Brock. It left her confused. What did he mean that it wasn't about money? That was literally the definition of tax evasion.

She hated all the tension. It also didn't sit well with her that she'd hurt him. God help her, she wanted to forgive him. She missed him––his smile, his humor, his touch. Now she regretted not hearing him out. Now she had even more questions after their last discussion, but it was too late. They had both drawn their lines in the sand.

The sound of an engine drew Ram's gaze to the parking lot. A pit of dread balled up in her stomach at Beth's arrival. She had delayed picking up her truck longer than she liked. At least Beth offered to take her, which also provided the opportunity to clear the air. The last thing she wanted was for Beth to be mad at her because of Brock.

Ram grabbed her purse, locked her door, and headed downstairs. The wind whipped her ponytail across her eyes. The air was stained with the scent of the coming storm.

"Thanks, Beth. You're a lifesaver. It's been hard being without a vehicle."

"No worries. Will you plug the address into my nav system?"

The map updated the various route guidance options, and then a woman's voice with a British accent provided directions. According to the display, Ram had ten minutes before arrival to clear the air with Beth. Even if she wasn't mad, she could still be disappointed in her. Ram abandoned what she had rehearsed and just led with her heart.

"Beth, I've been worried that I've upset you."

Beth shot her a side-eyed look. "What? You're doing a great job. I told you when you started that you had the flexibility to work remotely."

"No, that's not what I meant. I'm glad to hear you're pleased with my performance. What I mean is that maybe you're mad about what happened between me and Brock? I know you're protective of him. I don't want our issues to cause problems between us. I consider you a friend, and I don't want to lose that. I-I'm sorry, I know I'm rambling."

The turn signal started a series of ticks before Beth pulled into an empty parking lot. She jabbed the pause button with her finger to silence the automated directions.

"I understand, and we're fine," Beth's smile spoke volumes. "We are friends, Ram, which is why I butted into a personal matter between you and Brock. Some might say, like my husband, that it wasn't my place. I am disappointed that you two didn't work through your issues yesterday."

Ram inhaled a deep, steady breath through her nose. A small weight lifted from her shoulders. "Thank goodness, but I know this put you in an uncomfortable position. Remember when I told you about George, my ex? Well, he drained my bank accounts, and I felt so stupid for even giving him access. He used me, and that's been difficult for me to get over. I do care about Brock, but I can't continue in a relationship with someone I can't trust. I don't want to feel that way again."

Beth leaned her head on the headrest. "I see why you're hesitant. His past aside, did he ever do anything to show you that he was not an upstanding man?"

Ram shook her head. That was an easy question to answer. "He told me he desired to be a wealthy man. When he said he'd gotten arrested for tax evasion, that freaked me out. He took money that didn't belong to him.

"Did Brock actually tell you that he was wealthy?" Beth asked.

"No, but I figured it out. He once mentioned that he wanted to be successful and rich. So why else would you defraud the government to keep your money?"

Beth let her head roll to the right so she could look at Ram. "That may have been a young man's dream, but it's not why he went to jail. Oh Ram, you couldn't be further from the truth. Now, I understand why Brock's upset. He deserved to be heard, and now I'm afraid he'll never open himself up to you. If you want any chance of reconciliation, whether it's friendship or more, you may want to learn the truth."

Ram's stomach revolted again. Intrigued by Beth's perspective and her guilt over not hearing Brock out, she decided to take Beth up on her offer. Brock had fierce supporters in his corner.

"Yes, but how do you even know the details of his story?"

Beth sat upright, using her steering wheel to pull herself forward in the seat.

"Kurt and Rick are friends with Brock's lawyer, who recommended to his client that Destiny would be a good place to start over and rebuild his life. Two years ago, after serving a one-year prison sentence, he moved to Destiny. His wages are being garnished to pay back the hundred thousand dollar tax evasion fine. In addition, he does all types of side jobs to earn extra money to put toward his debt in ad hoc payments."

Ram let her gaze shift to watching the trees blowing in the wind. "He told me *most* of that already."

Beth turned to face Ram. "Here's the part you didn't give him a chance to tell you. He drained all his money and sold off his assets to take care of his sister, Gina, who had cancer."

Ram fisted her hands in her lap. "Is his sister alive?"

"No," Beth whispered. "She died while he was in prison, and he blames himself for her death."

"Oh my god, Beth, I had no idea. Why would he drain his accounts? Did she not have insurance?" Ram asked, a lump forming in her throat.

"Gina had insurance, but her doctor wanted her to be a part of an experimental cancer drug trial that held real promise. It had passed phase one and had moved into patient testing. Her doctor got her qualified, but her insurance wouldn't cover the experimental drug. Some insurers will cover drugs in that status, but not all. They tried to appeal the decision, but ultimately, she was denied. Brock called the pharmaceutical company, which finally agreed to let him pay out of pocket for these drugs. He told his sister that her denial had been overturned, and she had been approved. The only way he could pay for the expensive treatments was to use everything he had, his paychecks, savings, 401k, and eventually he sold his cars and house."

"Oh my God, Beth, this is horrible. He fought for his sister when the system had let him down," Ram said in a mere whisper.

Beth nodded. "He planned to declare and pay those taxes after she was in remission. Then the collection notices started to arrive. When IRS agents arrested him, he lost his job and the ability to pay for her continued care. He pleaded guilty, accepting a plea deal that included one year in prison and a reduced fine, all in an effort to reunite with Gina. Unfortunately, his sister's health declined, and she died right before he was released. This is why he blames himself."

Ram didn't say a word while she processed everything she had just heard. She covered her face with her hands. Her heart ached for Brock. What the hell had she done? She turned her back on the best thing that had walked into her life on speculation. Worse, she'd condemned him without knowing all the facts. Laney had been right. She was an idiot. What he did was wrong, but he did it out of love.

"What am I going to do, Beth? He hates me," Ram croaked out.

Beth rubbed her back to help calm her. "You fight like hell. People make mistakes, but forgiveness can happen. It won't be easy, but he's worth it. So are you, Ram."

Ram turned and hugged her friend. "Thank you for telling me."

Beth hugged her back, and when she sat back in her seat, Beth reengaged the navigation guide and continued down the road. The rain had finally arrived. The wipers barely kept up with the downpour.

The shop's workers scrambled to close early for the day so the employees could leave. Beth finally relented when Ram insisted she just drop her off as opposed to waiting. Ram promised to call her when she got home. In record time, she'd paid and was back on the road toward her apartment. Once she parked, she leaned forward to look up at the sky through the top of her windshield, hoping she would see some sign that the rain would pause.

"Girls Just Wanna Have Fun" started to play on her phone.

"Hey Laney, hold on a second..."

Ram dashed up the stairs to her door. Once she was under the overhang, she pinched the phone between her ear and shoulder. "I'm back. I just got back from picking up my truck. It's pouring here. I think the storm has arrived."

"I know, I'm watching the weather center."

"Laney, I'm an awful person. You were so right, why didn't I listen to you?"

"Are we talking Brock?"

In her apartment, Ram tugged some paper towels free from the roll to blot her face and hair. "Yes, and I royally fucked up."

She spent the next few minutes telling her everything she'd learned from Beth. Unshed tears pooled in her eyes. "I love him, Laney," she admitted.

"Oh, Ram, fear betrayed you. What are you going to do?"

Ram tossed her damp towels into the trash. "First, I'm going to apologize. Then, I'm not sure. I'm not sure if I can fix this, but I'm going to try. God, I hope I can."

A loud knocking at the front door interrupted her thoughts. Who would be out in this weather? A slight flutter of hope developed low in the belly, that it might just be Brock. Could she be that lucky?

"Hold on, Laney, someone's at the door," she said.

She twisted the lock. Tugging the door open, her flutter morphed into dread. The windows rattled from a loud blast of thunder. The rain fell horizontally, pelting her body and the floor. "George, why are you here? Never mind, don't answer that, just leave."

She stepped back to slam the door in his face, but his hand darted out, forcing it wide open.

"Don't be rude, baby. I drove here to be with you. I love you and I miss you," George said. He stood inside her apartment, dripping water and his lies everywhere.

"Uh, Laney, I need to call you back…"

She slid her phone in her back pocket as George waltzed into her place like he lived here.

"Where's the bathroom? I need to piss."

"Stop. You're not welcome here!" she yelled, following right behind him, but he didn't listen. He just prowled until he found what he was looking for.

She stood there, unmoving, a chill wiggling its way down her body. Several deep rumbles and flashes of light added to the creepiness of his arrival. When he finally reappeared, she pointed to the front door. "Get out, George, I want you to leave. You're trespassing."

"Baby, you're being emotional. Is it that time of the month?"

All she wanted to do was smack that smug look off his face. What a jackass. How did she ever find him attractive? Sure, he was handsome on the outside, but when he opened his mouth, attraction vanished. George was nothing more than a heartless shell of a man. Hearing his voice made her skin crawl. Her patience with him had run dry.

"What's the matter? Did your *soulmate* figure out you're a loser?"

"There's no reason to be nasty. I'm a man, baby. My dick steered me wrong, but I soon realized my future is with you," he crooned.

"How did you even find me?"

He snagged her arms and yanked her closer. "Laney loves snapping pictures and posting them to her socials, and of course, there's the news. It made locating you rather easy."

Finally, one honest thing he admitted to; he'd come because she'd won the lottery. How many nights had she lain awake thinking about what she'd say to him if she ever got the chance? Well, he took that away from her when he left her high and dry to be with another woman and all her money. Now she had a ton of anger to dump on him—from how he treated her and women in general, and from the rift between her and Brock.

His fingers dug painfully into her flesh. It might not be prudent to push him. He'd never been physical with her, but who knew what he would do if provoked? This man had a blackened heart and an agenda, which scared her.

She had to get rid of him, but how? He wasn't listening to her.

The lights flickered, followed by another big boom. This night was getting worse by the moment.

Chapter Seventeen

B ROCK HAD JUST FINISHED loading his groceries into his truck when his phone vibrated in his pocket. When he retrieved it, he saw Laney's name on the display. He almost ignored the call but thought better of it. Laney had no problem speaking her mind, but she didn't seem like the type to just call him out of the blue. If she wanted to talk about Ram, he'd end the call, but maybe it was important.

"Hey, Laney, what's up?"

"Brock, it's George. He's at Ram's apartment. Like he just showed up, which can't be good," she rattled off in a panicked voice. "I know you're mad at her and I don't blame you, but can you go over and make sure she's safe? Help her get rid of him. I'm worried."

Shit, that can't be good. That man was bad news, who had no business bothering Ram. George had driven a long way to find her, which meant he was motivated.

Thick rain drops beat against the metal frame of his truck.

"I'm on my way, Laney," he said in a raised voice.

"Thanks, I owe you."

He ended the call and drove faster than he should have to Ram's place. When he arrived, her front door stood wide open. He hustled up the stairs as another discharge of lightning flared behind him. An instant clap of thunder masked his footsteps as he approached. Relieved to hear her voice, he listened for a moment to assess the situation before he acted.

"Baby, we belong together," George sneered.

"Please, you're only here to get your hands on my winnings. Spoiler alert: you're not getting any of it. You're a despicable human being whom I want nothing to do with. And because of your bullshit, I misjudged an honorable man. I doubted Brock when I should have listened to him, and because of you, I've pushed the man I love out of my life."

Brock froze for a second. She had meant those words. *She loved me.*

"No," George shouted. He shook her like he could erase the comments she'd made. "Stop fighting me. Everything will be fine once we return to Knoxville."

"Stop it. You're hurting me. Get the fuck away from me, George!" she bellowed.

Brock burst into the apartment. "Release her now. The cops are on their way. You'll want to leave before you're arrested for trespassing and assault."

George shoved Ram backward. In the blink of an eye, he turned and lunged at Brock. Brock sidestepped his advance to deliver a direct hit to his face, feeling the crunch of bones beneath his knuckles. When George recovered, he swung at him again, but Brock evaded his attempt. In one fluid motion, Brock caught George's arm, twisting it up and behind his back.

"You're a dumbass. You must want to become someone's bitch in jail. Your two choices are to meet Destiny's finest or leave and never return. If you do return, you'll wish you never did," Brock snarled against the side of his face, cranking his hold on the man's arm a little higher until he cried out in pain.

"Leave. I'll leave," George panted, his voice a little higher than usual.

Brock released George, who bolted for the door and disappeared into the storm. Brock shut the door behind the man and locked the deadbolt. He pivoted and faltered at the sight of Ram, whose body shivered while tears streamed down her face.

"Are you okay?" he asked, his concern written all over his face.

Her hands covered her face, and her tears became sobs.

He sat next to her on the floor and wrapped his arm around her. "You're okay. Let it out, Ram."

As he comforted her, he thought about everything that had happened over the past few days. He now understood why she'd rushed to push him away. Her wounds were still fresh, but so were his.

When she regained her composure, he lifted her chin. "Let me see your arms," he asked.

She bent both arms at the elbows, giving him a view of her tender flesh marred with finger-shaped bruising. "These might bruise."

He propelled his body upward and extended his hand to help her to her feet. The moment her feet hit the ground, she wrapped her arms around him. "Thank you for coming. I don't know why you did, but I'm so thankful."

"Laney called me," he said.

Ram tightened her grip. "I know you're mad at me. I'm so so sorry, Brock. I want you to know Beth told me everything, but I should have heard it from you. I failed you, and I'll live with that regret for the rest of my life."

His chest tightened with an emotion he ignored. He didn't want her to live with regrets, and he truly believed that she was remorseful. He knew from experience that blaming yourself was not a healthy path to follow in life.

But he also didn't know what he wanted. His wounds were still fresh. He needed time to figure everything out and decide if they could move forward as a couple or if friendship was the only way ahead. "I accept your apology, but I don't know what else I can offer at this point."

Her gaze lifted to his, and it took everything in his power not to lean down and kiss those pouty lips.

"You promise? Because I plan to woo you back into my arms. It's going to be my mission to spend the rest of my life showing you how much you mean to me. And I mean all of you—ex-prisoner, hunk, landscaping god, and badass," she said with conviction.

It felt good to be wanted this much, but he wasn't going to string her along. "One day at a time, Ram. That's all I can promise."

The lights flickered again, and then everything went black. The only sound in the room was the hum of the motors winding down due to the loss of electrical power. Once his eyes adjusted to the darkness, he could make out her movements.

"I hope this is temporary," she said, moving to the skinny cabinet next to her refrigerator. She removed a flashlight, candles, a battery-operated radio, and matches.

"Wow, you're prepared," Brock said. He took the radio and fiddled until he found the local news station.

Ram lit the candles. "How long until the police get here?"

"They're not coming. I made that up because I had hoped George would flee on his own accord."

Ram's laugh made him smile. "Well, I totally bought it. I know I've already said it, but thanks for jumping in to help me. I've never seen that side of him. It frightened me."

"You don't need to thank me. I care about you and will always have your back," Brock replied. He meant every word. She mattered to him.

"I like the sound of that, but here's another favor. Will you stay the night? I'm still a little freaked out by his arrival and the whole no power situation."

"Done, but I need to get my groceries out of my truck before they spoil."

When Brock returned, they put everything in her refrigerator. She moved the candle to the coffee table and took a seat. He liked and had missed the familiarity of their being together. Spending time with Ram felt natural to him. The electricity was restored a few hours later, but they continued to sit in the darkened room, lit only by candlelight, enjoying the intimate atmosphere.

She wanted to hear more about Gina. At first, opening the part of his heart where he'd locked away his sister's memory hurt, but once he started sharing those stories, he couldn't stop. It became cathartic.

At some point, they had fallen asleep because the next time he opened his eyes, the sun had started to rise. He nudged Ram's leg with his foot. "Rise and shine, sleepyhead. It's almost noon, but we survived."

Drowsy eyes cracked open. Then, she slowly stretched like a cat waking from a nap. "No, roll the clock back so we can sleep a little longer," her voice was scratchy.

"I've got to get rolling to survey the damage from the storm throughout town, as well as head out to Burn Sand to see if their new landscape display survived Mother Nature. Do you want to come along?"

"Yes, I want to see it."

Brock and Ram spent two hours driving around Destiny, tracking all the damage he had to correct on Monday. Luckily, it wasn't as bad as it could have been—mostly branches with one fallen tree in the town square. There had also been some flooding in a few places where sand had been left behind. When they arrived at Burn Sand, he escorted her around to the backyard. Except for a few wayward plants that he righted, his creation had survived the storm.

He smiled when she gasped with excitement. "Oh, my gosh, you did a fantastic job! The coral reef and dolphins are beautiful. I love how all the colors came together. Do you mind if I take a few pictures?"

"No, go ahead," he said.

She fiddled with her phone as she walked around the area. "Did you send them any pictures?"

"No, Bernie likes theatrics. She'll want to see it live and in person so she can enjoy the visceral reaction or some shit."

Ram giggled at his comment. "Well, that's very worldly, but she's gonna love it."

When she finished, she walked to the edge of the yard, taking in the view of the magnificent ocean, which stretched for miles in front of her. The vision was akin to a siren on the edge of the cliffs. He retrieved his phone to take a picture of her. When he finished, he walked over and stood next to her. The view was breathtaking, the sea was calm, and the remaining clouds were wispy stragglers trailing behind the storm, like lost wanderers looking to chart their course.

"I'd like to have a home with an ocean view. I could spend hours watching it," she said.

"You could make that a reality," he said, not sure where her thoughts were headed.

"It's funny. You'd think having all this money would make life easier. And it does on one hand, but it also adds more ideas and options onto your plate, which you then spend time agonizing over whether you're making good decisions. I do have some plans I've been working on that I'd like to share with you, but I'm not quite ready."

"I'd be honored." Brock grabbed her hand. "Worrying won't help you make wise decisions. It just sucks the fun right out of it. Although I still think a financial advisor will help you manage that wealth, if you're concerned about spending too much."

She rolled her head from side to side in a playful manner. "A good Brock'ism. Okay, smartie pants, what's next?"

He thought for a moment. "How about an early dinner, and then I'll take you home?"

"Deal, but my treat. How about the Conch Shell Café?" she asked.

He nodded his head.

This is what he loved about spending time with Ram, what he had missed. It was easy. They had fun and could chat about anything or nothing at all. When she stood by his side, the world brightened. He could see them building a future together. He had never met another person who affected him so profoundly. The question that remained was whether his past would continue to bother her.

Chapter Eighteen

R AM KNOCKED ON BETH'S office door with two specialty coffee drinks in hand.

Beth and Rick had closed the Tipsy Pelican the day after the storm, allowing employees to spend time at home and take care of what was needed. Sleep-deprived but giddy, she had spent the rest of last night drafting her business plans for Destiny's newest shop, the Sand Dollar Florist Boutique. The logo she'd designed looked amazing, featuring a sand dollar with curvy font, but its meaning was what made it perfect. She'd completed a rough sketch a few days earlier, which featured an image of a sand dollar instead of using words, and in a curvy font, "Florist Boutique" appeared just beneath it, toward the right side.

The meeting with Mrs. Coventon needed to take place sooner than she had originally planned. The lottery office had sent her an email first thing that day letting her know the funds were ready to be sent after she signed a couple of new documents.

Upon learning this information, she wanted to meet with Beth to review her comprehensive timeline. The specifics would fall into place once she met with the various contractors and completed all the other moving pieces and permits.

She also wanted to update her on Brock. He had admitted he hadn't closed the door between them romantically. There was no doubt they would always be friends, but she wanted the fairytale ending.

"It's open," Beth shouted.

Ram twisted the knob, pushing it open, holding up her offerings. "I have updates."

Beth's eyes widened. "Oh, are you buttering me up, or is this good gossip?"

Ram smiled and took a seat in the chair at the front of her desk. "Both, but I'll start with the good news. I apologized to Brock when he came over to help me get rid of George. The best news was that he didn't reject me, so there's hope."

"Wait, back up. George came here?" Beth asked.

Ram sipped her coffee. "Yeah, he heard I won the money and thought I'd just take him back. Luckily, I had been talking to Laney, who then called Brock, and poof, that jerk was gone. When Brock went all alpha male on him, I'm not going to lie, it revved my engines—hot and sexy."

Beth rolled her eyes before snorting. "Do not ever tell him that or his ego will expand, and then you'll have him acting like Rick. I'm sorry about George, but Brock is protective of you."

"I'm prepared for this battle. Now here's the reason for the coffee."

Beth's face crumbled. "I can't handle it today if this starts with you giving your notice."

"Not yet. However, I would like to review my plans. I would appreciate your input and feedback on my proposed timeline, which includes my replacement. However, I'm hoping to stay here for a while, if you're okay with all of this. I meant what I said before; I'll be here until we have a replacement in place."

Ram reviewed her transition plans with Beth, as well as her business plan draft for her shop, making some revisions based on Beth's insight. Her ideas about how she'd handle this job while opening her shop worked for Beth. When they finished their discussion, she stood and paused.

"Hey, I would like to take my bonsai back. I have plans for that little guy."

Beth motioned with her hand to take it.

The next night, Ram came up with an idea to surprise Brock. She added those preparations to her list. When the time came for her to leave for the day, she dropped a stack of paperwork for Beth to review and headed to the shop space. Her dreams were about to come true, she thought, with her purse, briefcase, and bonsai tree in her arms. On her way to her appointment, Brock called to check in with her. Excitement flared, accompanied by a rush of endorphins. "Things are great. How goes the storm cleanup?"

"Better than I expected. Once I've completed all of those, I'll start working on another project. You were on my mind, so I thought I'd reach out. Do you want to have dinner tonight?"

Ram gave a fist pump. "I'd love to, but I'd like for you to come to the store first. Can you be here around five?"

"I'll see you then. Break a leg, Ram. Or, whatever you say when a person's rocking their dream."

She turned her car off, a huge smile covering her face.

An older woman came outside to greet her. "Ram, I'm Mrs. Coventon. How are you, dear?"

Ram extended her hand to the woman. "I couldn't be better. I also have good news. The money should be in my account in seventy-two hours."

"Okay. I happen to have the contract in my bag. Let's get this rolling."

Ram loved the space. She could envision the entire setup. After they discussed pricing, she signed the contract and gave her a check to cover a small portion of what was due until the winnings hit her account, giving her immediate access to the building.

Two keys sparkled in her hand.

She texted Laney some pictures, and within moments, her ringtone echoed through the empty space.

"Holy crap, is this the store? The space is amazing."

"Yes, it's all mine. Can you believe it?"

"Gosh, I may have to move to Destiny just to see your floral boutique come to life," Laney said in a cheerful whisper.

"Hey, will you send me that picture you took of Brock and me dancing? I want to use it too."

"Done," Laney replied.

The chirp on her phone confirmed receipt. "Thanks. I've got to run, I'll call you later. Keep putting good thoughts into the universe for me."

"I can't wait to hear how it goes. Oh, don't forget to wear your best lingerie set, just in case," Laney said.

Ram laughed, ending her call to tackle her to-do list. First, she had to take the picture to the drugstore to get it printed on thick poster board. The next stop would be the bank to get a form notarized, followed by picking up an order at the hardware store.

The final stop was to see the graphic designer who had created the artwork for her storefront. She wanted to order her signage, marketing supplies, and pick up a few things she wanted for later that night.

She checked the time on her watch and got moving.

Ram returned just after four, giving her plenty of time to set up, measure, and wait for Brock. She set up a folding table and placed the bonsai tree in the center and propped up the posters against the wall where she thought they might go. Once that was done, she placed the proposal on the table too.

After unloading her car, she set up the six-foot, rectangular folding table and placed the bonsai tree in the center. Then she removed the paper protection from the poster-sized pictures, propping them against the wall where she thought they might go. Next, she put the proposal on the table. The stickers were in their own bag, so she retrieved one.

Where had she put the hard hat? She looked through a few bags until she found it and placed the sticker along the front. When she put on the hat, it fell over her eyebrows. She fussed with the adjustment band in the back to tighten up the strap. When she looked up, she saw his truck parked along the curb.

Butterflies fluttered in her stomach when she saw him. He looked handsome in a blue T-shirt, khaki shorts, and flip flops. She rushed to the door to greet him.

"Welcome to Sand Dollar Floral Boutique," she greeted. She couldn't help but notice his gaze hadn't left her body.

"Sorry, I couldn't get past the hat," he said, his voice gravelly and deep.

She shrugged her shoulders. "Well, this visit is about dreams. I remembered you had one about me and a hard hat."

"Sweetheart, that was a fantasy—you know, a dream's counterpart, but with a carnal action."

Her body hummed in all the right places. Driven by need, she wrapped her arms around him until she could feel the warmth from his touch. Stepping back, she returned her gaze to his and pointed to the decal on her hat. "This is going to be the name of the store."

"That's perfect. I like the design," he said. He looked around, taking in the space. He pointed to his gift—the gifted bonsai tree sitting on the table—as he moved to the first grouping of pictures. "Whoever gave you that has great taste."

She came up behind him and nudged him with her shoulder. "He does. Both the man and the plant mean a lot to me."

"Why are these here?" he asked, squatting down to look at each print.

She fanned her hand across the space. "I envision a counter here with these prints hanging on the wall, highlighting your talents from the Burn Sand project."

"Why? What do those have to do with your shop?"

Ram approached him and took his hand. "That business proposal over on the table is for you. I want to bring you into my business. This area would be suitable for architectural landscaping projects, such as topiaries, wedding planning, or other special occasions. There's no pressure, but I want to build a future that includes you. I love you, Brock—all of you."

He stared at her, no doubt thinking about what she'd said. She didn't move a muscle, just holding his gaze and giving him time to absorb it all. The time had come to share what was in her heart. She had nothing to hide. Of course, she had hoped that he'd profess his love for her, but if he wasn't ready, that was okay too. She'd wait for him because he was worth it.

"This area over here is where I will put the register," she said, still holding his hand to take him with her. "And on the wall behind it, I want to hang this photo."

He picked up the photo and smiled. "I love this photo of us dancing. Laney sent me a copy, too."

She continued her tour. Showing him where she wanted a row of coolers to hold arrangements, plants, and individual stems for purchase, a table in the middle for displays, and off to his side of the shop, a working table. When they finished with the front of the store, she took him into the back, continuing to walk him through her vision for that space.

"Ram, this is spectacular. I'm eager to see it come together. I'll take your proposal with me and read it later," he said. "Right now, I have something to show you before dinner. Is that okay?"

"Of course," she replied.

When she had all the lights off, she removed her hat and placed it on the table.

Brock stood holding the door open, his keys in his hand. "Ram," he said in a husky voice. "Take the hat with you. I want you to wear it."

She bit her bottom lip between her teeth and smiled at him. "Your wish is granted."

She locked the door and followed him to his truck. He opened the passenger side before walking around the back and slid in on the driver's side. She'd never thought about it before, but she loved his manners. His mom raised him well and, in her heart, she knew his family would be proud of the man he had become.

Chapter Nineteen

B ROCK COULDN'T WAIT TO show her his surprise. The idea came to him as he cleaned up the damage from the storm, damage that wasn't permanent after he put in the effort to complete the task. Last night, he had realized that all of what had transpired between them was a fight based on misinformation and misperceptions. She had hurt him, and he allowed that hurt to color his emotions. Now he understood that her reaction came from her fear of what had happened between her and George, not because he was a felon or had been repulsed by his past.

He loved how she included him in her plans for the future—a proposal he couldn't wait to review. She had always been open and honest with him, but like him, she hadn't shown him her entire hand. But when he overheard Ram tell George that she loved him, it drove that point home. It may have taken him a while to get that through his thick skull, but eventually he figured that later was always better than never, when it mattered.

"I want you to close your eyes until I tell you to open them," he said.

She turned her head, giving him an assessing look. "Okay, my curiosity is piqued."

"Good, it should be. Now don't ruin my surprise. No peeking."

He slowed to make a U-turn in the middle of the road, then maneuvered his truck into a space against the curb with an uninhibited view of Destiny's center square with the small pond behind it.

"Open your eyes," he said. He smiled at her gasp. "Oh, Brock, I love the weeping willow. It's a great choice for a tree replacement."

He opened his door and moved to open her side. He waited for her to exit his truck with his hand extended. When she slid her hand into his, they walked together toward the tree and the Welcome to Destiny sign on one side, with a topiary heart on the other.

"This is for us, Ram. This weeping willow is a mash of our lives, past, present, and future. To honor those we've lost, along with the sadness and challenges we've survived. The willow's limbs represent the resilience and adaptability we've needed to get to this point as we find balance and harmony in our lives as we grow together."

"Oh, Brock, it's perfect," she said, a slight wobble to her words. "I love it, and I love you."

When he lifted her chin, tears pooled in her eyes. "It's not supposed to make you cry."

"Men," she teased. "These are happy tears. Now, what does the heart represent?"

He tugged her into a hug. "My love for you. I want to spend years watching you cry happy tears."

She tried to push out of his hold, probably to give him a sassy reply, but he claimed her lips instead. He poured all of himself into that kiss. She went soft in his arms, and she emitted that little groan he loved.

When he broke off the kiss, he cupped her face with both hands. "I also want to start over, if you'll give me that chance."

Her brows pinched together. "What does that mean?"

"I want to get it right with you this time. I want to take you to dinner. To share my story so you hear it from my lips. To answer every question you have. We have a lifetime to share every detail in between, but I want to do this right."

Her gaze moved upward, finding his. "Stay here."

She broke free and approached a couple walking their dog. Whatever she'd asked of them, they agreed, and then she handed over her phone.

"They've agreed to take our picture. Come on, Brock, let's pose. We can add this to our collection of memories, because I never want to forget this moment. This beats winning the lottery every day of the week."

When the pictures were over, Ram grabbed his hand and dragged him toward the truck. "I'm starving, and I can't wait to start our date. I was also hoping that maybe we could get to third base this time with a walk-off homer?"

"As long as you wear that hard hat, I'll perform all night long for you."

Ram fanned herself and blew him a kiss before she hopped up into the truck.

This would be his life, and he couldn't wait to live it with the woman he loved standing by his side.

The End

If you enjoyed their story, Brock, Ramona, and myself would love it if you would leave a review on Amazon, Goodreads, or other review sites to help readers like you find their story.

Turn the page for a sneak peek of the first book in the Love in Destiny series, Sunsets, Stick Saves, and a Honeymoon

by G K Brady.

&

a sneak peek of Trent's Redemption, a romantic suspense by Bailey Thomas

Sunsets, Stick Saves, and a Honeymoon Sneak Peek

Honeymoon for One

Lexi Campbell stepped from the shuttle bus and took a deep breath. The place was exactly as she'd pictured, right down to the lustrous open-air lobby, the swaying palms, and the sparkling blue water. So different from her home state of Colorado, yet equally breath-taking in its own way. She'd certainly hit it out of the park when she'd chosen the Sapphire Hotel as her honeymoon destination. Too bad she hadn't done as well picking the man who was supposed to be here with her.

Closing her eyes, she let the sea air caress her skin and wash away the pieces of Conrad that still stuck to her like staticky bits of plastic wrapper.

"Uh, miss?"

Lexi turned toward the deep voice that reminded her of gravel. *Agitated* gravel—to match the annoyance in the man's light eyes as he peered at her over mirrored sunglasses. This was the same guy who'd sprawled his big frame across an entire seat and had promptly fallen asleep, not only missing out on the beautiful tropical scenery sliding past the window but also making it impossible for anyone to sit beside him had they chosen to—not that the bus had been full, but still.

Lexi reminded herself—again—that not all men were insensitive narcissists who didn't flinch at breaking a woman's heart, and that she shouldn't be passing judgment on a stranger.

A different remarkable feature about this particular man was his shirt. It was covered with magenta flamingos against an eye-popping cobalt sky. Added to the mix were parrots in various shades of garish against electric green palm leaves. Lexi was as guilty as the next person when it came to questionable wardrobe choices, but if this guy had dressed to impress, he'd missed the mark. And that wasn't a judgment call—it was a fact.

"There's a bus full of people who'd like to get off and enjoy the view too," he informed her in a voice as dry as the crackers they'd passed out on the plane, "but they can't because you're holding up the line." A fake smile pulled the corners of his mouth and immediately dropped into a sour expression.

Clearly, she'd given this guy more benefit of the doubt than was merited. She was about to tell him where to shove his attitude when her gaze was pulled to the unhappy faces staring down at her from the shuttle's windows.

Oh God!

Mortified at her *own* insensitivity, Lexi quickly stepped aside. It wasn't like her to be so thoughtless, though Conrad would have argued otherwise. *"I swear, Alexis, sometimes you go through life as if no one else existed.*" Funny. Her ex could have been looking in a mirror when he'd hurled *that* admonishment at her.

The arrogant guest stepped off the bus and shoved his glasses back up the bridge of his aquiline nose. Sun glinted off his haphazard chestnut locks, lighting them with a hint of gold.

"Thanks," he tossed out, though there wasn't a single note of gratitude in his voice. He breezed past her without a backward glance.

Clutching her purse and carry-on in one hand and her suitcase handle in the other, she scurried toward the check-in desk as gracefully as one could with their hands full and a sandal missing its heel. Terrible Hawaiian Shirt Guy had beat her there. As she lined up behind him, she stumbled on her uneven shoes, falling against his muscular back before dropping to the floor like a sack of new potatoes. At least it *felt* muscular through the fabric of his short-sleeved kaleidoscope of a tropical button-up.

"Of *course* I trip and face-plant into a human wall," she muttered to herself.

He turned, slid his sunglasses down his nose again, and blinked. "Technically, I think I broke your fall. You're welcome."

Lexi peered up at him—*way* up. "Oh goodie. A hero *and* a smartass." Oh Lord! Lexi's mom would be *horrified* at her mouthing off to a stranger. She'd been taught better. Heck, she didn't even give her friends lip! A twenty-nine-year-old woman should have better control of her snark, but something about this guy stirred up her sassy side.

He didn't seem fazed by her sharp tongue, though. "Former hero, current beach bum. Smartass is permanent, though." He offered his hand, which she ignored, instead climbing to her feet with the grace of an elephant.

Gathering her dignity, she apologized. "I'm sorry. It's my shoe." His eyes traveled down to her feet and back up again. "I lost the heel on the airport people mover. There was this older woman, you see, and she was having a hard time getting off—you know how those things sort of throw you at the end. Anyway, I tried to help her and—"

He grunted and turned back around, pushing his sunglasses back into place and showing her his broad back. *Damn it!* She always babbled when she was nervous, though why this guy made her nervous was a mystery. Ever since Conrad dumped her seven months ago, her confidence had taken a plunge off the high dive and splatted at an all-time low. She used to be able to carry on conversations with attractive men without getting rattled. As a bridal magazine copywriter and sometimes-assistant to the magazine's photography department, she had been around some of the most beautiful humans on the planet. They were everywhere—even in Colorado. Talking to gorgeous men had been a common occurrence and, ironically, necessary mostly to put *them* at ease.

But like everything else in her life, that part of her had been broken too.

"You're not broken," her bestie's voice echoed in her head. *"So you were fooled and fell for the wrong man. It happens. He didn't deserve to lick the dirt off your shoes. You just need to get back in the saddle and get in touch with your inner Wanton Woman so she can use the hell out of a man. Many men!"*

Ha! Easy for Anna to say. She *had* her man, though Lexi wasn't too fond of him at the moment. He'd knocked up her best friend, which had kept her from taking Conrad's place on this all-expenses-paid honeymoon—the honeymoon Lexi had foolishly paid for a year ago, when she'd been *positive* she was getting married on New Year's Eve in Colorado's cold climate. A beach getaway had sounded like the perfect honeymoon. And sure, it had been a great deal ... because it had been *nonrefundable*. The hotel had taken pity and bent their rules, letting her postpone the stay for a year from the time she booked it—which explained why she was vacationing in the beach resort town of Destiny, Florida, during one of the hottest months of the year. Only after Lexi had locked in the new date did Anna learn she was pregnant. There was no backing out.

"Miss?" a clerk beckoned from the concierge's desk. Apparently, she had beckoned for a while because Mr. Smartass was being checked in by a different clerk.

He spared her a glance and a smirk. "Looks like you're holding up the line again."

Fuming, she hobbled to the counter. As she pulled out her driver's license, she repeated a mantra to stay calm and chive on. She was one step closer to a fabulous ocean-view suite and a week of tropical drinks and beautiful sunsets. Nirvana was near. Life was about to take a turn in the right direction. All she had to do was sit back, relax, and let opportunity in when it knocked.

Easy peasy, lemon squeezy.

Lexi unpacked, working out any wrinkles as she hung her clothes. She carefully laid her expensive lingerie into drawers—the luxurious bits of finery she'd purchased *before* Conrad dropped his bombshell. In the bathroom, she arranged her cosmetics and grooming essentials in the same neat order as at home. *A place for everything, and everything in its place.* Conrad used to laugh at her organization OCD, but she couldn't unwind until she'd put everything away. She'd always been wired that way. Work before pleasure. Except she didn't *have* any work anymore, but she wasn't going to think about that right now.

No, she had earned this vacation, damn it, and she was going to let herself—er, Wanton Woman—enjoy it. First, though, she and her alter ego needed to become acquainted—assuming she even existed.

When the first bars of Bruno Mars's "Count on Me" chimed on her phone, she quickly answered and plopped into a cushy lounging chair.

"Hey, girlfriend, I was just hearing your voice in my head urging WW to come out of her shell."

"Good! I hope she listens to me. So how was the travel? What's the suite like?"

"The travel was uneventful, but the suite! Oh God, Anna! The view of the infinity pool and ocean is to die for. The mattress is thick enough that the princess wouldn't feel an entire peapod, and the bathroom reminds me of a Roman bath." Lexi let out a wistful sigh. "I wish you were here to enjoy it with me. I swear, there's enough room for your entire family in here."

Anna came from a large Polish family. An only child, Lexi loved hanging around them so she could soak up the chaos, so different from her own life growing up. Her parents were professors, and dinner discussions had been quiet affairs that centered around the cerebral. Not that there was anything wrong with that—Lexi adored her folks—but she reveled in the banter and the unabashed affection Anna's family lavished on one another.

"So have you met any of this week's one-night performers yet?" Lexi could practically hear the waggle in her friend's eyebrows.

"Well, there was this guy on my shuttle." The image of a tall, dark-haired man with chocolate eyes and a brilliant smile floated through her head.

"Did you talk to him?"

"Well, no."

Anna sighed. "Lex, Wanton Woman's not going to have anyone to play with unless you put yourself out there. Promise me that as soon as we hang up, you'll throw on that slinky white sundress we picked out and take yourself to the bar. When you get there, you're going to *sit* at the bar—that's a neon sign that says 'My hoohah is open for business'—and order yourself an umbrella drink."

Lexi burst out with a laugh. "My *hoohah* is open for business? Anna, I'm not *selling* the goods."

"Well, you're advertising them. Especially after getting that Brazilian."

"It wasn't a Brazilian. It was a French bikini wax." *And it hurt like hell.*

"Okay, how about this for your delicate sensibilities? 'Down for love with the right slab of man meat. Applicants apply here.' Does that sound better?"

"Not by much," Lexi snorted. God, she missed her friend!

"That way you can interview the best candidates and pick from the bunch," Anna reasoned. "Or, if you have multiple choices that are too yummy to resist, schedule one for each night of the week. Better yet, set yourself up with a reverse harem."

"You've been reading too many smutty novels," Lexi deadpanned.

"Something you should consider, my friend, instead of your syrupy sweet historical romances, where the heroine faints the moment the hero dares to kiss her gloved hand. Real people don't behave that chastely, you know."

"They did in the nineteenth century," Lexi sniffed. "Besides, I don't remember how to flirt."

"Watch a YouTube video."

Lexi's heart sank. "I wish you were here. I need you to hold my confidence up."

"I wish I could be there too, sweetie, but you don't need me to hold up your confidence. Lex, you are an incredible woman who simply needs to find that gear inside herself and get it rolling again. And you know what? You took the first step by going to Destiny on your own. I'm really proud of you for that. And I believe down in my bones that good things are coming your way."

"Thanks, babe. You're the best."

"Now stop stalling and get down to the bar! Wanton Woman is *on* tonight!"

"Yes, ma'am," Lexi chuckled.

"And send pictures!"

"The only pictures I'm sending are of the delicious fruity drinks."

They hung up, and Lexi piled her hair on top of her head before taking a quick shower to wash off the stickiness of travel and the humid air. In the drawer she'd designated for underwear, she pulled out the beautiful black lace thong and bra set she had planned to wear on her wedding night. She forced back a surge of regret. She'd cried a river over Conrad, and he hadn't deserved a single one of her tears. Nor did he deserve the head space she was currently giving him to rain all over her idyllic honeymoon for one, so she banished the jerk.

As for the sexy undies, she didn't plan on showing them to anyone, but she wanted to feel beautiful and feminine.

After reapplying her makeup and spritzing on some perfume, she shimmied into the dress and slipped on her backup pair of high-heeled sandals. Not as practical as the first pair and probably too fancy for the hotel's laid-back vibe, but they added length to her legs and pushed her height from five three to five six. She was practically an Amazon.

Yeah, you keep telling yourself that, and maybe you'll believe it.

It was time to hit the meat market and fortify her nerves with some liquid courage … and a nudge from Wanton Woman.

I Am That Guy

Josh Wylder peeled off the hideous shirt his mom had given him. It looked like flamingos had mated with palm trees and barfed out parrots against a neon-blue ocean. He loved his mother, he really did, and he would never be able to pay her back for all he and his brother had put her through even if that aim was his sole focus for the rest of his life, but this shirt ... Maggie Wylder was an amazing woman with countless strengths, but fashion wasn't one of them.

"Ooh, the colors really bring out your eyes, Josh," she'd gushed. Then she'd added, "You're going to steal some girl's heart when you get to that fancy hotel." More likely scare her away, but he wasn't looking to attract anyone this week anyway.

He hadn't bothered asking exactly which colors Mom thought went with the hue of his eyes, unless she was referring to the hot pink and was ribbing him about being hungover a few mornings ago. Never mind that he'd had a really good reason to get wasted.

He held the shirt at arm's length, pondering whether to drop it in the trash and tell her it had been stolen. No, she'd only go out and replace it, and he didn't want her spending her dough that way. She'd spent plenty on him and his brother growing up. He and Bradley shared a love for ice hockey, and without any contributions from their absentee dad, that passion had strained their little family's meager reserves. Mom had always made sure her rambunctious boys had what they needed, though, even if the secondhand gear didn't fit quite right.

He and his brother had been fattening her bank account since their first big paychecks, but her single-mom frugality was so ingrained in her that Josh understood what it cost her mentally to splurge on this shirt—and "splurge" meant she'd bought off the full retail rack at Walmart.

Yeah, he owed her a fuck ton of good deeds, and he was woefully behind on the paybacks. He would do anything for her—like embarrass himself by wearing the damn thing. It seemed a minuscule price to pay for Maggie Wylder's endless selfless acts.

He riffled through his bag until he found his favorite T-shirt. Soft and gray—and probably a truer match to his eye color—it sported his brother's bicycle shop logo. Josh had worn it so many times now the logo was practically unreadable. Mom wouldn't be a fan of this particular wardrobe choice, but she wasn't here to judge, and he wasn't here to impress anyone. He didn't even want to be here. Why not be comfortable while he spent the week wallowing by himself?

Shucking his jeans, he pulled on an old pair of board shorts. A shove of his fingers to tame his hair and a pair of flip-flops later, he sauntered down to the bar, where he expected to spend the majority of his time for the next seven days—unless he got lucky with some nameless hottie looking for a no-strings fuck. Surprisingly, that didn't hold a lot of appeal, which was further proof of how down in the dumps he'd let himself sink. Then again, it had been a long time since he'd met a woman who got his motor revving. They all seemed to be ... the same. Hooking up had become monotonous. Downright boring. And since he'd gotten away from clubbing and partying, fewer interesting possibilities crossed his path anyway. Not that he was looking, but as he watched one buddy after another fall hard—and seem happier for it—Josh sometimes wondered what he was missing.

His brother's voice bounced around his brain. "Think of all the beach babes at the resort in string bikinis *everywhere*. Just tell them you're a pro hockey player, and you won't be able to peel them off you fast enough. You might even be able to get yourself a twosome ... a three—" Josh had cut him off there. Bradley had been living vicariously through Josh since his own career had stalled in the minor leagues, and his brother's imagination had far outstripped Josh's reality. Sure, he'd been dubbed "Wild Man" by his teammates for more than his acrobatic, unorthodox saves, but the moniker simply didn't fit his life *off* the ice anymore. And he was fine with that, even if Brad wasn't. At thirty-two, those days were in his rearview mirror—especially now that he found himself without a contract or a team.

And there it was again, reality staring him down. He'd worked his ass off to be the best goalie he could be, but it had garnered him a glove full of nothing.

Could he even call himself a professional goalie anymore? Philly hadn't renewed his contract, even for a backup role, which he would have groveled for had they given him any indication they wanted him. No other teams were trying to punch his dance card either, whether as a starter or a backup.

"Give it time," his agent, Herb, had told him when they'd spoken the week before. "There's always a lull right after a Cup run. Things'll pick up as we get closer to training camp."

Training camp for most teams started in early September—only six weeks away.

"Shouldn't they want to lock me up *now*?" he'd argued. "GMs and coaches want their rosters set *before* camp, right?"

Herb had waved him off, and for an instant, Josh had felt like he'd been marooned alone on Crazy Island. "You're making a mountain out of an anthill, son." But Josh wasn't convinced his agent was right this time. He hadn't been without a team since he'd first been drafted fourteen years ago. The fact that he didn't have a landing place for the upcoming season fucking sucked balls.

He needed to lock the thought away in a compartment for now—which meant it was cocktail time.

The bar was an indoor-outdoor space, an extension of the lush grounds beyond, where sun played on glossy palm fronds ruffled by a warm breeze. Josh picked a barstool with a panoramic view of the gardens and the bar area itself, which was filled with people seated at scattered tables. From his perch, he had a perfect front-row seat to human dramas and foibles—and he delighted in the fact that he was merely a spectator.

Happy hour had just started, so he ordered two rum old-fashioneds from a friendly bartender—Matt, according to his name tag—and settled in. A guy about Josh's age sidled up and pointed at the empty barstool beside him.

"Mind if I—"

"Go for it," Josh invited.

The guy extended his hand. "Neil Afton. Didn't I see you on the shuttle?"

Josh shook the dude's hand. "Josh Wylder. Maybe. I slept the whole way." Something about riding on a bus always made him fall asleep quickly, even when he wasn't tired—a habit he'd developed after years of team travel.

Neil looked around, a wolfish grin plastered on his face. "Really enjoying the scenery so far."

Matt delivered Josh's drinks and took Neil's order.

Josh tasted his cocktail. Damn, that was good! "So, Neil, what do you do?"

"I'm the chief financial officer for HelpFirst Healthcare."

A sign on the boards at Josh's home rink flashed in his mind. "No kidding? Aren't you guys one of the sponsors for Keystone Arena?"

"Yeah, that's us. I take it you've attended an event there?"

"I *am* one of the events there." Chuckling, Josh shook his head. "What I meant was I play for—"

The guy's eyes lit with recognition. "You're the goalie for the Philadelphia Forge, right?"

"Yep." *Was* the goalie.

"Sorry about your team's early exit from the playoffs. That had to be rough, but you're probably used to it after missing out the last bunch of years."

Josh was a competitor. He never got *used* to defeat. It left a bitter taste, and he downed half of his drink to wash it away. This was his first day of vacation, and he didn't have to drive anywhere, so why not?

"Yeah, winning is always preferred," he muttered. Losing was the norm when you played for a bottom feeder—which made them not extending him even more puzzling. He had the experience. He was a great goalie in the prime of his career. He was a leader in the locker room. And hadn't he put in the grueling rehab work after his injury? No matter what the coaching staff said, he was back to his old form, damn it. Why wouldn't they believe him?

So much for leaving it all behind.

Neil nodded. An awkward beat passed before Josh added, "Getting an early summer break has its perks, though." He gestured around the expansive space.

Neil readily agreed. "Can't argue with that. And if action's what you're after, there should be plenty to go around." He threw back his tequila, set the empty shot glass on the bar, and signaled Matt for more. "And speaking of action ..." Neil's eyes darted to the opposite side of the bar.

Josh followed his gaze and narrowed his eyes on the redhead who had blocked everyone on the shuttle and slammed into his back. She looked different. Maybe it was the off-the-shoulders gauzy white dress she'd changed into. It hit her mid-thigh and hugged her in all the right places—and she had all the right places for it to hug. Sandals with high heels accentuated shapely legs, and long auburn hair he hadn't really noticed before was brushed back, skimming her shoulder blades and revealing a heart-shaped face.

"Do you know her?" Josh asked.

Neil shrugged. "Not yet. I'm not into redheads, but I could make an exception for that one." He pointed toward a different woman who stood off to one side, seeming to survey the clientele. "That one's more my speed."

Unlike Red, this woman was a long cool customer with dark brown hair and eyes to match. Her tanned body was impeccably displayed in a red-and-white tropical number that exposed cleavage—cleavage that looked manufactured. She was gorgeous in an exotic sort of way, but an invisible sign flashing "High Maintenance" over her head was a turnoff. Josh had sampled his share of high-maintenance women, and the clues were unmistakable. *No thanks.*

Neil ogled her shamelessly, his grin exposing his pointy white eye teeth, and Josh nearly laughed out loud. "The redhead's all yours," Neil offered.

"No thanks, man. I'm looking for a quiet week. No drama." Josh wasn't going to touch this week, but look? Oh yeah. He could look *plenty*. Didn't cost anything and would definitely lift his black mood.

The redhead zeroed in on a table for two, where she took a seat, crossing her smooth legs and tugging at the hem of her skirt. She looked uncomfortable doing it, as if she wasn't used to wearing short skirts, though with *those* legs, short *everything* needed to be her go-to.

Neil's eyes remained pinned to the dark-haired woman. "You here alone?"

Josh nodded. "My brother was supposed to join me, but he came down with COVID and had to bail." Probably better that way because Brad would have been trolling hard, despite the fact his divorce wasn't final. Josh had been his unwitting "fishing" companion in the past, and it had caused friction between them when Josh had pointed out that Brad had a lovely wife at home. Might've explained why said wife was divorcing his brother's ass.

Their father's abandonment and the demise of his brother's perfect union were two of the main reasons Josh didn't believe in happily ever afters.

Neil yanked him back to the present. "I'm by myself too. If I can't convince that stunner that I'm the only man for her tonight, maybe you and I can have dinner together."

Why the hell not? "Sounds good."

Neil chuckled. "Hopefully luck's on my side."

Something told Josh Neil didn't need it. He polished off the rest of his drink, started on the next, and signaled the bartender to bring another round. As he did so, he felt eyes burning into him, and he looked up to find Red's gaze pointed his way. Not at *him*, though. She was lasered in on Neil. Josh stared at her a few beats, but her gaze didn't waver. If he could read a woman's mind—and he'd proved time and again he couldn't—he would've guessed she wanted to get to know his new companion.

The seat across from her remained empty. Maybe she was alone too and hoping someone—Neil?—would fill it.

Huh.

Tossing back what was left of his second cocktail, he scanned the rest of the crowd, purposely avoiding Red ... until his eyes ignored him and wandered back to her.

Read Lexi and Josh's story in
Sunsets, Stick Saves, and a Honeymoon
by G. K Brady

Enjoy this sneak peek of

TRENT'S REDEMPTION

Book 1 in the Mill Creek Mystique romantic suspense series

Chapter One

T HE RAPID KNOCK AT Trent's front door had him hoping that this unexpected interruption would spare him another lonely evening. Hastening his steps, he twisted the knob and sucked in a sharp breath. Nothing would have prepared him for this sight. His partner's sister and the woman he had dated. Margaret King's haunted green eyes stared back at him. Her blonde hair was thrown into a loose ponytail. Several strands had escaped and fluttered in the evening breeze. Even disheveled, she was still beautiful.

Dread settled in his gut, anchoring a weight to his chest as Dalton's last words filtered through his mind. *Promise me you'll look after her and keep her safe.*

"Maggie, what brings you here?" Trent's mind raced with possibilities, and none settled the growing dread that rotted in his stomach.

Her eyes widened briefly before she found her voice. "Can I come inside?"

"Of course, sorry," he stammered, moving aside and making a sweeping motion with his arm.

She hesitated for a second, then looked over her shoulder toward the driveway. Turning back, she met his gaze and released a deep breath. Remorse slapped him in the face as she entered his home. The last time he'd seen her was about ten months ago at Dalton's funeral. Not once had Trent reached out to see how she had adjusted to life without her brother. Now, the weight of his mistake stood in his entryway. Guilt riddled his body and his gaze shifted toward the floor because he'd let her down.

The subtle scent of oranges and vanilla floated by him as she passed. The moonlight shining through the open window cast a silvery glow across her pinched face. He clicked the deadbolt then flipped on the light before he sat on the sofa, waiting for her to join him. Her feet didn't budge, but her gaze circled the room.

Maggie raised an eyebrow, her eyes blank. "I'm sorry I didn't call first. I thought this discussion would be best in person. I can't believe I had to search the internet to find your address."

"I'm glad you're here, and I should have given you my address. There's no excuse for that..."

The tension in the room increased with every second of silence that followed.

"I-I don't know what to think anymore. You might think I'm crazy or worse, have overreacted to drive all the way here." Her voice sounded like sandpaper on wood.

Trent grabbed her hand and swiped his thumb softly across her knuckles. A rush of emotions flooded his system with that simple touch. He hated the strain emanating from her body. "Are you okay, Maggie?"

He released her hand and patted the spot next to him. The cushions dipped as she sat, her gaze lingering on the room and surroundings. "Why do you have scaffolding outside? Did something happen to your home?"

Trent smiled and shook his head. "No, I just finished renovating the interior and have decided to upgrade my roof. What's going on, Maggie?"

She turned to him, flashing a brief smile. "Good. I'm glad nothing bad happened to you. Could I have a glass of water?"

"You can have anything you'd like." He meant those words and vowed to himself to prove it to her. "But you need to tell me what's upset you. What made you drive all this way to find me?"

The single tear traveling down her cheek gutted him. Her resolve and strength may have had her sitting beside him, holding herself together, but her vulnerability undid him. He tugged her body against his, to feel her warmth and the pulse of her heart as he held her tight. To remind her she wasn't alone in dealing with whatever worried her. Even if his actions these last ten months told a different story.

A niggle of hope bloomed in his chest when she hugged him back just as fiercely. This wouldn't erase his absence from her life since the death of her brother, but maybe she'd see it as an olive branch to reconnect them to days long past. To the days when they were friends and all three of them spent time together.

When she sat back against the cushion, dark circles marred the delicate skin beneath her eyes. Trent's mind whirled with a million questions. Had someone hurt her? Had Maggie been with a man who threatened her? Why was she here? All of them remained unspoken because shame swamped his system. Not only was he a shitty person, but he'd broken a promise to his friend.

If only I'd taken out the shooter in the rafters, Dalton would still be here. Suffocated by the memories of that horrible day, Trent shot up off the sofa, desperately needing air and space. "I'll get you that water. When I return, how about you start from the beginning and explain why you're here? We'll figure this out together."

"Thanks. You're the one person I knew would understand," she said in a mere whisper.

Jesus, what had she been through that would make her run? The woman he'd known was full mirth and energy. He hated the mixture of defeat and uncertainty radiating from the depths of her green eyes.

"Here you go, Miss Margaret King." Trent handed her a glass of water.

"Ugh, call me Maggie, you know better. My parents called me Margaret, and that was when I was in trouble." She stared into the distance for a moment. "Maggie Moo was the nickname my brother preferred," she added with a slight wobble in her voice. "Sorry, I miss him so much. I just never thought I'd lose him after my parents died. I figured we'd grow old together. It's been difficult knowing I'm all alone in the world."

Trent's heart was clogged with condemnation. "Never apologize for missing him. Dalton loved you. He would've done anything for you. You were his little sister. Hell, I'd known him since training at Quantico, and I knew then, he'd be the biggest pain in my ass and best friend. His death left a hole in our lives." The words he left unspoken were that he'd abandoned her, too.

A soft giggle escaped her lips. "Yes, he could be a pain. He also tried controlling my life down to who I dated."

Trent nodded in agreement. "Yes, he had firm opinions on who should date you and why."

"If I recall, you did, too, since you cited your job as a complication of our relationship. Anyway, blood or not, you've always been a part of my family, which is why I'm here." She forced a slow steady stream of air into her lungs. "You were both logical and rational men who worked from facts to solve life's problems. I've lost count of how often I've endured a lecture about being observant and always aware of my surroundings."

He interjected, "A smart person assessed their situation and acted accordingly. That coincidences rarely, if ever, exist. Yes, I speak that same dialect."

"You are cut from the same cloth as Dalton, which is why I'm in Mill Creek. I've analyzed my situation and my findings have shocked me." She gulped the cool liquid. Straightening her spine, she continued, "Dalton made me promise—almost to the point of ritualistic chanting—that if I were ever in trouble and couldn't reach him, I should call you. I always thought he'd meant while he was alive..." Tears streamed down her face. "I think someone has been following me because I'm Dalton's sister."

Trent's eyes narrowed. She'd piqued his curiosity with that assessment. He then schooled his features so they'd remain neutral. "Why would you think that?"

"At first, I noticed a white van parked on the street facing my apartment. It appeared after Dalton's death. The days and times were random, but it was the same van. It disappeared for a while, then returned a few weeks ago. I can't explain it, but I got a strange feeling about it."

Maggie fidgeted, cracking her fingers one by one. He sat quietly while she fidgeted with nervous energy. He didn't want to add to her stress, so he gave her the time she needed to process her thoughts.

"How? What made it seem unusual?"

She lifted her gaze to meet his eyes and shrugged. "I only saw the driver and passenger twice, but I'm pretty sure they were the same men from the first time. This sounds crazy, I know it does, which is why I didn't report the van to the police. Those men could have lived in the complex or in the area. What happened the other night changed my mind, but instead of calling the police, I headed straight to you. This is personal, Trent, and it scared me."

"I'm glad you came to me." He gently urged her to continue by nodding and keeping his expression neutral. Deep down, his stomach knotted with apprehension over what came next.

A tiny smile crossed her lips. "God, you remind me of him, fierce and protective. I appreciate that you're not judging me—at least until I'm done."

"You're doing just fine, now, keep going."

"Early Saturday morning, I was working at my computer when the fire alarms went off. When I went outside to check, the adjacent unit had smoke billowing from inside. My neighbor appeared outside with her child, panicked, and talking into the phone about a grease fire and firemen coming. I ducked back inside my place to retrieve my messenger bag, which held everything that mattered to me and waited outside with my neighbor. After the firemen arrived and controlled the scene, I was informed that the fire was out, but it would be a couple of hours before I could return. I decided to head to our local coffee shop to hang out while the chaos passed. When I returned..."

The color drained from her cheeks. She lowered her head to stare at the carpet between her feet. "My front door was ajar, again, which I figured was so the firemen could finish their investigation. I caught a glimpse of that white van pulling away. When I entered, everything seemed fine...until I reached my office. Drawers were opened with papers and folders scattered across my desk and floor. Then, I noticed a knife stabbed into my desk holding a note that read, 'What did he know?'"

Trent snapped his brows together, his mouth drawn tight. He couldn't quell his reaction to what he'd just heard. The hairs on his neck bristled. He didn't know how, but he'd find a way to slay each and every one of her demons...or die trying. He owed Dalton that much.

"Why didn't you call the police? Do you know if anything was taken? Were other rooms searched?" Trent squeezed her hand a few times, bringing her gaze upward.

With her other hand, she reached for the glass and gulped the last few sips before she answered, "In my gut, I know this reaches beyond the police. The only 'he' in my life was my brother. My brain went into survival mode. I had to get out of my apartment and get to you. You'd know what to do. I-I didn't look any further. All I kept thinking was, this can't be good to have a knife stabbed into your desk, especially with how he died. I took my bag, hit the bank, and withdrew as much money as allowed. I left my car at the office and called a car rental company. I decided leaving my car behind was best. I stopped at one truck stop to rest, used only cash, then drove until I pulled into your driveway."

She sat still as if she had waited for him to say something. Processing what he had just heard shredded his insides. The last time they had spoken was at the funeral, and that encounter was strained, not ugly or mean, just distant because of him. This was opposite to how he and Maggie usually interacted. Instead, he struggled with his anger and self-condemnation while nursing the injuries he'd sustained that day alongside Dalton. As a result, Trent's job and assignment changed, which deprived him of retribution. He hated the exhaustion etched across her face. Starting now, he would atone for his wrongs.

"Brave and resilient is what you are." A surge of pride and respect flood his system. "You did damn good with disappearing off the grid and adapting in the face of adversity. You're far from an agent but acted cautiously and logically."

Fatigue, stress, and fear radiated from her, but he also saw a brief glimmer of relief. That was something he would build upon.

"Your brother would be proud. Hell, I'm proud of you. I'm also so damn sorry I haven't reached out before now. I own that. My apology doesn't change anything, but I hope my actions will. *If* you give me that chance. I'd say you read the situation right—a clusterfuck for sure."

Her eyes closed for a moment, and her shoulders dipped as tension seemed to fade from her body. Something deep inside Trent's stomach twisted painfully. Had she thought he might deny her his support and protection? Of course, why wouldn't she? It wasn't his intent, but he'd basically removed her from his life. Another epic screw-up to add to his list that he needed to fix.

He cupped her chin. "I understand why you weren't sure about coming to me for help, so I'll clarify that misconception now. I will always protect you, Maggie. You have my word."

She shifted her head from his grasp and stabbed him in the chest with a finger. "You hurt my feelings, but I'm not blameless either. You have to promise you won't put yourself in jeopardy in any way. I can't stand the thought of losing another person."

The painful truth behind those words constricted his chest. The vibrant woman he had known seemed to have retreated somewhat. Trent snatched her hand, loving how buttery soft her skin was under his fingertips. "Give me your keys. I think it's best to put your rental in the garage for now."

She stood and dug into her front pocket to retrieve the key ring. "Thanks for allowing me into your home, especially with my trouble in tow."

Trent extended his palm and caught the keys. "You always were trouble. I'll give you the grand tour first and point out the highlights from my renovation."

"I thought you liked living out of boxes. You know, afraid of commitment."

"Smart ass," he lamented. "I'm working on unpacking everything."

He couldn't imagine what she thought when she arrived but was glad she'd come. He started in his kitchen, explaining how his friend Kane had updated everything to stainless and gas.

"This is amazing. I love the gas stovetop. That refrigerator must keep you fed for months. It's huge."

"I've heard that bigger is always better," he deadpanned.

She rolled her eyes and protested, "Seriously? You haven't changed one bit."

He flashed her an exaggerated wink and guided her through the rest of the house. When they reached the master bathroom, he showed her his second favorite feature from the renovation: his walk-in shower with multiple adjusting heads that also produced steam. He owed Kane for this gem, too. Her small whimper when she spied the shower didn't go unnoticed. Trent also hadn't missed how closely she followed him the entire time. He'd do anything to diminish the worry radiating from her body. He ended his tour with the room she'd be using and the bathroom.

At the door to the bathroom, he paused and met her eyes. "Why don't you shower in my bathroom while I move the vehicle? You can give me a woman's perspective on my shower."

She leaned her head against the doorway and sighed. "A shower sounds heavenly, but I'll use the guest bath. Will you grab my bag from the front room and put it on the bed?

"Sure, do you have anything in the car you need?"

Her mouth twisted into a frown. "No, I didn't pack any clothing or even think about bringing my bathroom supplies. In my haste, I went with the less is more theory. Do you have a toothbrush and paste? And if I could borrow a few things to wear, that would be super. Walking around naked might be kind of awkward."

He groaned internally as his mind conjured several inappropriate scenarios involving her sans clothing. Built like a goddess, with her curves and creamy skin, he'd love nothing more than to see her naked. He caught her staring at his reflection in the bathroom mirror and knew he'd been nailed. His traitorous cock stirred behind the confines of his pants. This woman still caused his mind and body to want more from her. Definitely his cue to leave.

"I'll put a T-shirt and a pair of sweatpants on your bed. Leave your clothes outside the door, I'll wash them for you. We'll go shopping tomorrow to fill in whatever else you left behind."

She opened her mouth as if to speak, then clamped her lips together as she moved into the bathroom.

"What's on your mind?" he asked.

"Do you have any cereal or yogurt? Something easy to fix."

He put both hands on his waist and cocked one eyebrow. "You can have whatever you want. When did you eat last?"

Her eyes narrowed, and her mouth gaped. "I-ah, a granola at the truck stop."

He shook his head. "You're my priority. That includes food, sleep, protection, and whatever else I've forgotten to mention. Get that through your thick, stubborn, and beautiful head." Trent punctuated his point by wrapping her in a crushing hug. He wasn't sure what else to do, a move so familiar from all the previous times he and Dalton had visited between assignments or while on break.

He sighed as her curves melded perfectly against his frame and in all the right places. A surge of possessiveness roared to life within him, and not only did it startle him, but it also made him back away, breaking their connection

"Shower, then kitchen," he said in a tone that encouraged no debate.

He headed down the hall and heard the snick of the door as it closed behind him. Needing to put space between them, he'd take care of her car. This woman in his home was Dalton's sister. The same baby sister his partner proclaimed off limits to any man who worked in a risky profession. Dalton was adamant that Maggie should marry a man with a stable job, allowing him to come home every night. A man whose existence wasn't nestled in danger, with the potential to cause her harm because his job encompassed every aspect of his life. Trent had squashed his attraction to her because he hadn't wanted to ruffle Dalton's feathers. Even though he hadn't been exempt from Dalton's censure, he had to agree with the man. She deserved better. She deserved a marriage where her husband would be around every damn night. Whose job wouldn't risk her safety or threaten their lives. A fact of his employment he couldn't offer.

~ * ~

Relief washed over Maggie's body the moment Trent agreed with her assessment. That she hadn't overreacted. She never should have doubted that he'd support her, but hearing it from his lips alleviated her apprehension. The warmth from his embrace grounded her. If she could press the rewind button, she'd rather go back to when Trent held her in his arms. There was a familiarity to it, and she'd missed the simplicity of knowing someone had her back.

She'd gotten to know him when she went to college in Washington, D.C. and had chosen to live in Dalton's place instead of on campus. Her brother brought Trent home during break when they were both at Quantico. Not only had they become partners but friends. It wasn't like he was home often with his career, but it gave her an excuse to be close to her brother. She and Trent had dated a few times, but he had ended saying he didn't have time for a relationship due to his career. Her brother would never answer her question, but she would put money down on the fact he interfered.

When Trent smiled and flashed the bluest eyes she'd ever seen, it could melt the panties right off a girl. Never in her life had she experienced such a strong reaction to another person. It also didn't hurt that he was devastatingly gorgeous at six feet tall with his athletic build and all those well-defined muscles. His touch still made her girly parts tingle.

She'd cranked the shower tap to the left. When the bathroom mirror fogged over from the steam, she tugged back the curtain, adjusted the heat, then stepped inside. The hot spray pulsed against her tired muscles and sluiced down her body. She visualized removing Trent's shirt off his body to reveal raised pectorals and a ripped abdomen that flowed into a trim waist with sculpted hips. She bit her bottom lip and moaned. Well, that was what happened when one was sex deprived and surrounded by male hotness.

She adjusted the dial until a cold blast of water jolted her system. That daydream would be her little secret. She needed to stop this line of thinking. He probably had a bevy of beautiful women on speed dial. The type who looked perfect even after a torrential rainstorm. The exact same type her brother had circling him at all times. A girl could dream, couldn't she?

After stepping from the shower, she dried off and slathered on some lotion she found in the cabinet. She finger-combed her hair and mentally added an actual one to her list of things to buy. There was nothing like a shower to make a person feel human again. Towel wrapped around her body, she padded to the bedroom he assigned. As promised, sitting on her bed were the clothes and the items from her car. She removed a stuffed animal from her tote and kissed the cow on its nose before putting it back inside. She'd give anything to hear Dalton call her by her nickname one more time.

As she made her way to the kitchen, she took in his home. It had the perfect blend of cabin and modern.

The center of the room had a wooden dining table with four chairs, and in front of one chair sat a grilled cheese sandwich, her absolute favorite. Especially when she was having a crappy day.

Trent looked over his shoulder holding a spoon. "You look more relaxed. The tomato soup will be ready in a minute. These are my go-to choices when I need comfort food."

Her insides melted like the cheese in the sandwich.

"Mine too," she said. The part she kept to herself watching a hot man cook for her did wicked things to her body. Good grief, she needed to get a grip. He was being nice, not offering her a night of decadent sex. Or a life of love, marriage, and children. The fantasy train needed to stop so she could disembark because that destination did not exist.

The last few months had changed her. She had to find a way to survive before her grief and despair consumed her entirely. Being around Trent has created a few sparks in the recesses of her mind, reminding her of the woman she had been and what they had shared.

"Are you for real? A good-looking man who can cook and isn't afraid to admit that grilled cheese and tomato soup have the power to cure most things in life. I think I've died and gone to heaven," she tossed out and took a seat at the table.

He rolled his eyes and huffed dramatically. "I hate to burst your bubble, but men can do many things these days. I can even load the dishwasher and do laundry, but I draw the line at ironing."

Maggie burst out laughing. "Ah, I needed that. It's been a while."

Trent ladled soup into a bowl. "Feel free to laugh anytime. It suits you very nicely. I also happen to appreciate the eye candy comment."

Did he just flirt with her? She took a bite of her sandwich and moaned. "This is delicious."

"The secret is mayonnaise instead of butter. It's how my mom makes them. Tonight, I want you to promise me you'll rest. I don't like seeing those dark circles under your eyes."

"I'll try, but it's hard to get my brain to stop churning over everything." She blew on a spoonful of soup.

"Well, I promise to keep the boogie men away. Hey, one question, though. Something you said earlier confused me. You said you left your car at the office. Do schoolteachers refer to their classrooms as offices now? Are you still teaching?"

She put down her spoon. "No. I quit teaching."

His eyebrows knit together as he processed what she said, but to her relief, he didn't question her any further. She didn't want to get into it tonight. Her love of teaching had died after she buried Dalton. The burden of life's truths wore her down, and she couldn't handle deceiving those precious faces daily.

Trent filled in the prolonged silence. "We can talk about all of this tomorrow after you get some rest."

"Okay," she said between a spoonful of soup.

"Oh, one more thing. I'm meeting some friends for breakfast tomorrow. I want you to come. Afterward, we'll head to the store to pick up whatever else you need."

Maggie took a big gulp of water. "I don't want to impose."

"I see your listening skills haven't improved," he muttered sardonically. "We're meeting them tomorrow at eight. I'll have your clothes folded and waiting for you outside your door. You'll love the Knotty Pine Tree. The food is delicious, and I want you to meet my friends,

Kane and Annika. They're good people; you can trust them. Besides, your smart actions put distance between what happened in Dallas and what happened here. It'll give us some time to figure it all out."

There was a time when meeting new people and being a social butterfly came naturally, but that part of her died when she put Dalton in the ground. Maybe she should label her life accordingly now. BD—before Dalton—and AD—after Dalton.

The scaffolding outside the kitchen window reminded her of a skeleton in the moonlight. She hated the nights the most. All her fears and problems grew into large, creepy monsters that caused her constant worry that whoever left the note would find her.

Chapter Two

B ELLS JINGLED AS TRENT held open the door of the Knotty
Pine Tree for Maggie to enter. The delicious scents of bacon,
coffee, cinnamon, and freshly baked bread surrounded him. It was
slower than usual for a Tuesday morning, but he wasn't going to
complain.

Placing his palm on Maggie's back, he guided her toward the
rear to his favorite booth in the corner. This table allowed him to
sit with his back to the wall with views of the entire restaurant.
The two big windows along the side wall gave him a perfect line
of sight to Main Street. He waved and nodded to practically every
customer in the diner.

She slid into the booth and then followed her so they sat side by
side. He needed caffeine to jump start his system. Sleep had evaded
him last night. He mulled over every detail she'd relayed and
documented those events, creating a timeline. What she told him
last night blew his mind and dredged up memories he preferred
to keep buried. After breakfast, he'd call Noah Parker, his friend
and analyst at the FBI, to enlist his help with several items.

"This place is amazing, and everything smells so good. I love all
the old license plates and pictures decorating the walls. Is this the
history of Mill Creek?" she asked.

"Yes, this diner is one of the original landmarks. The Sullivan family has owned it since the beginning."

"Wow, imagine all the changes they've seen over the years."

He turned to the approaching woman. "Were your ears burning, Sally?"

The older lady waved off Trent's attempt to stand. "Let me guess, you were discussing my good looks and how amazing my food is?"

Her husband hollered through the metal window that separated the front of the restaurant from the back. "Whose good food? Hey, Sheriff, Sally, I've got a question when you're finished."

She winked at Trent then turned her attention toward Maggie and held out her hand. "I'm Sally. My husband, Peter, and I own this diner. I haven't seen you around here before. Are you planning to take this hot bachelor off the market?"

A nice shade of pink suffused Maggie's face. He was about to jump in and save her from Sally's noisiness, but she beat him to the punch.

"Oh, I know, right? He's totally hot, but he's too stubborn. Besides, we're practically family. So, I'm solidly in the friend category. I'm Maggie, by the way. It's nice to meet you."

Not liking one bit that he was the punchline or what she'd said, Trent rolled his eyes at both Sally and Maggie who were laughing.

"I like her. She's a keeper." Sally winked then announced, "When everyone arrives, I'll circle back to take your orders." She sauntered toward the next table of waiting guests in her section.

Trent couldn't agree more, but that could never happen. Maggie's intelligence, matched with her sense of humor, made her special. Not many could diffuse Sally's style of interrogation with such ease and decorum. Maggie didn't miss a beat and, in the process, made a new friend. When she spoke, she gestured with her hands. With each move, her body vibrated against his, causing a zing of electricity to pulse through his system. *Friend category, my ass.*

She had the body of a man's dreams. This woman next to him, with her expressive eyes, would test his restraint at every turn. He liked seeing glimpses of the women he knew. Not just the startled and reserved woman who'd shown up on his doorstep. Seeing how she'd dropped her guard a few times gave him hope. Maybe they could help each other work through the gigantic hole Dalton's death had left in their lives. His mind traveled back to that awful morning.

The pulsing vibration of metal against the wood of a nightstand had roused him from sleep.

Snatching his phone off the nightstand, Trent glanced at the display and answered, "Can't even go a weekend without me?"

"It's those blue eyes. They've mesmerized me," Dalton cooed over the line.

Trent glanced at the alarm clock before turning over to see if he'd awakened the woman lying next to him, but she was still asleep. Maybe he could coax another orgasm or two after he ended this call.

"Let me guess," he whispered, "you're bored waiting for your flight from Dallas? Sorry, man, I'm otherwise occupied."

"Oh, you're man-whoring," Dalton drawled.

"Nice try, but the intent and expectations have been defined, so I'd call it a win-win."

"Whatever. Hey, I flew home last night from visiting my sister."

Trent bolted upright then turned to put his feet on the floor. "You left early. What the hell is up? Did you piss off Maggie?"

"Relax, I hadn't seen Maggie-Moo for a while, and I needed to take care of some family business. It's the protector in me. Although, she was just as shocked as you by the visit. Apparently, being unpredictable doesn't come naturally to me."

Trent ran his hand through his hair and smiled at the thought of Maggie giving her brother an earful. She never liked it when big brother played the overbearing and intrusive role. Her passion and beauty were a lethal combination that managed to always keep her brother on his toes.

"Besides, if I recall, you're always blathering that I should live outside my comfort zone."

He snickered. "Right. Remind me to call NASA before the debriefing meeting to report that you've been abducted by aliens. You sound like Dalton, but that's where the familiarity ends."

"Pull up your skirt, man, and find a damn pair of pants. I have something important to show you. It's big and not something to discuss over the phone. Meet me in the parking lot of the old, abandoned railroad warehouse."

When the bells jingled again, Trent snapped out of his reverie in time to see Kane and Annika enter the diner. He could tell by Kane's wide eyes that Maggie's presence confused him. Trent stood, shook Kane's hand, then hugged Annika. "Kane, Annika, this is Margaret King, Dalton's sister."

Maggie waited to extend her hand until they had taken their seats. "It's nice to meet you both. Please call me Maggie."

"I'm so sorry for your loss," Annika replied in a solemn voice. "Trent loved Dalton like a brother."

Trent tugged Maggie against his side, unable to resist comforting her when tears fell down her cheeks. She leaned into his side before responding in a wobbly voice, "Geez, I try not to cry within the first two minutes of meeting people. It's just...talking about him is still hard."

He squeezed her shoulder, showing his support. "It's only been ten months. Besides, I don't think there's a time limit on grief."

Kane flashed a sincere smile before studying the menu, giving Maggie a couple of minutes to compose herself without the prying eyes of newcomers. "How long will you be visiting?" he then said.

Maggie turned to Trent, as if searching for how to respond. He winked, and she returned her attention to Kane. "Well, I seem to have some bad luck following me around lately, and Trent is willing to help me exorcise those monsters."

Kane's gaze shot up from his menu to Trent before sliding to meet Maggie's. "I'm sorry to hear that, but he's the best at exorcisms or other pesky problems. Would it be better to postpone our breakfast? We don't want to interrupt if you need to speak privately?"

Trent winced as he removed his arm from Maggie's shoulder, absently rubbing the spot where he'd taken a round. "Nope, we're good. So, did you two pick a wedding date?"

Kane expelled a hearty laugh and nudged Annika. "See, I told you he would want to know dates. He's a planner, sweetheart."

Annika nodded. "How does Labor Day weekend sound? We'd marry on Saturday, in our meadow. Afterward, we'll start construction on our home."

Sally stopped by to take everyone's order and fill their coffee cups.

"Sounds like a great day. Does this mean no monkey suits since we'll be outside?" Trent asked, waggling his eyebrows at Annika.

She pinned him with a stern expression that faded into a devious smile. "I would never pass up the opportunity to see you strutting around in a tuxedo. That alone will make the day special."

"Traitor, and after all I did for you," he grumbled.

Maggie leaned forward and held out her hand to Annika. "Can I see your ring? And, please, you have to send me a picture of him in a tux."

Annika beamed with pride, immediately sticking out her hand. "It's a deal, and if you're still here consider this your invitation. Then you can see him in person."

Trent shook his head and wrenched his face into his best look of horror at the women's antics.

"Oh my, it's beautiful! Congratulations," Maggie exclaimed, ignoring him.

"Well, that's if your father doesn't kill me, Annika. We still have to tell them what happened," Kane murmured while he nudged her with his shoulder.

Before long, the women chatted while he and Kane discussed his plans for the house he wanted to build for Annika. The conversation stopped when the Sally appeared with her arms full of plates and condiments stuffed in her apron pockets. Once she served the food, the only sounds at the table were forks and knives scraping across the plates.

"Oh, my God, this brioche French toast is sinful," Maggie crooned between bites. "Nothing will fit when we go shopping for clothes because I'm going to eat all of this goodness."

Her face softened in pleasure, and her tongue darted out to lick a spot of powder sugar off her bottom lip. A bubble of warmth formed in Trent's stomach as he watched Maggie smile and laugh. It reminded him of lazy Sunday mornings when Dalton and Trent visited Maggie and went out to breakfast before returning to their jobs. This was what he had hoped would happen this morning—normalcy. A reminder of what life was supposed to be like, not the current shitstorm that had enveloped her world. The same sentiment applied to Annika, who had barely survived her own ordeal.

"Trent...Trent?" Maggie elbowed him in the ribs, jarring him from his thoughts.

He turned to look at her, hoping she'd throw him a bone since he'd zoned out and missed a key part of the conversation. At the moment, he couldn't think of one single reason that kept him from checking on Maggie during these last ten months. What the hell had he been thinking?

"Sorry, my mind drifted to the day's tasks. What did I miss?" Trent asked, not missing that everyone stared at him as if they didn't believe a word he'd spoken.

Annika jumped in and saved him from further embarrassment. "I have an idea. I'll take Maggie shopping while you and Kane do whatever you need to do. Could we meet at the sheriff's station in about an hour?"

Trent glanced at Maggie, who seemed comfortable with the idea but also looked at him for input. "Sounds good to me. What do you think, Maggie?"

A smile covered her face. "Sure. I don't want to keep you from work."

Kane pressed a kiss to Annika's temple. "We're making a quick trip to Los Angeles. It's time for me to meet them, and we have much to discuss."

Trent motioned to Sally for the check. "That should make an interesting first impression. What time do you leave?"

Kane palmed his wallet. "Not until we arrive, but we're aiming for two. A perk of owning a jet. I need to pick up the deed to our property. You officially have a neighbor."

Trent glanced at the check as he listened to Annika and Maggie discuss their shopping strategy and which stores they should visit.

"Breakfast is my treat." He slid out of the booth and offered his hand to Maggie. As soon as she stood, he gave her his credit card. "Buy whatever you need, and if there are any problems, tell them to call me at the station."

Maggie nodded her head. "Okay, but I'm paying you back, Sheriff Jacobs. And that's on the record."

He gave her his best attempt at intimidation and then watched as she walked toward the exit. Once she left the restaurant, he gave the cashier the check.

Kane waggled his eyebrows. "I know that look—"

"Zip it, lover boy," Trent shot back. "Today's your lucky day. You get to ride with me. I'll even let you ride in the front. And, before you ask me again, no, you still can't use the siren."

Kane let out a loud whoop as he followed him to his service vehicle. Trent rolled his eyes at his friend's exuberance. This man who was raised with a silver spoon in his mouth had missed out on so many boyhood experiences. Maybe, for Christmas, he'd buy Kane one of those toy police cars that had sound. Annika would just love him for that one.

~ * ~

Maggie liked the quaint old-town style of Mill Creek and how Main Street preserved its charm of days long past when horses and wagons roamed the streets. The stores, restaurants, and hotels were constructed from logs and had tin roofs. A long sidewalk made from wooden planks ran down the length of the storefronts. Some even had hitching posts and watering troughs out front. The well-worn boards were smooth and groaned with each step from years of use. Each store's large picture window displayed items for sale, amid seasonal decor.

Annika wrapped her arm around Maggie's and tugged her toward the door. "Rayna's Outpost is amazing. I would call it more of a boutique, but she does have everything from outdoor clothing to sexy lingerie. It's become one of my favorite places. Oh, and I love the lilies she planted outside her store in that big box. Afterward, we'll head to the drug store."

"That's an old feedbox for animals," Maggie answered, before removing her sunglasses and opening the big door.

Inside, it resembled a big city department store rather than an outpost, but also had an eclectic blend of clothing. Definitely trendy, but the selections were cool and not pretentious at all. One day, when she wasn't buying the bare necessities, she'd come back and browse. She immediately liked how the clothing was not segregated by size; each rack held all the sizes in one spot. It was inclusive. There were so many cute items she wanted to try on, but now wasn't the time. She took her handful of practical items to the dressing rooms.

Annika rapped on the dressing room door. "Hey, you disappeared quickly. Did you see this dress? It's sexy, and the color makes your eyes pop. I love this shade of orange. Oh, and I found these cute tops and shorts."

Maggie's eyes widened into large saucers at the mound of clothing Annika held in her arms. "Uh, I don't need sexy lingerie. I'll just grab a multi-package of underwear. This is really about getting the basics since I didn't have time to pack."

"You should always have options. Besides, maybe I'm wrong, but it seemed that Trent couldn't keep his eyes off you. If you catch my drift." Annika waggled her eyes.

"I'd call that worrying. We've already dipped our toes into that pool. It didn't work out."

Oh, she'd love nothing more than to seduce him. When he ended things, she'd been crushed, but didn't want to lose him as a friend. Never had another man's touch made her body ache in all the right places. It was enough to make her brain short circuit.

She smiled at Annika. "He's beyond awesome, which makes me happy to call him a friend. Plus, I have no doubt he's dating someone or has at least had several women vying for his time and attention. He's never lacked for company, if you know what I mean."

Annika moved closer, held up her elegant hand, then started ticking off items one by one with her fingers. "I had concerns about Kane. He was too wealthy. Too handsome. His parents were mean. I had too much baggage, but here I am."

"Seriously? That's horrible, and you're so nice. Why wouldn't anyone like you? Plus, you're gorgeous."

Annika winked at her. "Thank you, but I'd kill for some of your curves or Marilyn Monroe's. I'm not picky. As for the dating part, I didn't see him with anyone when we stayed with Trent over the summer. It never hurts to have secret weapons at your disposal, just in case you two decide to try again. Here, try these outfits on. If not for Trent, then do it for yourself. You never know when Mr. Tall, Gorgeous, and Single will present himself."

Maggie giggled as she took the pile of clothes into the fitting room and closed the door. She liked Annika, and more importantly, she liked shopping and hanging out with a friend. She'd missed these types of interactions and didn't even realize how much until today. It had been too long since she had a little girl time. "All right, give me a few minutes to see what fits."

When she finished, she came out carrying the stack of clothing she decided to buy.

On her way to the cashier, Annika added a baby-doll nighty to the pile. "What? I'm just making sure you don't have to walk around naked. You know, friends don't let friends be naked, especially when there's something this cute to wear." She batted her eyelashes.

Maggie rolled her eyes and snorted out a laugh. "Oh, you're a funny girl. Thanks for coming with me. This has been fun. It also beats worrying about all of the not-so-fun things."

Annika pulled her into a hug. "I know, but you're in good hands. Trent is one of the main reasons I'm standing here today. He never gave up and kept digging thanks to his gut instincts."

She'd like to sit down and hear Annika's full story someday. It seemed they shared a common bond, and knowing Maggie had someone to talk to helped ease the tension. She'd missed being with her friends and being social, but those indulgences also came with a healthy dose of anxiety. Your happiness could be torn from your grasp in the blink of an eye.

She had to face the fact that some of her hardships from that isolation were self-inflicted. When Dalton died, she'd cut herself off from everyone. She didn't think she could handle losing one more person she loved. It was lonely, and she had kept a tourniquet on her heart.

Maggie gave the saleslady Trent's credit card. "You and Kane remind me of my parents—best friends who were madly in love. They always fought for what they wanted. There was a time when I wanted to have that same type of relationship."

"Then you should keep working toward that goal. Life is too short sometimes, so no time like the present." Annika replied solemnly.

Relieved that the transaction had gone through without a glitch, Maggie collected her bags and followed Annika toward the drug store. As they strolled down First Street, Maggie took in everything Mill Creek offered, including all the friendly residents who waved or offered a greeting along the way.

Annika pointed between two buildings. "See that park? Every Saturday night they play a family movie. Practically, everyone in town goes and picnics."

"That's a cool idea and a great use for that space."

"Maybe you two will get the chance to go. I think your visit will be good for Trent. I'm almost certain he blames himself in some capacity for Dalton's death."

Maggie thought about what Annika had said. *Why would Trent blame himself?* "That doesn't make any sense. Did he say anything else about it?"

Annika pushed the door open to the drug store and held it for Maggie. "Not really, but it was the way he said things and acted—or maybe what he didn't say."

Once inside, Maggie found a cart and added everything she needed to it, along with a few extra items she found along the way, including her favorite lotion. While the cashier rang up and bagged her purchases, she turned to Annika and asked in a whisper, "Did you share that with me so I'll encourage Trent to talk about Dalton?"

Annika pressed her lips together before she answered, "I think he's struggling with survivor's guilt. It's an educated guess, but I'm pretty confident in my assessment. If you decide to push, don't let him hide. He'll come up with many excuses, so stand strong and push right back."

They strolled back toward the sheriff's office in mutual silence. What Annika said made sense, but Maggie didn't know if Trent would open up to her. Afterall, he'd chosen to shut her out of his life. "I remember how shaken Trent was at Dalton's funeral. He'd kept to himself and barely said a word to me. I'd chalked it up to grief and that he'd only been released from the hospital a few days before his service. It was an unbearable situation, right down to the fact I wasn't allowed to see my brother's face one last time to say goodbye. I can't imagine how Trent felt."

"Why was his casket closed if that was so important to you?" Annika stopped moving to face her.

"The FBI demanded that his casket be closed. I never asked why. I figured it had something to do with protocol since he was killed in the line of duty."

"Oh, that's horrible." Annika gasped.

Maggie had gone stony. "The day was horrible. Trent could barely stand or walk. He'd remained in the back of the church. The pew reserved for family members had only one occupant which was me. It was a miracle that he'd survived. One of the bullets nicked a major artery." Her mind returned to his apology last night about not reaching out to her sooner. *More guilt? Maybe Annika has a point.*

They resumed and ascended the concrete steps to the sheriff's office. Eagerness washed over Maggie to see Trent's new domain. The place he'd come to when his life crumbled. The fact that he was the sheriff of Mill Creek County made her smile. It also hit her that she had never really thought about all he'd lost until now. Being overwhelmed by grief didn't excuse her self-centered actions. She'd never reached out to offer him solace or support.

The scent of wood and oil hit her nose the moment she entered the building. The hardwood floors shined but creaked and moaned under her steps. The hand-carved wooden railing separating the waiting area from the main office was beautiful. Squirrels, pinecones, and trees covered the surface. As she moved farther into the building, she saw that the open cubicles and desks had modern computers but really old phones. Flat-screen televisions hung on various walls, displaying local and national news feeds. The space was functional, and she liked the blend of past and present.

Kane stepped out of an office in the back. "Hey, ladies, I see you were successful given the number of bags. Have fun?"

Annika held up her bags before placing them on an empty desk. "Maybe a little. Did you two finish your chores?"

Kane kissed his fiancée on the forehead. "Yes, it's official, Trent has new neighbors. We own the meadow."

"Yahoo," Annika cheered, before a gigantic smile plastered across her face.

A woman with a beautiful mess of auburn hair piled on top of her head with several tendrils framing her face approached. "Hi, you must be Maggie."

Annika and Kane spoke at the same time before Kane stopped and motioned for Annika to proceed. "This is our friend, Margaret King, and this is Trent's assistant, Aimee Lang."

Aimee extended her hand. "It's so nice to meet you. Trent asked me to keep an eye open for your arrival. Can I get you anything to drink while you wait? He's finishing up a call."

"No, I'm good, thanks," Maggie said and shook Aimee's hand.

Aimee had a beautiful smile that made her hazel eyes sparkle. That, paired with her curvy figure, and her friendly disposition made her a total knockout. She motioned to a desk behind her. "I sit right there, so if you change your mind just holler. Kane, Annika, safe travels. I'll see you next time you're in town."

"Are you leaving now?" Maggie whirled around to ask Annika.

"Yes, we're scheduled to leave Boise at four. I had so much fun today. Call me if you need anything." She hugged Maggie first, and then Kane hugged her.

"Thanks, I will, and I had fun too." Maggie stood motionless as Kane and Annika headed toward the front of the building hand-in-hand then disappeared through the doorway. She had to admit, she really did have fun today, and what surprised her most was how she forgot about her drama for a while.

Aimee broke the silence and gestured to the closed door. "Trent's ready. You can head on back."

As Maggie headed toward the big office, she noticed the bank of file cabinets along the wall that had recently been delivered since the packaging still clung to each unit. At the sheriff's door, she turned the knob and crossed the threshold. Her insides warmed at the sexy sight that greeted her. He'd rolled his sleeves up to his elbows, exposing his muscular forearms that flexed and bunched as he moved stacks of folders. *Good Lord, this man is still a looker, and he has handcuffs.*

"Ah, just the woman I wanted to see. It doesn't seem like you encountered any problems using my credit card, although I did have Aimee call ahead to several shops and provide advance authorization."

Maggie took a seat. "Thank you. It would have been embarrassing if someone thought I stole the sheriff's credit card."

He arched an eyebrow and grinned. "Lucky for you, I have a key to the jailhouse."

"Who's this pretty lady?" A tall, lean man dressed in uniform drawled from the doorway.

"A beauty who's off limits to you. Miss Margaret King, this is my deputy, Lance Charles, who has quite the reputation in town with the single women."

Trent's reply made her heart flutter. It kind of sounded like he'd staked his claim on her. *Silly?* Hell yes, because she knew he wasn't being possessive of her. He was being protective. She'd almost forgotten that Trent would have the same reputation. Maybe not serious relationships, but it had always been something her brother teased him about.

Lance extended his hand. "Guilty, but the pleasure's all mine. I can't help it if I'm dashing and charming."

"I've always liked a humble man," Maggie replied.

A smile split his face. "I like this one. She'll keep you in line."

He gave her hand a brisk shake before withdrawing. Then, he proceeded with various updates before heading out on patrol. Once Lance left, she watched Trent type something into his computer.

"Your desk is beautiful." She lightly trailed her fingers over the intricate carvings. "Did the same person who carved this desk do the railings out front?"

"No. This was given to my father when he worked in New York for the Federal Deposit Insurance Corporation. He gifted it to me when I was elected sheriff. I don't know who did the railings."

"Wow, that's special, and I bet he's proud of you."

"I think so, but I also know I've made my parents worry too much. They're both happier with my new career." Trent moved the mouse on his desk, clicking it every so often.

A lump formed in her throat. "I think that comes along with the whole parenting thing and when you love someone."

His smile didn't quite touch his eyes. "Something like that, anyway. Did you get everything you needed, or do we need to make another stop on the way home?"

Home. She liked the sound of that more than she should, even if his context was vastly different from what she wanted it to mean. "No, I'm good for now. How does it feel working in the same building as your grandfather? I like that you've kept a lot of the original charm."

Trent perked up, his smile now touching the corners of his eyes. "It does remind me of my grandfather when he was the sheriff. The only things I've upgraded since my arrival are associated with technology—the security system, jail monitors, the office computers and monitors, and I've even had a few flat-screen televisions installed. I like being able to watch real-time updates from around the world. It was something we had at the Bureau. The old phone system is next. That thing is archaic right down to the tape answering machine."

Maggie giggled. "Can you even buy cassette tapes anymore?"

"Couldn't tell you. My predecessor, who took the position after my grandfather, used his remaining budget on updating the jailhouse before retiring so I can't give him too much grief. He spent his money wisely, but that antiquated phone system had to go. Next, I need to finish evaluating my team and fill in the gaps as needed."

"Are you happy wearing that star?" She studied him intently, looking for signs of distress.

"Being able to help others is who I am and is what I need to do."

Her heart clenched at his declaration. He hadn't answered her question, but what he said spoke volumes. Knowing him the way she did, it was what he hadn't said that bothered her the most.

"Aimee's great," she blurted, switching topics.

"Agreed. I haven't regretted hiring her from the minute she started. She's a great addition to my team and keeps me in line. So, you ready to head out? I've taken care of everything urgent for the time being and thought I'd cut out early to give you a tour of my town before we head home and talk."

"Lead the way." Maggie stood and followed him out the door.

She wanted to hear his assessment and what he'd learned today. She also wanted to bury her head in the sand and delight in this moment. It had been so long since she'd enjoyed the genuine camaraderie of friends. She couldn't believe how easily her old self had risen to the surface. Being around a familiar face with a link to her past melted away the carefully crafted protection she'd erected. What did it hurt to live in the moment because she trusted Trent? She would just have to keep her heart out of it. When she returned to Dallas, she'd transition back into her carefully constructed life of isolation. It was her safe haven.

Trent would keep her safe. She was sure he'd already analyzed her situation to a gnat's ass of detail. Like he said, she put distance between her problems in Dallas by coming to him. This glimpse into her old life made her want to prolong those feelings for just a bit longer.

~ * ~

"What the hell do you mean they can't find her? It's been two days. She's a civilian who lives alone. My order was simple, monitor Margaret King's apartment and report to me. Now that she searched the web on that name, the reason couldn't be more important. We need to find out what she knows." Michael Mason, Falcon's leader, simply known as Talon, exploded. "The two men you assigned were supposed to be highly skilled in surveillance. Their orders were to surveil and bring me information. Now, I have no information or person, so what does that tell me? Nothing! Why is she missing?"

"The bitch must have run. She's not in Dallas, or my team would have found her." Talon's thug whined in defense of his men.

"Don't refer to her as a bitch again. She's a lady who deserves respect. That will serve as your only warning. Now, if you and your men would have done their jobs this discussion would be moot. I've grown very fond of Miss King and losing her is a big fucking problem," Talon admonished in a tone that remained low, and menacing.

The hired gun, clearly not understanding the dangerous line he was close to crossing, continued to push. "Listen, Talon. These guys are commit—"

"Enough! Here's what will happen," Talon commanded, turning toward his operations manager who sat at the conference table. "The men this idiot assigned were sloppy." He jerked his thumb toward the thug. "If I can't trust them to surveil Miss King, then why would I asked them to bring her to me? She could be hurt, which would disappoint more. I won't tolerate this type of disrespect or ineptness within my organization. I need to make an example out of their mistakes."

"You're bat-shit crazy, these men are loyal—"

Talon whirled on the goon. Fists clenched, he punched and punched until his knuckles hurt. A red haze filtered across his vision which carried the coppery scent of blood.

"I'm not crazy, and I'll never tolerate disrespect," he spat while slowly climbing to his feet. He pulled a handkerchief from his pocket and wiped his face and hands clean before tossing the cloth onto the body. "Get rid of that trash, permanently."

"Sure thing, Boss, but next time let me know, and I'll throw down a drop cloth," his operations manager quipped.

Talon's breath sawed in and out of his chest from his exertion as he strode out of the conference room.

A chipper female voice echoed down the hallway behind him. "Talon, I have good news."

He turned to greet his administrative assistant who'd been with him since he formed Falcon. The extent of her knowledge was that he ran a security consulting business.

He forced a smile to his face. "I could use some good news today."

"Your man found the admitting hospital for that poor mother and son who you heard about on the news." She handed him a piece of paper with all pertinent information scrawled on it. "Oh, and I almost forgot, the husband is dead. I shouldn't say this, but I think he got what he deserved."

Another good reason to have a government worker on his payroll. Talon refused the note. "I agree. Please make the necessary arrangements to pay both hospital bills in full. Use the same account as before and use anonymous as the name."

Her smile radiated her happiness and eagerness to deliver a struggling family some good news. "I'd be delighted, but I don't understand why you don't put your name on it. It's such an extraordinary gesture."

Talon saw his second-in-command walking toward them. "Sometimes it's better to believe in miracles." He dismissed his assistant and turned toward Darren Waltz, who followed him into his office.

Waltzer, as he was known within the Special Forces community and within his team, was a brutally efficient soldier who now pledged his loyalty to Talon via a carefully negotiated contract. His tactical skills and cunning made him a lethal threat to anyone in his sights. It didn't take long to recognize those abilities, which was why he rose to the rank of second-in-command. Since then, Waltzer had formed two tactical teams of mercenary soldiers who operated under his orders. Oh, yes, they were all expensive as hell, but worth every penny.

Talon motioned to the man to take a seat. "Today hasn't gone as I'd have liked…"

"Yeah, I passed by the conference room on the way here. I've asked one of my men to help tidy up the place," Waltzer replied, taking a seat in a chair opposite Talon's desk.

"Get Alpha team ready to roll. I want those men that thug hired hunted down and executed. Before your team pulls the trigger, make sure those thugs know the particulars. Send me the video, I have plans for it. Also, find out what they did to make Miss King run." Talon slapped the man on his back as he moved toward his desk.

"Roger that, I'll instruct my men. Do you want them to take over King's reconnaissance?"

Talon nodded. "Start with her brother's partner."

"One more thing," Waltzer said, "I highly recommend changing protocols since we're unsure about the extent of exposure—"

Talon slammed his hand onto his desk. "This is my organization, and I'll decide how we move forward. Your role: hired help."

A slow smile spread across the man's face. "Understood. But you pay me for my observations too, which is why I'm going to press. This obsession with that woman is becoming a problem. If I feel my men are being put in danger by your decision-making, we're out."

Talon's jaw clenched, but he restrained himself from saying more. He'd love to wipe that smirk from his face, but now wasn't the time. He needed this man and his skills. "Noted. But watch your fucking tone."

Talon waved his hand dismissively, pleased when the big man stood and exited his office. He needed time to think. Letting his anger get the better of him wasn't acceptable. His success had come from being strategic, patient, and diligent. His boss had used those qualities to describe his strengths while in the CIA, alongside his exemplary service record and numerous commendations. Talon had understood valor and honor, which was why he didn't cross that line with Waltzer today when he had stood up for his team.

The problem, Talon didn't believe in that philosophy any longer. It died the day the CIA deemed him expendable for the greater good, the day his boss pulled out that weapon, shot him three times then left him for dead. He vowed on that day, and every grueling day of his recovery afterward, he'd make the government pay for their arrogance and betrayal. Just as his father had.

Talon had monitored Maggie again for less than a month when his IT team informed him she'd performed a search on that snitch's name—Bart Schamko. Nothing had surfaced since Dalton and Schamko's death, so Talon was confident he'd handled the problem. Now the big question in Talon's mind: had Dalton given her this information and instructed her to wait? How much did she know or have?

All good things come to those who wait. His mother's words echoed in the back of his mind.

He slid open a desk drawer and rummaged around until he found her photo, one that had worn edges and yellowed with time. He ran his index finger over his mother's face. His thoughts drifted back to when he was a small boy helping her make chocolate chip cookies.

Ah Mom, I miss those days. Hey, I have some news for you. I know I have told you numerous times that I'd never marry, but I found a woman. And to think she's Dalton's sister—life couldn't get any better.

He rested the picture of the woman over his heart and stared out the window. First, he had to locate Margaret King. Oh, how he loved a good game of cat and mouse.

Chapter Three

TRENT EXHALED AS HE pulled into his driveway. The destruction zone, as he referred to it, had grown since this morning. Between the mess and the crew, the timing couldn't be worse.

The reason behind her escape and the long drive to his doorstep worried him. Eighty-percent of his mind and gut told him that Falcon was behind it, but he had to remain objective until he knew for sure. Over the years, he and Dalton had made plenty of enemies.

Scaffolding had now been erected on all sides of Trent's home to assist the roofers. Alongside his driveway, a big dumpster sat for the old roofing materials and debris. Tired of living in a state of chaos, he'd be happy when this project was over. Almost everything he owned was packed in boxes or closets for safekeeping. The process of unpacking and putting the house to rights had stalled. At some point, he needed to prioritize that, but for now it was Maggie.

She slipped out of the truck and opened the rear door to gather her shopping bags. "Wow, things change quickly around here, including the temperature. We get summertime storms in Dallas, but it doesn't get cold, just more humid."

"The weather out here can change on a dime," he replied, rounding the front of the truck.

"Thanks for the tour. I enjoyed seeing the town through your eyes and appreciate the time you carved out of your schedule."

He loved the twinkle of joy that sparkled in her eyes. "It's a great town. Plus, it's good to have a general idea of what it offers since you'll be here for a bit. I'm going to check out today's progress, then change out of my uniform," he answered, then headed toward the side of the house.

She hollered to be heard over the rustle of leaves. "I'll help with dinner in a minute."

The hard slap of plastic whipping in the wind caught his attention. The crew had secured tarps over most of the pallets, leaving him one to cover. The lone wooden platform sat exposed with the underlayment. The sky transformed from light gray to darker as big black clouds billowed in the distance. A cold gust swirled around him and skittered down his collar. The weather could be unpredictable in the mountains.

Heavy with moisture, the air had him hastening his steps to move fast if he wanted to finish grilling dinner before the rain hit. He found a cover for the pallet in the garage, then stopped to turn on the grill before heading into the bathroom to wash up and change. After slipping into a pair of jeans and a Henley, he left his boots by his bed in exchange for a pair of flip-flops. Afterward, he stored his service weapon in his gun safe.

Cold air pressed against his body as he removed the meat and vegetables from the refrigerator. He carried the platter of food outside to the table next to his grill. Heat warmed his face as he rotated the lid backward. He added the steaks one by one after removing the butcher paper. The meat sizzled on the hot grates before he sprinkled a liberal amount of seasoning on each.

He thought back to how he reacted when Lance flirted with Maggie. Trent's possessiveness shocked him. The thought of Lance pursuing her bothered Trent. Man, he needed to pull himself together. Any red-blooded man would flirt with her, and he couldn't beat up every single one who did. She wasn't his and never could be. That had been settled long ago. Now, he needed to get his body aligned with his brain.

He added the ears of corn while he reflected on his jealous behavior, which was more protective now that he looked at it. Yes, he wanted to safeguard Maggie and meant what he said to Lance. She might not like Trent being overbearing, but she came to him for protection.

He rotated the corn, not wanting the ears to burn. The wind increased in power and howled through the trees. The smell of rain stained the air. The storm had gained speed as it moved across the mountain range. He loved this time of night when the setting sun left behind an array of brilliant colors streaking across the sky. The purple, orange, and red colors were framed by gray and black billowing clouds. In the distance, a flash of lightning added to the scene. His mind drifted off while he watched Mother Nature's show.

When he woke up in the hospital and was told Dalton hadn't survived, a part of Trent had died that day, too. He vowed that he'd stop at nothing to topple Falcon the day he was discharged. What Trent hadn't realized at the time was that the injuries he sustained would require so much rehab. When he learned he'd been removed from the case due to his compromised identity, he'd lost his head. That decision robbed him of avenging Dalton's death.

Trent rubbed at his shoulder, trying to ease the ache from the cold—a parting gift from Falcon. Trent's arm and leg always told him when inclement weather approached.

Falcon cost me everything. A flicker of movement caught Trent's eye, and he glanced upward to see Maggie approaching. *Well, almost everything.*

"It's getting cold." Her beautiful voice penetrated his sullen thoughts. "Want me to bring you a sweatshirt?"

"No, thanks. I've got the grill to keep me warm. Did you get everything put away?"

"I did. Having a few things to wear that aren't four sizes too big is nice. So, tell me, Trent, do you think I overreacted by coming here?"

He wouldn't pretend he didn't understand the context of her question. He also wouldn't sugarcoat it. "No, and I've got a bad feeling, but coming here was smart. What do you know about Falcon?"

Her eyebrows scrunched together as she searched her brain. "I assume you're not talking about the bird, so I'd say nothing. Should I?"

"Did your brother talk about his job or assignments with you in any detail?" Trent opened the lid and rotated the ears of corn again.

"No, I've heard snippets of things over the years but didn't pay attention. He certainly didn't divulge any details. Why? Who or what is Falcon?"

Trent turned toward Maggie. His mind raced with how to summarize the case. "It's the last assignment we worked together. Falcon had been in play for several years. This organization supplied military grade weapons and drugs to the Middle Eastern and African warlords. The US government wanted this group dismantled because America's finest were being killed by their own weaponry peddled to the highest bidder. So many agents across multiple agencies and organizations invested their lives to infiltrate this group. Those deep cover assets endured the daily routine of watching these monsters act like gods and kings. Not to mention all the horrific acts they had to carry out to keep their covers intact."

Maggie's eyes widened. "What? I don't know what to say, that's horrible in so many ways."

Trent grabbed his tongs and flipped the steaks. The aroma of grilled meat made his mouth water. "It's a necessity to bring down these types of organizations. Your brother and I were responsible for following the money that would eventually tie suspects to weapons and drugs. The only way to decimate Falcon was to deplete their funds. Intel gathered suggested that Falcon's leader was an American, either from the military or a covert agency, but his identity remained unknown at that point. All we have is his code name: Talon. The two biggest problems—the leader of this organization never surfaced, and following the trail of money had been almost impossible, but we're making progress. This cartel ran a tight ship and had countermeasures for practically every scenario."

Her mouth gaped, and her gaze darted back and forth. "What are you saying? That this group is who killed my brother? Do you think they were the ones to leave the knife? Oh, God."

"Slow down. At this point, all we know is what you've told me. Yes, whoever left that knife is tied to Dalton, which probably means it's tied to the FBI. Falcon makes the most sense but could be any of our past cases. It could also be something entirely different, although I would bet on the former." He had wanted to talk about this earlier today, but she had seemed so happy, and he hadn't wanted to darken her mood. "I have more questions for you, but how about we tackle them after dinner?"

A loud boom of thunder caused her to jump. "Holy smokes, that sounded close. Uh, sure. After dinner. Do you want me to prepare the salad?"

Trent nodded at her. "Everything's on the counter, and I have several bottles of dressing in the refrigerator. The steaks will be done in a few minutes."

Her hips swayed as she walked toward the house. He appreciated her candor and direct questions. Man, he couldn't believe she was here with him. They still clicked and melded together as if they hadn't spent time apart. The only difference was that her brother would never join them. She tried to mask the pain, but he had the secret decoder ring. Those green eyes told a story all on their own.

He would do anything to erase that pain. Even now, she still calls to him on so many levels. He'd never been so drawn to a woman, and letting her go wasn't easy.

"Where's your mixer?" she hollered from the screen door.

Now, what was she up to? "Cabinet, next to the refrigerator."

He wanted to ask why but figured she didn't supply a *because* for a reason. Excitement bubbled in his body. He liked the thought that she had a surprise for him.

A flash of lightning, followed by another boom of thunder, made him look toward the sky. Large raindrops pelted his face and body. Again, the sizzle of electric energy split the sky, followed by the deep, resounding rumble that hastened his actions. The storm was escalating, promising to deliver a wicked show.

He removed the steaks and corn from the grill and covered them with aluminum foil before placing them on the platter. Holding the plate in one hand, he turned the barbeque off before dashing toward the house.

As if she read his mind, Maggie met him at the door and took the dish out of his hands. "You're drenched. Wait here. I'll get you a towel."

She moved with a sense of purpose, but he heard a suppressed giggle trail behind her as she went to find him a towel.

~ * ~

Maggie damn near swallowed her tongue after returning with a towel. Trent had stripped off his wet T-shirt to reveal a chiseled chest that was a ten on the drool index. Raised pectorals with tiny, hardened discs strained from the cold air. Tiny goosebumps dotted his flesh. His chest was sheer perfection, with a slight dusting of hair that traveled down from his navel to disappear into the waistband of his jeans.

She couldn't help herself. She lightly trailed her fingers up his stomach, over every ridge of hard muscle that contracted under her touch. He emitted a low groan that sent shivers down her body. The fresh cool scent of rain and mountain air clung to his skin. She wiped away the excess moisture with the towel before giving it to him altogether.

A lopsided grin formed on his face. "If you don't close that mouth, you'll catch a fly."

She caught her bottom lip between her teeth and tilted her head upward to look him in the eyes. "Your body is a work of art, and my hand acted on its own accord."

A heated blush worked up her neck at her brazen comment. She looked away from him and started to retreat, but a warm hand gripped her arm to halt her movement. His touch sent jolts of electricity directly to her core. Her heart pounded against her ribs, and pinpricks of excitement tingled across her body. Anticipation rippled throughout her body while she waited to see what would happen next.

"Thank you," he drawled. "And it doesn't hurt to have a good-looking woman tell me she can't keep her hands off me."

Maggie chewed on her bottom lip. "I appreciate that, but I know you're not interested in me *that* way anymore, right?"

He emitted a growl from deep in his throat, her only warning before he snared her wrists and maneuvered her so her back slammed flat against the door. The press of his much larger frame against hers was deliciously erotic. Her chest heaved, not from fear but excitement. He stole her breath.

He moved one of her hands downward between their bodies until it rested on his jean-clad erection. "Does this feel like I lack interest? I've been in this state since you arrived. You, Margaret King, are one sexy, smart, and beautiful woman."

Desire flooded her system, making it difficult to think. She trembled, and her nipples hardened into tight peaks that rubbed against the satin of her bra. A hot rush of arousal pulsed through her body. Oh God, what had this man unleashed inside of her?

She slid her hand slowly up his length, hating the denim that separated them. He stared into her eyes, lust darkening his pupils, and even his breathing increased. Her tongue darted out to moisten her dry lips. She never wanted anything more in life than this moment right now.

"So much better than a dream," Maggie whispered, not intending to voice that sentiment.

He ground his erection against her belly. "Yes, I crave you. You tempt me in ways I've never experienced. Your body is a wonderland of possibilities because I know you can handle my need to love hard and with abandon. Do you understand me?"

His breath feathered against her lips right before he covered her mouth with his. The kiss wasn't soft or gentle; it was raw and untamed. It represented all their missed opportunities and that telltale of what might have been.

Her body burst to life, every nerve-ending zinging with happiness. A flash of light crackled, followed by a boom that seemed to rattle the house. The lights flickered briefly before the room went dark.

In the absence of the soft electrical humming of the refrigerator, the only sounds were their ragged breaths mixed with the rain pounding against the house.

Trent stepped back and cleared his throat. That moment faded into the darkness, along with his touch, the second he retreated. "Storm's getting worse. I should get flashlights and candles. And some dry clothes."

Maggie blinked as he fled, and the room went still as the hottest and sexiest moment of her life evaporated right before her eyes. She wanted to cry and scream with frustration. She wanted that damn kiss and whatever it brought afterward. She needed Trent Jacobs like a flower required water.

Her body shivered from the absence of his body heat. A profound and unwelcome feeling of loss slammed into her chest—a feeling she despised. What had changed his mind? Did he have another woman? Of course, he did. He always had someone, except her when he had the chance.

Her mind whirled with how to handle the awkwardness of the situation. Her head waged a war with her heart, and it sucked. She wasn't prepared for this intense resurgence of attraction. Worse, she wasn't sure she could resist it. She sensed his reaction was honest, but she didn't understand why he shut down. Then, something Annika said drifted in the back of Maggie's mind. *I think he's struggling with survivor's guilt. He'll come up with many excuses so stand strong and push right back.*

A word she would not use to describe herself was coy. She preferred strategic games, like trying to sink your opponent's war ships, a game she and Dalton played for hours when they were children. As a teacher, that description would get you eaten alive by her students. She had to be firm yet loving in her quest to develop all those precious minds.

Maybe Trent needed that approach too. Blame stopped growth and only eroded the truth over time.

Trent padded back into the kitchen a few minutes in dry clothes and with a handful of lighting options. She accepted a flashlight and silently headed to her room to put on a pair of sweatpants and channel her strength. It was time to remind herself why she had come there. She hadn't expected the flood of memories and emotions that had inundated her, which was naïve on her part. They had history together, and with Dalton, and nothing would ever change that, nor would she want that.

The smell of sulfur penetrated her nostrils when she returned. Several candles burned, and a small pile of spent matches sat on the table. The soft flicker of light danced off every surface in the kitchen. It made the setting for dinner romantic, though that wasn't the objective. The storm caused all sorts of things to flap and flutter in the strong winds.

"What would you like to drink?" he asked, putting the salad she had prepared on the table.

"Whatever you're having is fine with me."

He took two wine glasses from the cabinet and the bottle of wine from the counter. They ate in silence while the bug screens rattled against the windows in between the rolls of thunder. Flashes of light illuminated the scaffolding erected outside the windows, creating an ominous scene.

"My steak is cooked to perfection." She forked another bite into her mouth.

"I can't wait to see what you made for dessert." The smile he flashed revealed his joy as the candlelight flickered against his skin creating a soft glow. He truly was a handsome man.

"How do you know I made dessert?" She scrunched her forehead with feigned confusion.

He hunched his shoulders and cocked his head to the side. "I'm pretty good at investigative research. For starters, nothing we've eaten so far has needed a mixer, which leaves dessert or breakfast."

She sensed him relaxing a bit, the easy banter flowing between them. That made her feel better and took some of the awkward out of the evening.

"Hmm, is that what you think?" She raised her eyebrows at him. "You'll just have to wait and see, Inspector Jacobs."

His cellphone chirped, drawing his attention from her and to the screen. "Hi, Mom." He listened for a few minutes and smiled. "Yes, it's storming here. I'm home. I do love your lasagna, but I'll have to take a rain check. Dalton's sister is visiting, and I'm helping her out with a few things."

She loved how his love for his mom reflected on his face. He didn't seem to want to rush her off the phone, but also didn't want to have a long conversation. A pang of longing hit her in the chest, knowing she'd never get a call like this to have dinner at her parents' house. When they died in her senior year of high school, the immediate loss and pain was horrible, but losing Dalton almost killed her.

"Yes, she's doing well. I think she'd love your lasagna. It might take a few weeks to sort everything out, but if your schedule is open, we'll come for dinner." He winked before mouthing, "Sorry."

He finished the call and put his phone back on the table. "It seems we have a standing invitation for dinner and she's happy you're visiting. I'll start a fire in the living room while you serve up your surprise. This storm sounds like it's going to last a while." He placed their dishes in the sink and left the kitchen.

The ingredients for dessert sat in the refrigerator. As she made the final preparations, she thought back to all the family dinners she had as a child. They would laugh and share stories about their day. It didn't matter if it was over a pizza or a full-blown meal. All that mattered was they were together. She missed those precious moments the most.

The pain in her chest deepened, causing her to squeeze her eyes shut to stop the flow of tears. Now even her dinners with Dalton were gone. Rolling her head back and forth, she sucked down a deep breath and held it for several seconds. Now wasn't the time, she needed to focus on this threat and what it meant. She entered the living room with her treat in tow and leaned against the wooden frame to enjoy the view.

Trent waded up newspaper, the muscles in his back flexing, before he picked through a stack of kindling to find smaller pieces for the base. Once he'd erected a pyramid-shaped pile, he struck a match. Smoke tinged the air. He pressed the flame to the paper, and the edges changed color from orange to brown and then black before the material crumbled to ash. Just like life, vibrant and colorful one minute and gone the next.

Trent sat staring at the flicker of light.

"Penny for your thoughts?" she asked.

He ran his hand through his hair and sighed. "Many, but I'll start here; I crossed the line earlier and I'm sorry. It's just...having you here...it's... never mind."

"Finish that sentence, Trent." She entered into the room and set the tray with the wine, strawberries, and bowl of whipped cream on the coffee table. "Please."

He stood and placed the screen in front of the fire before moving to the couch. The second his butt hit the cushion she knew he'd buried his thought. The fire started to crackle, filling the dreaded silence that had blanketed the room. She refilled their wine glasses with the bottle of red he opened for dinner. The glow from the flames flickered across his face in a golden hue. He looked like a Greek god.

"Overwhelming. That's a good way to describe it. Let's sit on the floor while we talk." Trent moved the table forward giving them more room between it and the sofa.

She plucked a berry from the pile, swiped it through the fluffy cream and hummed with delight. The sweet juice combined with the velvety texture of the cream melted onto her tongue. It didn't escape her notice that he watched her every move. Plucking another strawberry, she dipped it into her white fluff enjoying another burst of flavors. The simple act of sitting in front of a fire to enjoy a stormy evening with him calmed her, but it also made her feel alive. A dangerous acknowledgment, but one she'd worry about tomorrow.

"Don't eat it all," he groused, before plunking a berry through the concoction and popping it into his mouth. "Delicious. I like that you made this for me."

"You're welcome, but it's not that hard to make." She winked. "So, what did you want to discuss?"

"Did you happen to take a picture of the knife and note?"

"No. Honestly, the thought never crossed my mind. I should've, but I freaked out and left."

He popped another berry into his mouth and spoke around the bite. "You did the right thing. I just wanted to know. Can you describe the paper used or the knife?"

She moved her gaze to the flames and watched them dance. "I'm pretty sure it had a black handle. The blade wasn't too large. More like a steak knife, but wider and sharper looking. The note was scrawled on a sheet of paper from my memo pad."

"That's good. Do you have any details about the van besides the color, like make or model?"

"Yes, and I even have the license plate number. I had planned on giving you that last night after dinner, but I was so exhausted it slipped my mind. I'll get that for you. I never really saw the two men up close. They wore baseball caps and always seemed to be looking down."

"That's my girl. So, a sketch artist is out, but the rest of that information is useful. Does anyone know why or that you've left town?"

Maggie rubbed her forehead. "I didn't tell anyone I was leaving town. I emailed my boss stating that I needed to use some vacation days."

Concern washed over his face. "I'm contacting my friend from the Bureau, Noah Parker, to help us. I'd trust him with my life. I want him to pull traffic footage from around your apartment to look for white vans. In the meantime, I'll run those plates, but I'm sure they'll come back as stolen. Whoever left that note is tied to Dalton."

"I agree."

The fire crackled and hissed in tandem to the rolling thunder in the distance.

"Do you think he'll find the van in any of that footage?" She reached for another strawberry.

"I hope so."

A sudden clap of thunder rattled the windows and caused her to jump. "Sorry, all of this makes me jittery. I'm not fond of horror movies, yet it feels like I'm starring in one. None of this makes any sense to me. I'm virtually a nobody. I'm not social anymore. I stick to myself."

"I remember a bubbly, funny, and stubborn woman. Even the stories Dalton told me about you in high school matched that description. What do you mean by 'sticking' to yourself?"

"You know, stayed at home by myself. It annoyed me when everyone always asked me how I was doing or told me it would get easier. It made me want to scream. I was tired of perfecting the art of loss."

Trent nodded. "When did you decide to quit being a teacher? I thought you loved teaching."

She shrugged and sighed. "After Dalton died, I couldn't teach anymore. All those innocent third graders would look at me daily, full of life and happiness. I couldn't deceive them any longer. I didn't view the world through that same lens. Now, I'm a freight auditor. I can work from home. Plus, I can take on as much work as I want to help fill the downtime. I live a boring life."

"I don't like that you've isolated yourself. Trust me when I say this, living in the shadows is not your place. Just like giving up on people is not the answer. You're too bright and caring. Why would you do that to yourself?"

Her shoulders slumped. "Something deep inside changed when he died. I guess the world became unstable, and all the bad you two talked about became real for me. Trusting people seemed harder. Losing those I loved devastated me. I'm tired of that cycle. I miss him...and I miss my parents. My heart has been ripped from my chest too many times. Now it's irrevocably broken."

Her voice cracked, and hot tears ran down her cheeks. "I can't risk that type of loss again. To me, the solution was easy: no love, family, or friends equaled no more loss."

"I should have reached out and been there for you instead of leaving you to grieve alone." He slid her trembling body into his lap and cradled her in his arms. "I miss him too, but hiding won't stop the pain."

"No, but it prevents future pain. Watching your family dwindle to nothing as they're violently ripped from your life, rendering you the sole survivor, is brutal. Words like 'traumatic' and 'devastating' only scratched the surface. Therapy helped some after my parent's death, but it also drilled home the concept that everyone goes through the cycles of grief differently, and there isn't a right or wrong way to grieve. Doing what I need to do to survive isn't wrong, which is why I found a quiet corner and stayed there after Dalton."

It was on the tip of her tongue to ask him why he'd been so distant during the funeral, but the warmth of Trent's arms and the rush of her tears prevented her from asking. In an odd way, it felt like she'd finally been given the chance to purge her grief with someone who understood the profound impact of losing her brother. This moment could have only been shared with one person, and his arms were wrapped tightly around her. This night belonged to the memory of her brother. Tomorrow belonged to solving the puzzle of who had threatened her.

Trent's Redemption, Book 1 in the Mill Creek Mystique romantic suspense series is out now.

Acknowledgements

This project became clearer to me after a passionate meeting with DL Croisette. The idea for this world and series came from a group of talented writers who were on a retreat in Florida, using their free time to daydream and brainstorm this story.

I loved the idea of a shared world where each author created their standalone story set in the beachside small town of Destiny, Florida. I couldn't commit quickly enough to join this talented and amazing group: GK Brady, DL Croisette, Judy Kentrus, and Cindy Kehagiaras. I'm proud of what we've built and have enjoyed every moment of our collaboration. I'm ready for a sequel so I can bring Laney's story to the forefront. Anyone interested?

The writing world is a solitary space, for the most part. Still, I've been fortunate with building a network of dedicated professionals and enthusiasts who have helped me grow and refine my stories. I've also gained some exceptional friends along the way. The laughter, tears, and things we've learned from all our meetings are priceless. I'm honored to have found these individuals, along with my friends who have supported me unconditionally in my journey.

Living in the fantasyland of happily-ever-afters is one of my favorite pastimes. The things I've learned through research, my imagination, and the experiences I've had or outcomes I wish had been different in my life give me the freedom to escape, and I hope the stories and adventures I create offer my readers the same freedom.

Life's struggles are never fun, and we've all had our hurdles and sucker punches to handle and process. I have, too, and I'm looking forward to a book release when I don't have to add an In Memoriam line or three into my dedication section. This has happened in every book I've released to date. To everyone reading this, I'm sending you hugs, sunshine, and strength because I must believe it does get better.

Speaking of great support, brainstorming, feedback, and everything in between, I want to personally acknowledge a few individuals whose unconditional love and support mean the world to me. Jordanne, for your detailed insight and feedback. You are both a cheerleader and a critic, and I can always rely on you for anything. A Fabulous Production has been my go-to resource for formatting, layout, and graphical support for social media. They are professional, creative, timely, and exceptional in all respects. If you need these types of services, I highly recommend them. Cindy, your verve is infectious. Having you in my corner is priceless, and I adore you! To Trisha, whose unwavering support, feedback, creativity, laughter, insight, and giant foot, which lovingly kicks me into new, uncharted waters, are the best. You make the world a brighter place, my friend. My Vicki Jean, who has always stood by me and motivates me to chase every dream I've had. And to my ride or die, my infinity and beyond, life with you is never dull. It's filled with adventure and laughter, and if I ever got a do-over, you're a no-brainer.

A huge thank you to my ARC Stars. I appreciate your willingness and time to read my story and provide your insightful feedback. You are amazing, and I'm honored to have you on my team.

Lastly, but certainly not least, thank you to my wonderful readers who chose to read this book. I hope my story provided you with a brief escape from reality, leaving you with a smile on your face. I truly appreciate your support!

XOXO,

Bailey

BOOKS BY BAILEY THOMAS

ROMANTIC SUSPENSE

Mill Creek Mystique Series

Trent's Redemption
Hidden Identities
Breaking Point
Kane's Reckoning (Coming Soon)
Legally Bound (Coming Soon)

 Available in Audio

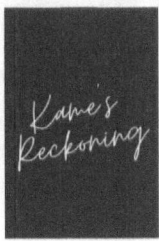

CONTEMPORARY ROMANCE

Sand Dollars, Secrets, and Starting Over

Part of the Love in Destiny romance series

Torrent of Hearts

Also available in the Pack Your Bags short story collection

As an only child, Bailey Thomas' active imagination and adventurous nature always kept her busy. Now, she channels those creative powers into storytelling.

Living in the Southwest, Bailey splits her time between crafting heartfelt stories and indulging in her favorite pastimes—whether it's devouring books, marathoning shows, or catching a game.

Life is too short, so Bailey tries to live by her motto of finding adventures that make you smile. She loves to hear from her readers. You can find and connect with her at the links below.

Website/Blog:
baileythomasauthor.com
Instagram
instagram.com/Author_BaileyThomas
BookBub
bookbub.com/authors/bailey-thomas

www.ingramcontent.com/pod-product-compliance
Lightning Source LLC
Chambersburg PA
CBHW030104260626
47156CB00008B/2511